HOME SWEET MESS

ALLISON ASHLEY

Cover Design: Elizabeth Turner Stokes

This book is a work of fiction. Names, characters, places, and incidents are the
product of the author's imagination or are used fictitiously. Any resemblance to
actual events locales, or persons, living or dead, is coincidental.

First Edition June 2021

For Jeni and Susan

This story touches on cancer, infertility, and child neglect. If these are sensitive topics, please read with care.

CHAPTER ONE

Jeni Bishop was disturbingly familiar with the sounds her neighbor made during sex. To be clear, it wasn't intentional on her part to be within earshot of the woman's early morning amorous exploits.

Not at first anyway. But by this point, it was a matter of principle.

Jeni sat on her front porch, hands wrapped around a mug of steaming coffee, the wooden swing swaying lightly in the subtle breeze. Growing up on a farm, her day had begun before dawn for as long as she could remember, and the habit of rising early refused to be purged from her system.

That had been rough during college, but now that nights of staying out until two or three in the morning were few and far between, these quiet hours were her favorite part of the day. Or they had been, before she moved to Kansas City for a job opportunity exactly one month ago. If she'd known who she was moving in next to, she might have reconsidered this particular location. Or asked her landlord to waive the security deposit, at the very least.

Now, four weeks in, Jeni had come to expect her morning

solitude to be interrupted at least twice a week. Last week it had been four.

Same guy, but still. *Four.*

Jeni didn't mind that the lady was getting laid or even how often. It was the fact that she refused to keep it private, in a neighborhood where the houses were stacked nearly on top of each other. Also, because she seemed to require an open window to reach her big finale.

Didn't most people get busy at night? Well, maybe she did that too, but it was evident she appreciated a certain kind of wake-up call.

"Yes."

Jeni nodded along with the words of affirmation the woman was so generously offering.

"Ohhh…don't stop."

Yes, don't stop. Just get it over with, already. Jeni took a sip of coffee.

A low, rhythmic thumping joined the feminine moans. A headboard, maybe?

Jeni sighed and wondered why the idea of sleeping with the window closed was such a distasteful notion to her beautiful, energetic, and probably limber next-door neighbor. If the double-paned glass was firmly latched, the entire neighborhood wouldn't get an earful. As the closest neighbor, Jeni might still hear *something*, but it would hopefully be muffled to the point she might have assumed it to be a cat or a dying squirrel.

A woodpecker, maybe.

"*Oh…*"

Jeni circled a hand in the air in front of her, as if to say *keep going*. Almost there.

"Oh!"

Jeni very nearly set her cup down to clap but decided against it. All was silent now, just as she liked it.

Inhaling deeply, she closed her eyes and took in the fresh air.

The late August morning was warm, but it wasn't uncomfortably hot yet. Just as in her hometown in Nebraska, she wouldn't be able to enjoy these mornings come winter, which was one reason she stubbornly refused to give up the ritual now, no matter how irritating her neighbor had become.

She spent several minutes in the quiet, thinking about nothing in particular. She'd had a good stretch of meditation before her neighbor burst onto the stage, and now Jeni just wanted to take advantage of the moments she had left before getting ready for work. As a social worker for Child Protective Services, there was no telling what she'd walk into today. While she harbored a deep passion for her job and couldn't see herself doing anything else, it was far from easy and she'd learned the importance of balance early on. This house—the first place she'd ever called her own—was her safe place to relax and unwind.

She inhaled deeply, and her shoulders softened as she sipped her coffee.

A few minutes later, a screen door creaked open and slapped shut against the frame. Startled, Jeni snapped her head around.

A man stood on the porch of her neighbor's house, head bent forward as he worked one of the buttons on his shirt.

Wow. He got out of there quick.

She hadn't seen this guy before. The four-timer from last week had been large, dark, and sexy. Very Jason Momoa-ish. Irritating as the interruptions were, Jeni had given props to her neighbor, and this one wasn't bad either. Wavy blond hair, tall but not excessively so, lean build. The stylish, leather sneakers he wore with his button-up shirt and jeans created a boyish quality. The men before him had worn pressed slacks and gleaming oxfords as they entered and exited the craftsman-style house, looking like high-level executives who had come straight from the downtown boardroom for a romp in the suburbs.

This guy wasn't her neighbor's typical style, and Jeni wondered what it was about him that made her bring him home.

The man looked up and to the left, his gaze landing on Jeni. She tensed momentarily, mildly embarrassed to be caught observing him. None of the previous men had noticed her. For a moment she was tempted to jerk her gaze away and act like she knew nothing. That she had no idea what and who he'd been doing just minutes before.

The man's eyes darted to the open bedroom window, a mere eight feet from the edge of Jeni's porch, and a slow, knowing smirk spread across his face.

That arrogant expression immediately irked her. Instead of diverting her gaze, Jeni narrowed her eyes at him, as if to say, *I have every right to be sitting here, and yes, I heard everything.*

The guy winked at her and called out, "Join us, next time."

That embarrassed her, and her mouth dropped open. She had limited experience with men (the experience was less than stellar) and couldn't remember ever receiving a proposition like that.

He laughed and walked down the sidewalk with long, confident strides to a silver, older model pick-up truck parked along the curb. A white sticker in the shape of the Hawaiian Islands stood in stark contrast to the tinted back window, the shapes shrinking and blending together as he pulled away from the curb and drove off.

Jeni sat there, staring at the place on the street his vehicle had just vacated.

The screen door squeaked a second time. Her neighbor stood in the doorway, a colorful silk robe draped across her voluptuous body and long blond hair piled in a messy bun atop her head. Her cheeks were flushed, and her lips carried a small smile as she lifted a glass to take a sip of water. Her hip held the door open, and she clutched a cell phone in the opposite hand.

Her eyes leisurely moved around her front yard before she turned to go back inside. When she did, she faced Jeni for a moment and paused to offer a wave. Jeni forced herself to smile and wave back.

This was the extent of their interactions, infrequent as they were. A smile or wave. Jeni didn't even know the woman's name.

Her neighbor opened her mouth like she might say something, but the phone rang. She held it in front of her face, looking at the screen. A voice squawked through the speaker, but Jeni couldn't make out the words.

"No, not right there," her neighbor said, squinting at the screen. "It's not centered. Move it a little to the left." She walked into her house and the screen door closed behind her. But not before one last sentence. "Yes! Right there."

Jeni couldn't contain the laugh that escaped as she stood up to go get ready for work.

That's what she said.

Jeni gave herself one final check in the mirror before heading out the door. For a minute she allowed her mind to compare the reflection staring back at her with the woman next door.

Her neighbor was fair in hair and complexion, while Jeni was brunette with gold irises hidden behind thick-framed, tortoise-shell glasses. Jeni certainly didn't have the voluptuous body her neighbor flaunted; her build instead spoke to life growing up on the farm and a love of athletics—softball in particular. Her nose and cheeks were covered in freckles from so much time in the sun.

The other woman had a steady stream of boyfriends crossing her threshold, while Jeni was the only one coming through her door at the end of the day. She didn't mind, honestly. She thrived on the knowledge she was doing things completely on her own. She was curious though. What might that be like?

If it's anything like what you had before? Not worth it.

Jeni shook her head, attempting to snap out of the vortex of comparison because it never did her any good. She straightened and checked herself one last time. She might have been a tomboy growing up, but today in her white blouse, pencil skirt, and nude heels, she looked every inch the professional woman she'd become.

Traffic was particularly heavy that day, and her twenty-minute commute to the welfare offices on State Avenue took twice that long. She wouldn't complain though. After a serious accident in high school, she'd endured long months without the ability to drive, and the freedom she had behind the wheel of a car was something she'd never take for granted again.

Employees typically parked in the large lot across the street, and she circled the first few rows, hoping she'd catch a visitor leaving. The only location she'd be guaranteed a spot was in the back, and her choice of shoes didn't seem like such a good idea anymore.

Just when she'd decided to give up and accept the walk—and the blisters—a car pulled out of a space on the first row.

Yes. Jeni slammed on the brakes and jerked her car in reverse, turning the wheel to start down the line of cars. A silver truck approached from the opposite direction, and Jeni flipped on her blinker. Either not noticing or not caring that she had staked her claim, the driver whipped the oversized vehicle into the parking spot she was waiting for with an ease that might have impressed her if she hadn't been so pissed.

Swallowing her frustration, she sighed and started moving forward again, her eye passing over the image of Hawaii on the window of the truck as she passed by.

Wait.

Her gaze darted to the rearview mirror, and sure enough, a blond man with a phone pressed to his ear exited the truck. He walked quickly across the street, toward the businesses that lined the sidewalk near her office building.

It had been just a glimpse, but it had to have been the guy

from this morning. Jeni pursed her lips in irritation and drove to the back of the lot.

The second she arrived at her cubicle, the heels came off. The morning went quickly, and she spent hours at her desk reviewing case files without so much as standing to stretch her legs. Her boss, Sandra, a boisterous woman with gray hair and red glasses who reminded Jeni of Oprah Winfrey, passed by a few times on her way to the conference room and was the only soul Jeni spoke to the entire morning. There must have been some sort of meeting because every so often a burst of voices would reach Jeni's ears when the conference room door opened.

"What's going on in there?" she asked Sandra during a pass by her desk.

"We're meeting with a nonprofit organization, Fostering Sweet Dreams. Have you heard of it?"

"No, I haven't."

"They take donations of cribs and beds for foster families to use when they take children in. It's been around for a few years but has grown a lot over the past year. We meet with them every once in a while to discuss logistics, such as drop-off locations, transporting the items, and choosing which families receive the donations."

"What a great idea," Jeni said. One of the top reasons they had trouble placing children in homes quickly was a lack of the tangible items required in an available home—like a bed or a car seat.

"FSD has been a huge blessing for us," Sandra said with a warm smile. "Are we being too loud? The director is a personal friend, and he and I can get a little rowdy when we're together."

"No, not at all. It's nice to hear laughter," Jeni said and meant it. Too often the office was filled with the heartbreaking sound of a crying child.

Jeni resumed her focus to the pile of case files on her desk, full of photos, intake forms, and notes made by her predecessor and worked tirelessly to familiarize herself with the children she was now responsible for.

She had a home visit that afternoon with a family fostering a six-year-old boy whose mother was in prison on drug charges. Based on the file, the foster parents were some of the best the agency had at their disposal, and the boy had been with them for two months so far. Hopefully it would be a relatively painless check-in.

Her stomach grumbled, and she glanced at the clock, surprised to see it was past noon. She was expected at the foster family's home at one, and she hadn't brought lunch. She grabbed her purse and hurried outside, hoping she could quickly get in and out of the only lunch spot within walking distance.

Jeni ducked into the deli, relieved to see that the line wasn't terrible. The store was small, and the people lined up for the cashier blocked her access to the refrigerated case that held pre-wrapped sandwiches and boxed salads. She took her place at the end to wait, pulling out her phone to enter the client's home address. She planned her route as she took a step forward every few minutes, and when she was at the edge of the food display, she slipped her phone back into her purse.

Glancing past the guy in front of her, she noticed there was one vegetarian sandwich remaining. She internally did a fist pump. This place made the *best* in-house hummus and didn't skimp on applying it to their veggie sub. It was a little far to reach yet, so she folded her hands in front of her and looked up.

The guy in front of her turned to the side and bent over slightly to peruse the available lunch options.

Jeni blinked and stood a little straighter, her brain whirring to process the signal her retinas were sending—this was, in fact, the guy who'd high-tailed it out of her neighbor's house at six-thirty this morning. And subsequently stole her parking spot.

Dressed to impress, he now wore a crisp, white dress shirt, navy slacks, and dark tan leather oxfords. His thick, blond hair was maybe a smidge too long but had a perfect wave many women would kill for. A clean-shaven, sculpted jaw set off high cheekbones and long, dark lashes—which were particularly noticeable from the profile view she had at the moment.

He was…different, up close. If she was being honest with herself, he was one of the most attractive men she'd ever seen. She revised her earlier thought that he wasn't up to par with the other men her neighbor invited over. He might be tied for first place with the Jason Momoa look-alike.

He smelled nice too. Clean and fresh and with a hint of some masculine cologne.

Too bad he seemed like an arrogant prick.

"Excuse me." He reached for a salad just beyond her elbow. Okay, so he had *some* manners. It was in that moment that she saw the flash of blue, giving her the full effect of his masculine features, and her breath caught in her throat.

She'd always had a thing for blue eyes. Maybe she'd judged this guy too quickly. She was forming an opinion on shockingly little information, after all. Why she was even forming an opinion about him at all was beyond her, but…here she was.

But then, he put the salad back and picked up the last veggie sub, turning to face the cashier to signal he'd made his final choice.

Oh, hell no. He wasn't taking her parking place *and* her favorite sandwich. Her internal filter was apparently on break, and Jeni couldn't stop the word that blurted from her mouth.

"Seriously?"

The guy didn't turn at the sound of her voice, likely not realizing she was talking to him.

A small voice in the back of her head reminded her of her propensity to become more than a little irrational when she was hungry, but she ignored it.

Jeni tapped his shoulder. "Excuse me."

He looked back, and when his eyes landed on her face, his expression was pleasant but blank. "Yeah?"

He didn't recognize her. Probably a good thing.

"Are you a vegetarian?" she asked.

His brow furrowed. "Um. No?"

"Oh. Well, you chose the last vegetarian sandwich."

His frown deepened, and his chin moved back an inch. "So?"

A voice called out, "Next in line, please."

Jeni quickly waved at the heavyset lady behind her, gesturing that she should go around. "We're not ready yet."

The man's eyes went wide, and he swiveled his head around, looking confused as hell.

"It's just, I don't eat meat, and I was going to buy that sandwich," she said, beyond caring that she seemed like the one out of her mind. "If you're not a vegetarian, maybe you could choose something else. The ham and cheese or the roast beef?"

He blinked, looking between her and the food case. "No, this is the one I want." He spoke slowly, almost like he wasn't sure she understood English. "Now, if you'll excuse me." He shot her an irritated look and marched up to stand behind the woman Jeni had allowed to precede them.

Jeni's mouth dropped open. She stepped forward and grabbed his sizeable bicep—and damn if it wasn't like granite. She released her grip as if she'd been burned. "You're really not going to give it to me?"

He peered down at her like he couldn't believe she was still standing there. "I'm really not."

She let out something between a huff and a grunt. Her face heated, and she fisted her hands at her sides.

What a *jerk*.

As he paid for his food, she belatedly realized she still had nothing to eat and swiped a yogurt parfait, the first meatless item she saw. She basically threw cash at the employee and ran outside, crossing the street to the parking lot.

He walked with casual, long strides toward the silver truck, sandwich in his hand. She jogged up behind him.

"Seriously, guy?" she said. "It wasn't enough to ruin my morning?"

The guy stopped short and, in slow motion, turned on his heel. This time, when he met her eyes, there was recognition. His full lips slowly spread in a grin. "I thought you looked familiar. I can't comment on yours, but I had a great morning."

"I heard."

His smile widened, and she had the urge to stick her tongue out at him.

"Was there something else you wanted from me? I already extended an invitation for you to join in next time."

Jeni snorted in disgust. "All I want is that sandwich."

"Just how hungry are you?"

"On a scale from one to ten? Seventeen."

His eyebrows shot up. "Wow. You're one of those people who get hangry, aren't you?"

"I don't see how that's relevant. All damn day you've been everywhere I turn, messing with my routine. Even if I put aside this morning's noise disturbance, you took my parking spot *and* stole my food."

Confusion passed over his features. "I don't know about the parking spot, but I paid for this sandwich. And unless you're willing to offer me something in return, I'll take it and be on my way."

She grimaced at her sad-looking cup of yogurt. She held it out to him.

He sighed, shaking his head in mock sadness. "Not what I had in mind, I'm afraid. You have a good day, now."

Jeni could only stand there in consternation as he got into his truck. He backed out, and when he put the truck in drive, he held up his hand in a wave that would have appeared friendly to anyone passing by.

Jeni knew better, and she nearly offered him a single finger in return.

Could this day get any worse?

As it turned out, it could. After a perfectly mundane experience at the planned home visit—in this job, boring was good—she returned to chaos at the office. A set of twins were in the holding room, and Sandra, who rarely got directly involved with placements anymore, pulled Jeni into the fray. They were four years old and inconsolable. One was a little boy with red hair that looked as if it hadn't seen a pair of scissors in a year or shampoo in a month. The other was a girl who wore a winter hat despite the midday heat in the nineties. Both were thin and dirty.

"These two were walking down a major street," Sandra said in a low voice. "The police picked them up and, when they took them home, found their father high on something and completely out of it." She touched the cross hanging from her neck, the only outward sign she was bothered by the situation. Sandra had been around long enough to curb her reactions. "I don't have a foster family with two beds. They'll have to be separated."

Jeni's stomach dropped to the floor. In the room next to where she and Sandra stood, the children clung to each other, fear in their eyes and tears running down their cheeks.

When she and her twin brother Andrew were that age, they were inseparable.

"What can I do?" Jeni asked.

By the time she walked out of the office several hours later, she was beat, physically and emotionally. Part of her wanted to just go home and run a hot bath, but she'd been looking forward to this evening. She had plans with one of her favorite people in the entire world. The fact that Andrew lived in Kansas City was an added bonus to the job offer at Child Protective Services and made the decision to move incredibly easy.

She sent a text to let Andrew know she was running late, but the silver lining was she'd missed rush hour traffic. After she'd settled into the booth with a Boulevard Wheat in her system, Jeni started to relax a little bit. Andrew sat across from her, sending a text message.

"Talking to Caroline?" she asked flatly. She wasn't a fan of the girl Andrew had been dating the last few months. He'd brought her to Nebraska for a long weekend in May, and she'd been standoffish and moody the entire time.

"No, she's out with some friends tonight." He didn't look up as he spoke. "I invited my friend, Logan. I hope that's okay. He should be here soon."

"Sure." She'd heard a lot about Logan over the years but had yet to meet him. "I need to meet some people. So far, the only friends I have are you and my sixty-five-year-old boss."

"You've been busy, little sister."

Jeni rolled her eyes as she did every time he called her his *little sister*. She was a measly three minutes younger than him.

"Started you off running, didn't they?" he continued.

She nodded, though Andrew was in the same boat. He was in law school and interning at the District Attorney's office and working way too much for what he was being paid. Jeni had barely talked to him since moving day. She said, "The girl they hired me to replace was supposed to be around for another month to train me, but last week she went into pre-term labor. Left a ton of stuff half-done that I'm having to work through."

"That sucks."

"Yeah. This afternoon was rough. I was late to meet you because—"

Andrew sat up and waved a hand in the air. "Sorry, hold that thought. There's Logan."

A light, pleasing scent of cologne reached Jeni's nose as Logan approached their table from behind her, sitting down to Andrew's left.

"Hey, man," the guy said, giving Andrew a slap on the shoulder. "Glad you texted. I really need a beer after the day I've had."

Jeni looked at the newcomer and blinked, hoping her eyes were playing a trick on her. "You've got to be kidding me."

CHAPTER TWO

L ogan looked across the table and laughed.

"Do you know each other?" Andrew asked.

"No," they said in unison. Logan definitely did not know the beautiful brunette he'd encountered twice that day. But he damn sure wanted to.

She didn't appear amused, and Logan curbed his laughter.

"Uh, okay," Andrew started, appearing unconvinced. "Logan, this is my sister, Jeni. She just moved here...what was it, a month ago? She's a social worker for Child Protective Services."

Logan sat a little straighter. She worked for CPS?

"Jeni, this is my friend, Logan Davis," Andrew continued. "He's from Kansas City and is a social media manager for the Chiefs."

Logan flashed his most charming smile and held out his hand. "Nice to meet you, Jeni."

Jeni didn't return the gesture—the smile or the handshake. "The Chiefs? As in, the Kansas City Chiefs, the NFL team? Strike three."

"Huh?" His hand still hovered above the table.

Her unique gold eyes flashed. "You had one more chance with

me, and maybe—*maybe*—we could have been friends. But that's it. You're out."

Andrew bounced his gaze between them and opened his mouth to speak, but Logan let his hand drop to the tabletop and cut him off. "Dare I ask what my first two offenses were?"

Andrew frowned and lifted his beer to his lips just as Jeni offered a scowl eerily similar to her brother's.

"One." She held up a finger. "The loud sex this morning."

Andrew lurched forward and spit his drink out on the table. Logan calmly clapped him on the back without taking his eyes from Jeni's face. Her cheeks flushed, and she pushed her thick-framed glasses higher up on her adorably freckled nose.

"*What* sex?" Andrew ground out between coughs.

"Not sex with me," Jeni clarified, tossing a few napkins in her brother's direction.

Technically, Logan had extended an offer. Probably best not to bring that up.

"My neighbor," Jeni said, as if that would explain everything to Andrew. She turned back to Logan. "Second was the dick move you pulled at the deli this afternoon."

Whoa, were they going so far to call it a dick move? "Hold on—"

"And now," she interrupted. "I find out that you work for the Chiefs. The only thing worse would be if you worked for the devil." She lifted her eyes in thought. "Or the Oakland Raiders."

Still struggling to compose himself, Andrew found the strength to muster up a nod of agreement at the last comment.

Not surprising. "I should have known she'd be a Broncos fan like you," Logan replied easily, elbowing his friend. The way this introduction was going, he needed a drink before it continued. "I think I need that beer." He glanced down at Jeni's empty glass. "Can I buy you another? I can't in good conscience let a beautiful woman be without a drink."

"Pump the brakes with the flirting, man," Andrew said. "That's my sister."

Shit. "Right, sorry," he said. "Habit."

Jeni's face contorted like something smelled bad. "You're obnoxious."

"That opinion would be widely refuted around town," Logan replied, raking his fingers through his hair. This girl needed to loosen up. "That's a no, then?"

"I'll have a Guinness," she said. "It's the least you can do."

Logan grinned and winked at her before sliding out of the booth. "What about you, Andrew? Need another?"

"Seems like that would be a good idea."

"Great." Logan crossed the room to the bar, which stretched along the back wall, processing what just happened. He couldn't believe that woman was Andrew's sister. The entire day considered, Logan would say he'd never met a woman so frustrating.

Or so frustratingly arousing.

And not only was his body sending confusing signals, so was she.

He could have sworn she was checking him out in line at the deli before she demanded he hand over his lunch.

Logan thought of himself as a gentleman and a chivalrous one, at that. His mother taught him well. But that deli made the *best* hummus, and he'd been thinking about it all morning. He'd wavered for a split second to consider a salad and avoid the carbs, but he just couldn't. He wanted that hummus, and she wasn't the only one who got hangry. So when she made her audacious request, he couldn't bring himself to do it.

Andrew spoke so highly of Jeni, and she worked in child welfare, a career Logan couldn't put any higher on a pedestal if he tried. It was a beautiful thing for her to be doing and surely meant she had compassion and kindness somewhere in that nicely shaped body of hers.

He couldn't be sure, though, with her hostile attitude. She'd obviously decided she didn't like him.

All because of sex and hummus.

Oh, and because of his job. His dream job, no less, one he'd never imagined landing at the age of twenty-seven. What kind of woman held a man's job against him anyway? Was he not supposed to eat or pay his mortgage? She didn't want him to pay the taxes that went back into the system and ultimately paid *her* salary at the child welfare office?

The bartender approached. "What can I get you?"

"Two Guinness drafts and a Michelob Ultra, please."

The bartender nodded and moved down the counter. Logan leaned his elbows on the bar to wait.

"Thirsty?" came a feminine voice.

To his left sat a woman with long, black hair and a sultry smile. She was probably ten years older than Logan, but that didn't bother him.

He smiled and angled his body toward her. "Will it disappoint you they're not all for me?"

One dark eyebrow raised. "Michelob Ultra for your girlfriend?"

"No, that's for my friend who worries about his physique more than any woman I know. I don't have a girlfriend."

The woman rotated on the stool so that her body faced him and crossed her long legs. "That's good news."

Well, all right then. He moved closer and held out his hand. "I'm Logan."

This woman didn't hesitate to slip her thin hand into his. "Amber. Nice to meet you."

Logan considered asking if he could buy her next drink, but he didn't want to bail on Andrew. That irritating sister of his, maybe. But nah, better not.

The sound of glasses being set down on the bar pulled his attention away from the woman. He paid for the beers and looked at her again. "I'd love to chat more, but I'd better get back to my friends."

The woman stood and sidled up next to him. She smelled nice, like some sort of fruity perfume. She slid a business card across the wood countertop. "If you want to meet up sometime, give me a call."

Logan smiled and slid the card into his pocket. "I'll do that."

He tucked Andrew's beer bottle against his body with his forearm and grabbed the pint glasses. He carefully made his way back to the table where Andrew and Jeni sat, setting the drinks on the table.

"Jeni was just filling me in on your...interactions today," Andrew said.

Logan sat down. "In vivid color, I'm sure."

Jeni pulled her beer to her side of the table. "Just telling it like it was. I was almost to the part where you took the last vegetarian sandwich and wouldn't give it to me."

Andrew laughed at that. "Did you ask nicely?"

"Yes, did you ask nicely?" Logan echoed.

Jeni scowled.

"How about this?" Logan said. "I'll buy you lunch another day. You name the day and place, and you can order whatever you want. Will that make up for it? Andrew, you can come too."

Andrew regarded his sister with a raised eyebrow and took a swig of his beer.

Jeni seemed to consider that for a moment, taking a long sip of her own beverage. "No, thanks. Looked like you already picked up a date at the bar for this week anyway."

Logan wasn't sure which part of that sentence disarmed him more—her reference to his friendly offer as a 'date' or the fact that she'd noticed him speaking to the woman at the bar.

"Not so fast, I'll take a free lunch," Andrew said.

"Only if Jeni comes," Logan said. "I don't need to woo you,

man. She's the one who doesn't like me, and you know how much I hate that."

Andrew nodded. "It's weirding me out. And also kind of refreshing."

"What is?" Jeni asked.

"The fact that you're a woman and you don't seem to be a fan of Logan. Ladies usually love this guy." Andrew chuckled wryly. "He's a great wingman."

"Gross," Jeni said.

"I'm here for you buddy," Logan said, and Andrew laughed again.

Jeni scrunched her nose. "Seriously, stop talking about picking up women with my brother."

"Fine. So, lunch then?"

"I'll think about it."

Logan shrugged and took a long drink of the smooth, dark beer, eyeing Jeni as she did the same.

Andrew looked at Logan. "You'll have to excuse my sister. We grew up in a small town where we knew everything and everyone. She hasn't had to make new friends in a while, and I think she's forgotten how." Jeni set her glass down and opened her mouth to object, but Andrew kept going. "You're my two favorite people in Kansas City, so I hope you can start over and get along."

"Favorite? Really? Wow, thanks, man," Logan said with a sincere nod of gratitude.

"Of course I'm your favorite," Jeni said. "I'm the only member of our family you can stand to be around for more than ten minutes."

"That sentiment runs both ways," Andrew shot back. "Don't even try and deny it."

Logan waited a moment to make sure this sibling confrontation was complete before he once again held his hand out to Jeni. "He's right. Let's try this again. Fresh start?"

Jeni regarded his hand, and just when he thought she would refuse him a second time, reached up and shook it firmly. "Okay."

The table was silent for a moment before Andrew spoke again. "Before Logan got here, you were about to tell me about something that happened at work this afternoon."

Jeni's face turned downcast for a moment. Then she straightened, and her expression shuttered. "You know. The usual drama —stoned parent, two toddlers roaming their neighborhood alone in a rough part of town. Couldn't find a foster family with beds together, so they had to be separated."

Logan's breath caught in his throat, and the blood drained from his face.

Usual drama.

Stoned parent.

Couldn't find a foster family.

He swallowed thickly while Jeni continued.

"Took some time to get them situated, and that's why I was late."

He watched her closely as she spoke and got the feeling she wasn't as unaffected as she seemed.

"That sucks," Andrew said.

"They were twins," Jeni added. She and Andrew exchanged a look of sympathy and understanding.

Logan sat in silence. As an only child, he didn't understand the bond between siblings, much less twins.

"Poor kids," Andrew said. "I don't know how you do it."

"Someone has to." Jeni took a sip of her beer, once again averting her eyes.

"How long have you been in social work?" Logan asked.

"I finished my Master's in May, but I did a lot of interning and shadowing during school. So, I guess you could say two years."

She was pretty new to the gig then. How long would she last?

Knowing better than to voice that thought, Logan nodded tightly and looked away, lifting his own beer to his lips.

"What exactly do you do for the Chiefs?" Jeni asked.

He was thankful for the change in topic. "Mostly I manage the posts on the team's social media pages, especially on game days during the season. I help analyze which posts bring in the most online traffic and try to figure out why then plan a strategy for the next game day."

"Logan's a social media guru," Andrew put in. "Didn't you do an internship with one of the big ones?"

"Twitter," he said. "I almost stayed in San Francisco for a job there, but—" He almost mentioned his mom and quickly changed direction. "I decided to come back here."

"I don't understand Twitter," Jeni said.

"I like how succinct it is," Logan said. "Short, sweet, and to the point. Each social media outlet has their place though. I hit a different demographic with all of them."

"What got you started with that anyway?" Andrew asked. "The social media stuff, I mean. I don't think you've ever told me."

"I guess I've always been interested in what connects people. Whether it be for a conversation, like Snapchat, a shared goal or interest like Instagram, or even things like friendship or relationships. I started studying communications with a dual major in Advertising and Public Relations and then got that internship. Even though social media and marketing is what I wanted to do, when I moved back to Kansas City the only job I could find was at an ad agency, so I did that for a few years."

"How did you get stuck doing marketing for the second-worst football team in the league then?" Jeni asked.

"You do realize the Chiefs were ranked above the Broncos at the end of last season, right?"

"Irrelevant."

He laughed and glanced at Andrew, who shook his head.

"I wouldn't start with her, man," Andrew warned.

Logan snorted. He could handle her. "Actually, official rankings are the one relevant way to measure a team's talent and success—"

"Just answer the question, Logan," Jeni said.

Logan blinked. Was her haughty attitude irritating or hot? "I work for the Chiefs because I want to, and I jumped at the chance when a position came up a few months ago. They've been my favorite team since I was thirteen, and my dad was their biggest fan."

Her expression softened a little.

She probably wouldn't ask about his dad, but just in case, he kept going before she could. "It was the first thing we really bonded over, and I've followed them religiously ever since. That won't change, so we'll just have to agree to disagree about football."

The semi-gentle look on her face disappeared, and she pursed her lips. "We can disagree, but just so you know, I like to win."

Yeah.

He'd gathered as much.

CHAPTER THREE

Andrew: I'm hungry. How about that free lunch today?

Unknown: It's only 9:15.

Jeni: I assume the third person on this text is Logan.

Unknown: The one and only.

Jeni snorted, the sound immediately lost in the chaotic office, and saved his number into her phone. She clicked over to her Outlook calendar and took stock of her day.

Jeni: I can get away for lunch, just have to be back at 1:30.

Logan: Same.

Andrew: Yessss

Logan suggested a ramen place downtown. Jeni didn't have much experience with Asian cuisine, having grown up in a tiny farm town in Nebraska.

Potato salad and coleslaw? Expert.

Buttermilk biscuits from scratch? You betcha.

Ramen? She only knew of the square kind wrapped in plastic

with a full day's worth of sodium content. But she was all about trying new things.

That had kind of been the whole point of leaving Nebraska in the first place.

The morning went quickly, and at exactly noon, Jeni walked into the restaurant.

Logan waited just inside the door. He wore a pale blue dress shirt with fitted slacks, no tie. Two buttons were open at the neck, revealing a sliver of tanned skin underneath. His wavy blond hair was in perfect disarray, and his blue eyes pierced her like a knife.

A tremor ran through her, and she hated herself for it.

She did *not* like Logan Davis like that.

Yes, she'd agreed to start over with the guy. But that had really just been a show for Andrew. She didn't intend to spend more time with Logan than she had to.

But shit if he wasn't gorgeous.

A tiny, aggravating part of per brain suggested he might be useful in her quest to try new things, and she quickly cancelled the thought.

Nope.

"Hey," he greeted.

"Hi."

"Andrew's not here yet. Should we get a table?"

"Sure."

The restaurant was small, and Logan walked right past the hostess stand like he owned the place. One wall was lined with a long, wood-top counter with several black-shirted chefs just beyond, preparing food for the onlookers. Each barstool at the counter was full, and Logan went the other direction, where several leather booths lined the opposite wall. Muted conversation and the hiss of raw food hitting a hot grill filled the room.

The second they sat down, a man with a wide smile approached the table.

"Logan! Good to see you. You've got a date with you, I see." The man spoke quickly and tossed a wink in Jeni's direction.

Logan's voice was even and smooth. "Sam, this is my friend, Jeni. We've got one more, so if a guy named Andrew comes in, send him back here."

"Sure, you got it." Sam handed Jeni a menu. "I'll let you look, and I'll be back."

Sam hurried off, and Jeni arched an eyebrow. "Bring a lot of dates here?"

"I bring a lot of everyone here." Logan leaned back and crossed his arms. "It's the best."

"Mmhmm." She picked up the menu and realized the server hadn't brought Logan one. "Do you know what you want?"

He nodded. "I get the same thing. Sam knows."

"Oh. Well, what should I get? I've never had fancy ramen before."

"They have an entire section of vegetarian bowls. That's why I suggested we come here." He leaned forward and reached over the top of the menu to point. "Are you vegan?"

He'd considered her dietary preferences when choosing the restaurant? Maybe he really was trying to make up for stealing her hummus. "No."

"I recommend the garlic tofu, add black mushrooms."

That sounded good, but she took her time reading the menu anyway, hoping to find something else on her own. Finally, she closed the menu, set it down, and said grudgingly, "I'll try it."

"Did Andrew say he was going to be late?" Logan asked at the exact moment both of their phones vibrated on the table.

Andrew: Sorry guys, I've got a killer headache and am heading home. Rain check.

Jeni looked up and met Logan's eyes. He frowned, and she

wondered how well he knew her brother. Andrew never got sick, even with something simple as a headache.

Jeni: You okay? Need anything?
Andrew: Just my bed and a dark room. Call you later.
Logan: Take care, man.

"Guess it's just you and me," Logan said unnecessarily.

"We don't have to stay."

"Come on," he said. "I'm not that bad, am I?"

"I don't know. Maybe I should ask the last woman you brought here."

He laughed and slid his phone across the table. "You can call her if you want. I didn't, like, sleep with her and never call again. Despite what you might think, I'm not an asshole."

"If you say so. I'm still undecided."

"I haven't made up my mind about you either, if we're being honest. Good thing we've got an entire lunch hour to talk. Let's call it a friendship date."

"Are we friends?"

"I don't think so. Not yet, at least. I don't think you've ever even smiled at me."

"I've smiled at you."

"Not once. I'm kind of wondering if you know how to move the muscles in your face that way."

Jeni glared at him.

"That expression I'm familiar with, thanks."

She turned her head to the side and closed her eyes. This guy was going to drive her insane. She took a deep breath and returned to face him, revealing her teeth.

Logan choked and swallowed. "What is that?"

Her perpetual frown—perpetual when she was around him at least—returned. "A smile."

"No way. It was...I don't even know. A grimace? A grit? Can

you think of nothing that makes you happy, or does your skepticism of me overshadow everything else?"

Jeni considered that. A lot of things made her happy—Broncos football. A foster child finding a forever home. The sound of a softball hitting the catcher's glove when she threw a strike or three.

Damn, she missed playing and made a mental note to look for a rec league around here.

In the corner of her eye, Logan's countenance changed. She lifted her gaze to his face and found him smiling. White, straight teeth and a dimple filled her vision, with a slight wrinkling of skin near his eyes. Her heart paused in its pumping duties, and she suddenly knew what all those women saw in him.

"Why are you looking at me like that?" Her voice sounded a little breathless.

"You're smiling at me."

She took stock and immediately shut it down. "Was not."

"Was too." His smile widened.

Jeni snorted. "Whatever. One of your eyes is smaller than the other."

"Excuse me?"

"It's like the left one is kind of squinting."

Logan gaped at her, tilting his head a little to the side. Probably trying to hide his weird eye.

Jeni grinned.

"You're smiling again. Are you laughing at me?"

She lifted one shoulder. "It's nice to find something imperfect about your appearance."

"It's nice to…hold on. Are you saying you find me attractive?"

"I might have. Before," she said. "And just for a second. Now I think I'll start calling you Squinty."

He grumbled something under his breath, just as Sam came by and took their orders.

Logan went back to the subject at hand. "Why do you have to make this so hard?"

"Come on, I was just teasing. Isn't that what friends do?"

"I guess. Your brother makes being his friend the easiest thing in the world. So far, I can't say the same for you." He was right, Andrew was one of those guys who could befriend a brick wall.

"Andrew lets people in easily. He's an open book. Just because I don't lay all my cards out there when I first meet someone doesn't mean I don't want to be friends. I just...I don't know. Things have been different, since..." She trailed off. She used to be good at friendship and meeting new people. In high school she'd been energetic and outgoing and could strike up a conversation with anybody. She knew exactly when and why that had changed, but she wasn't going there. "I'm just more reserved than Andrew, I guess."

"Says the girl who marched up to a stranger on the sidewalk and demanded he give her his lunch."

"I can be reserved *and* get hangry. They aren't mutually exclusive. I wanted that hummus."

Logan lifted one corner of his lips and let out a small sound of pleasure that sent a zing straight to her core. "One of the best things I've ever put in my mouth."

"That's what she said."

He threw back his head and laughed, and Jeni found herself smiling for the third time. Maybe she *could* do this. She smoothed a hand down her hair, pulling her long ponytail over one shoulder. He watched her, and for a second, she met his striking blue eyes before looking away.

"What do you think of Kansas City?" Logan asked.

"I like it so far. It's completely different from the town I grew up in, but I lived in Omaha during my Master's program and it feels a lot like that. You're from here, right?"

"Yep."

Jeni waited for him to expand on that.

He didn't. "What made you want to work in child welfare?"

"That's a story."

Logan shrugged. "We've got time, and I want to hear it. From what Andrew's told me about your family, it doesn't seem like it could be from personal experience."

"You're right. I was lucky with the family I was born into. Until my senior year in high school I wanted to be a teacher. But that changed halfway through the year when Andrew and I were in a car accident. I needed surgery so I was in the hospital for a while, and because I was seventeen, I was in the pediatric ward. There was this little six-year-old girl named Ella in the room next to me. I overheard the nurses talking, and based on her injuries, they suspected they were inflicted by her parents."

He shifted in the booth, the leather creaking, and nodded for her to continue.

Jeni had rolled her own wheelchair into Ella's room several times a day to play or watch TV with her and had felt an overwhelming desire to protect her. Along with an even more overwhelming feeling of helplessness. She'd been a kid herself and couldn't do anything for the girl other than befriend her. "Sometimes I could hear her crying through the wall at night. I always had someone from my family with me, but I rarely heard anyone other than nurses in there with her."

Logan was quiet, but she knew he was listening. His face lost some color, and she felt bad for turning the conversation down such a dismal road. But he'd asked how she chose her career path, and this was part of it. She nudged his foot under the table.

"The story is about to get better," she said with a small smile.

He took a deep breath. "Is it?"

Jeni nodded. "The orthopedic surgeon who performed two of my surgeries was also one of Ella's doctors. He and Ella formed a unique bond, and he and his wife were registered foster parents. They fostered her after she was discharged for several months and ended up adopting her." She smiled, thinking of the happy girl Ella was now. Jeni's dad and the surgeon were old college buddies and kept in touch, so Jeni had received updates about her over the years. Ella's happy ending pushed Jeni to keep doing what she did. It was hard, challenging, and didn't pay nearly enough, but it was her calling.

For better or worse.

"That is a happy ending," Logan said, though his voice sounded strained. His eyes were on the table. "But she'll never forget the darkness of the first years of her life."

"I'm sure that's true," Jeni agreed. His reaction made her wonder what darkness lurked in his past. "But her future is brighter because of the intervention of some caring people. That's why I wanted to do the same and make a difference in as many children's lives as possible. Sometimes that just means getting them out of a bad situation temporarily while their parents get their shit together. Other times it means getting ugly to keep them from ever going back where they came from."

"I bet you're effective at the second one."

Her spine stiffened. "Meaning?"

Logan gave her a bland look. "You're intimidating as hell. Surely you know that."

She paused. Was that true? The way he said it, it sounded strangely complimentary. "I don't mean to be. I'm competitive, that's for sure. Assertive, maybe, and straightforward."

"Intimidating," he repeated.

Her mind conjured up an image of two people facing off for dominance. "I don't see you running in the other direction."

"I like a challenge."

What the hell did that mean? Before she could ask, Sam walked up and delivered two steaming bowls of noodles. The scent of salty broth was immediately comforting, as if her mother had just delivered chicken soup to her bedside when she had a cold. Noodles were arranged with colorful vegetables and a soft-boiled egg on top, creating one of the most visually appealing meals she'd ever seen.

"Wow," she said. "Thank you, this looks delicious."

"Enjoy," Sam said with a grin and departed.

Jeni skipped the chopsticks and picked up a fork, winding several noodles around the tines.

"Tastes delicious too," she said after the first bite.

"I'm glad you like it."

They ate in silence for a moment, and Jeni wracked her brain to think of something to say. She didn't usually mind silence, but for some reason with Logan, it felt awkward. "I wanted to tell you that, terrible employer aside, I think your job sounds cool. When you put it like you did—wanting to connect people over shared interests like the camaraderie of football—it puts it in a new perspective."

"It's fun, which is more than I can say for the advertising job I had before. My accounts were a funeral home and an automotive group that owned several car dealerships. Football's so much better."

"Do you have access to game tickets?"

"Sometimes. I bet I could swing it when the Broncos are here in a few weeks, if you wanted to go."

Her eyes widened. "Really?"

"Sure."

Jeni met his blue eyes and irritation flared. She pursed her lips. "I hate it when Andrew's right."

Logan cocked his head sideways at the change in topic. "What do you mean?"

"I had a terrible first impression of you and judged you based on that first day. But Andrew insists you're a good guy and everyone who meets you likes you. I didn't believe him at first."

A slow smile spread across his face. "And now you like me?"

"It's under consideration." She switched to a spoon to ladle some of the broth. "Ask me again when you hand me those Broncos tickets."

He laughed. "Well, I like you. Even if you are a little crazy."

Jeni looked down and smiled, a little surprised at how much she enjoyed that. "Crazy but likeable? I'll take it."

CHAPTER FOUR

Logan only saw Jeni twice over the next month, but he thought about her more than he cared to admit.

She met him and Andrew for lunch once and joined them at McNellie's one Friday night, which might have bothered him if it were anyone else. It wasn't as easy to meet women when you already had one at the table. But not only was Jeni more like one of the guys, Logan also found he wasn't as interested in working the room that night.

Jeni was an enigma. There were times she came across as fun and witty and others when she seemed closed off and introverted. She was still prickly and sometimes a little defensive, and he wasn't quite sure where they stood on the friendship scale. But he sensed there was more to her than she let show and wanted to dig deeper. He was drawn to her and didn't know why.

Maybe because she was fucking hot. Thick, soft-looking brown hair that fell to the middle of her back, those cute freckles canvassing her nose and cheeks that somehow made her seem softer than she probably wanted to come across, and a body meant to drive men to the brink of insanity.

But he wasn't supposed to notice any of those things, her being Andrew's sister and all.

Andrew was a good friend—maybe the best guy friend Logan had ever had. Friendship with guys had never been something Logan was very good at. Sure, he knew how to shoot the shit and talk about sports, cars, and women. He could play a round of pool and throw back a few beers and tell jokes with the best of them. But real friendship, where you could actually talk about things? Be there for each other? That wasn't something he'd had much of growing up.

Come to think of it, it wasn't limited to men—he didn't have women friends either. He could flirt, woo, and appreciate spending time with them in and outside of the bedroom, but moving on to complex layers of intimacy wasn't easy for him.

Logan wanted deeper relationships but hadn't quite figured out how to get there.

He wasn't sure why it clicked with Andrew, but it did, and their friendship felt effortless from the start. Maybe because Logan had met Andrew when he was older and away from all that shit he'd dealt with as a kid.

He'd expected to like Andrew's twin just as much as he liked Andrew, maybe even more simply because she was a woman.

That hadn't exactly worked out like he thought it would. But he was getting there.

Today was Sunday, and the Chiefs were on a bye week, freeing up Logan to watch football as nothing more than a spectator. He'd still have to keep an eye on social media activity during the games, but things would be more relaxed than usual. Before he'd landed the Chiefs job, he'd spent most Sundays watching football with Andrew, and it felt like old times. Except for one thing.

Logan sat in the passenger seat of Andrew's truck, a little confused as to how they'd gotten here. "Remind me why we're watching the game at Jeni's?" He didn't mind, per se. He just hadn't expected it. They'd always watched games at Andrew's.

"Jeni's TV is bigger than mine. She doesn't mess around on game day, and since I told her we were coming, she'll have all sorts of food made. It used to be an all-day affair at our house growing up. She'll probably have more beer options too."

Logan had noticed that the evening he met her. She'd ordered a Guinness, and he'd had the strangest urge to leap across the table and kiss her right then and there. Most of the women he had drinks with preferred cocktails, fruity wines, or light beer. Jeni's taste for a good, strong stout was apparently a real turn on.

Who knew?

Andrew shot him the side-eye. "We don't have to go to her house if you don't want to."

Logan sort of wished Jeni didn't live next door to Cassidy, because she hadn't spoken to him since he'd texted her after spending the night. Even more, because now he thought of that evening as the night before he met Jeni.

That was weird, right?

"It's fine. I don't care where we go. I bet she'll be laughing with you and insulting me in under fifteen minutes."

He'd said it as a joke, but Andrew grimaced. "I feel like I should apologize for her. She hasn't been very nice to you."

Logan shrugged. "I've had worse."

It had been a while since he'd met a woman that got him worked up like Jeni usually did, it was true. Women typically came at him with flirtatious banter and sexy smiles rather than glares and snarky comments.

But he figured he could handle one feisty Jeni, no problem. Oddly enough, he kind of liked it.

"Still," Andrew said, "like I told her, I'm disappointed you two don't get along all that well. I really thought we'd all be good friends. You and I get along great, and she and I are so similar. I don't get what the rub is between you two."

"We're cool," Logan said. "Really. I don't mind being around her, and she can tolerate me. But I'd have to disagree—she's not like you at all."

"What do you mean?"

"She's mean, for one," Logan said with a half grin. "Presumptuous and opinionated. Kind of rude. Loud and excitable but also a little uptight. And unapologetic about all of the above." Andrew's eyes narrowed the tiniest bit, and Logan realized he might be offering a little too much information. Only someone who'd thought about Jeni a lot would have a list of qualities locked and loaded. "None of those are words I'd use to describe you, my friend."

Andrew sighed. "She's had a rough few years. Don't get me wrong—she's always been strong-willed and stubborn. But the rudeness and negativity aren't part of the Jeni I know. I think her divorce really messed her up. She's been pretty closed off since then, and I worry it will affect her making new friends here. She hardly knows anyone, and my first attempt to introduce her didn't exactly go well."

Logan did a terrible job hiding his shock. "She was married?"

Why was he so surprised? He barely knew her.

And she definitely barely knew him. Few people did.

"Yeah." Andrew pulled into the driveway of her small, craftsman-style house. "The guy was a real dick."

Logan stayed quiet as they got out and walked to the door. His eyes darted to Cassidy's house, and he was relieved to see her car wasn't there. Running into her now would be awkward as hell. Andrew knocked, and Jeni opened the door. She planted her feet in the doorway, blocking entrance.

Her brown eyes slid to her brother. "Did you ask him?"

Logan took in the woman standing before him, his eyebrows raised. She wore tight jeans that hugged her sculpted legs like a second skin and a loose-fitting Bronco's jersey that had the opposite effect on the top half of her body.

No problem. His imagination filled in the gaps.

Her hair was piled on top of her head, and he wondered how the hell she got all of it up there. Her thick-framed glasses perched on her nose, and she gently gripped the right side with her thumb and forefinger to scoot them closer to her face.

Andrew tilted his face up in exasperation. "No. You're ridiculous."

"Is there a password?" Logan asked.

Jeni looked at him. "The Chiefs aren't playing. You aren't rooting for the Raiders, are you? If so, you're not welcome here."

He almost said yes just to get a rise out of her. "Probably not."

She narrowed her eyes. "Okay. Come on in, Squinty."

Logan grunted and followed Andrew inside. This was going to be an interesting afternoon.

"Squinty?" Andrew asked.

"Don't ask," Logan muttered.

Jeni's house was small, similar to his own. The wood floors creaked under his weight as they passed through the living room, which was like a cross between a man cave and a typical feminine living space.

Man cave: massive flat screen dominating the far wall.

Feminine touch: floral curtains hanging at the windows.

Man cave: framed John Elway jersey.

Feminine touch: coasters and candles on the end table.

Man cave: overstuffed leather couch.

Feminine touch: colorful throw pillows on said couch.

Logan supposed the room was on par with the woman herself —a contradiction. Putting Jeni in the social construct of "typical woman" would be akin to attempting to force a square peg in a round hole.

The space was a little messy too. Not dirty or unclean, just a little disorganized. Several pairs of shoes dotted the front room, books cluttered the coffee table, and a discarded sweatshirt was balled up in the middle of the couch. Probably how he'd find it if he dropped by unannounced, as if she was comfortable enough with her brother and his annoying friend not to impress them with tidiness.

Jeni led them to the kitchen, making a sweeping gesture with her hand. "Help yourselves. Beer and sodas in the fridge, water from the sink if you want it. I've got some layer dip that's almost ready, but it'll be best if we let it chill for another thirty minutes. Chips are in that cabinet." She pointed to a slow-cooker on the counter, and the aroma of barbecue and spice was so delicious Logan could almost taste it. "Pulled pork is ready. Buns are there if you want to make a sandwich. And in the cookie jar are some chocolate chip cookies I made yesterday." She looked at the clock on the wall. "Game's about to start," she said, and walked out.

Logan cut his eyes to Andrew, who had a satisfied grin on his face.

"See?" Andrew said.

"Impressive," Logan admitted. Maybe she wanted to impress them a little bit. Especially with the pulled pork—he wasn't likely to forget she was a vegetarian. She must have made that just for them.

The kitchen walls were bright yellow, a color he'd always associated with sunshine and optimism. Not what he would have expected to find in Jeni's house. But the natural wood shelving and open-concept cabinetry seemed strangely perfect for her, displaying mismatched dishes and an array of eclectic drinkware.

Andrew pulled the layer dip from the fridge—apparently he didn't want to wait—and grabbed two plates from a cabinet. He handed one to Logan. "Have at it, man."

Both men loaded their plates with food, selected beers from the fridge, and settled themselves in front of the television, the sweatshirt still untouched and crumpled between them. Jeni was already curled in an armchair nearby, her eyes glued to the screen.

The Broncos game was first on the agenda, followed by Green

Bay. Even though the Chiefs were Logan's favorite—had been since he was thirteen—he and Andrew were in a fantasy football league with some other guys, and he had several players to keep an eye on today.

Jeni remained quiet during the first few plays of the game, and Logan wondered how much she really knew about football. He hadn't met too many women who—

"False start!" she yelled, two seconds before the flag was thrown.

Andrew leaned in Logan's direction. "Just a head's up—Jeni gets a little fired up."

"Do not," she said.

Andrew snorted.

"You're one to talk," she said. "You're the one who broke the coffee table during the 2014 Super Bowl."

Andrew grimaced.

"What about you?" Jeni turned her amber-colored eyes on Logan. "Are you one of those people who just sits there quietly during a game? The Chiefs suck, so I wouldn't blame you if you did."

Logan kept a carefully neutral expression, refusing to be needled. "I get excited when the time is right."

Her eyes remained on his for a moment, like she was deciding whether it was worth it to say anything else.

The three chatted a little during the first quarter, and Logan maintained active surveillance of Twitter and Facebook activity. When it was almost half-time Jeni, mid-sentence, leapt off the couch and stabbed a finger at the television. "Pass interference!"

Logan shook his head. "Incidental contact."

She glared at him. "Bullshit. Jones grabbed his arm."

"He was competing for the ball."

"By ripping Cortado's shoulder out of socket?"

Logan regarded her for a moment. Her cheeks were flushed,

eyes wild, and threads of hair had begun to fall loose. "Remind me never to play a board game with you."

She waved a hand of dismissal and sat back down, crossing her arms in front of her chest. "Seems like you'd just be on your phone the whole time anyway."

Logan stiffened. "It's my *job.*"

"Whatever."

Two minutes later she was up again. "Face mask!"

Logan turned wide eyes on Andrew.

"Told you," Andrew said around a mouthful of food.

By the third quarter, her voice was getting hoarse. The Broncos were down by seven, and the quarterback was moving the ball all wrong.

"He's rushing it," Logan said.

"He's trying to make a play," Jeni defended.

"Fast doesn't always get the job done."

"That's what she said," she said without inflection.

Andrew shook his head, and Logan burst out laughing. Her attention was back on the game, like what she'd said had been completely second nature. She hadn't even thought about it.

Logan's laugh quieted, but a small smile remained on his lips.

Who was this woman?

Logan was relieved when Andrew stood and said he was ready to head out just after the evening game started. They'd been at Jeni's house most of the day, and Logan didn't know how much more of her he could take.

If he could just sit and look at her, that would be one thing. But listening to her alternate between yelling at the television, trash-talking the Chiefs, and arguing with anything that came out of his mouth, well, he wasn't sure it was worth the view.

"Seriously?" Jeni looked incredulous. "It's only halfway through the first quarter."

"I know," Andrew said.

She must have heard something in his tone that Logan didn't pick up on because concern flashed across her face. "You okay?"

Andrew wrinkled his nose a little. "I don't feel that great actually. Maybe I had one beer too many, I'm not sure."

Jeni stood up and moved to stand in front of her brother, peering into his face, like she'd be able to visually inspect him for illness or injury. "Why don't you just stay here tonight?"

Andrew shook his head. "I drove Logan here."

"Don't worry about me, man," Logan said. "I'll get an Uber."

"No, I'm good. I'm just really tired."

"You've been working too much," she accused softly.

"So have you," Andrew returned.

She rolled her eyes. "I'm not so tired I'm ready to go to bed at eight o'clock."

Andrew shrugged and glanced at Logan. "Okay if we head out?"

Logan rose from the couch. "Sure. But really, it's fine if you just want to crash here. It's not a problem for me to get a ride."

"Yeah, Logan could just go next door," Jeni put in. "Sleep in my neighbor's bed tonight."

Andrew's eyes went wide, and he grabbed his plate and empty beer bottles before escaping to the kitchen.

Coward.

Logan considered defending Cassidy, but a comment with innuendo would probably bother Jeni more. "That's not a bad idea actually. But only if you come too. Cassidy wouldn't mind."

"Cassidy?"

"You don't even know her name?"

Jeni shook her head. "We haven't officially met. You sure you'd be welcome? I haven't seen you back there since that day I met you, but there have been others—"

42

The surprise Logan felt at that must have shown on his face because she stopped short.

"Didn't know that part, did you?" she asked.

Logan blinked. He hadn't thought about it, really. He and Cassidy had worked together at the same advertising agency before he'd quit for the Chiefs job, and at the time they hadn't been able to act on mutual attraction. They lost contact when he left, but he ran into her at a bar one night, and they ended up talking. He was hoping for more than a one-night thing, but she'd made it clear the next morning she wasn't looking for anything serious. He hadn't considered her reason was that she liked a variety of men, rather than just one.

He didn't have room to talk since he wasn't exactly known for long-term relationships himself. He wanted one someday though. Maybe that was the difference.

"No," he finally admitted. "But it's not my business. It's her life."

Jeni made a murmur of agreement, and the low sound did something funny to his stomach. "She's a lively one, that's for sure."

Logan tilted his head to the side. "Are you jealous?"

"Jealous?" Her pitch rose. "Please."

"Sorry to interrupt this catfight," Andrew said as he walked back into the room. "Can we go now?"

Logan's shoulders relaxed when he turned to his friend. He hadn't realized how tense he got when talking to Jeni. "Shit, sorry, man. Let's go."

Jeni focused her attention on her brother. "Can I box up the pulled pork for you before you go? Do you need anything else? I've got Tylenol. Water for the road?"

"Nah but thanks."

"You seemed fine earlier," she said, a question in her tone.

Did she feel guilty she hadn't noticed? Logan's attention had mainly been on her that afternoon, instead of football or Andrew.

Something about her provoked him more than he was used to.

"I was. It came on really fast. Something similar happened last week, and I woke up the next morning feeling normal. I think I just need to get some rest."

Her eyebrows pinched together. "Text me when you get home, okay?"

Andrew nodded, and they left. He was quiet on the drive home, and Logan kept side-eying him. His friend didn't look well. Logan didn't say anything, but by the time Andrew pulled into his driveway, Logan felt a little uneasy leaving him alone.

"You don't look good," Logan said.

"I feel like shit."

"Are you sure you're good to drive home?"

"Yeah. I'm fine."

"Just call if you need something, okay?" Logan wasn't convinced, but Andrew was a grown man and could make that call for himself. "Thanks for inviting me today." He held out his hand, and Andrew shook it. Andrew's palm was sweaty, warm, and unsteady when he pulled back.

Something wasn't right. "Dude, you sure you're okay?"

"I don't...I don't know."

Logan paused for a moment then got out of the car and went to Andrew's side. He opened the door. "Trade spots with me."

Andrew nodded weakly and slid out, shuffling to the passenger side. He leaned his head back against the seat, not saying a word as Logan drove him to the emergency room.

CHAPTER FIVE

An hour after the guys left, Andrew called. Jeni picked up on the first ring.

"I thought I told you to text me when you got home! It's been—"

"Jeni, it's Logan."

"Logan? Why are you calling me? Is Andrew all right?"

"He's okay, but I brought him to the ER—"

"Which one?"

"Saint John's."

"Room?"

"Fifteen."

"I'm on my way."

She'd never moved so fast in her life and walked into the hospital sixteen minutes later. She burst into the room and rushed to her brother's bedside. "Andrew?"

An IV was in his arm, and a large bag of clear fluid hung on a pole beside him. His face was pale, and he kept his head against the pillow as he spoke. "I got lightheaded when we got to Logan's house and wasn't sure I could drive. He thought I should come here. So far everything has been negative, like flu and strep. There are a few more test results we're waiting on."

She wanted to be reassuring. "I'm sure it's just a virus or something. I feel terrible I didn't notice you weren't feeling well."

"He seems a little better since they gave him medication and started the fluids," Logan put in.

Her eyes darted to him for the first time. He sat in a chair against the wall, hands in his lap and eyes worried.

"Thank you for bringing him."

Logan nodded.

"You don't have to stay," she said. "I won't leave."

"I want to," Logan said then looked at Andrew and added, "If that's okay."

"Sure." Andrew closed his eyes.

Relief filled her. She didn't mind being here alone with her brother, but it was nice to have someone else with her. She couldn't put her finger on it, but she just had a bad feeling. Something seemed off.

In that moment, an older man in a white coat came into the room. His face was serious, and he slid the glass door closed behind him. "Andrew, I have the results of your lab work. There are a few things that concern me, and I'd like to admit you to run some additional tests."

Jeni's hand went to the blanket-covered mattress for support, and out of the corner of her eye, she noticed Logan move forward in his seat.

Andrew swallowed. "Okay, but what do you mean? What was concerning?"

"Your white blood cells are abnormally high, and your red blood cells are very low. I'm surprised you were able to walk in here on your own."

"I had help," Andrew admitted, glancing at Logan.

"What could that mean?" Jeni asked the doctor.

"There are a lot of possibilities. It still could be an infection, a virus like mono. The lymph nodes in your neck are enlarged, so that's high on my list of what could be going on."

"I had mono in college," Andrew said. "Can you get that more than once?"

"It's possible. It's rare, but when it does resurface, it's usually pretty debilitating."

That could explain it. Jeni was glad to have a possible answer.

"I want to be honest with you that it could also be something more serious," the doctor continued. "Some of your white blood cells were atypical, or unusual in appearance. Along with your recent history of night sweats and fevers, I want to biopsy one of the lymph nodes and perform a bone marrow biopsy to rule out lymphoma or other blood disorder."

Jeni's stomach dropped, and for a second, she thought she might vomit.

Lymphoma? Andrew might have cancer?

Both Andrew's and Logan's faces had paled. Jeni probably looked the same. They were three ghosts in an emergency room.

"I'm sorry I couldn't give you better news or more definitive news. We'll know more in a day or two." The doctor pursed his lips and tipped his head at Andrew. "Someone will be by shortly to transfer you to a room, and another physician will take over. They'll give you more information about each procedure before they do anything, all right?"

"Um. Okay, thank you." Andrew's voice shook slightly.

Things moved pretty quickly after that, as the nurse came in immediately after the doctor left. They rolled Andrew to a room on the sixth floor, and a resident came in to introduce himself and explain the bone marrow biopsy. Evidently it would be done right there in the room and was a relatively simple procedure to draw tissue from the bone in Andrew's pelvis.

Jeni and Logan were asked to leave during the procedure, and they walked down the hall to the empty waiting area, Logan a few strides behind her. He crossed the empty room to a row of chairs against the wall and sat with his elbows propped on his knees, his head in his hands.

Jeni absently filled a cup of water. She walked to where Logan sat and stood next to him, downing the contents before setting the empty cup on a side table. Her legs felt wobbly, and her eyes burned with unshed tears. Her chin began to tremble, and she knew they wouldn't be contained for long.

Logan stood and opened his arms to her.

She immediately turned away, not wanting him to see her cry. She inhaled a shaky breath and exhaled, the whoosh of air coupled with a soft sound of anguish. Her arm dropped to her side, and she sniffed, hot tears streaming down her cheeks.

A hand gently brushed hers, the touch light and tentative.

Jeni relaxed a little and closed her fingers around his, taking some comfort in his gesture. Her initial withdrawal had been more reflex than a true desire to be alone. Maybe he sensed that.

She kept her hand in his but didn't turn around and face him, and they stood there for several moments. She took a deep breath, and the clean scent of him surrounded her. For this brief moment, they put aside their disagreements and sarcastic banter.

Jeni had no idea what would happen next, whether they'd receive news that it was nothing serious or if their lives were about to change forever. But she did know one thing, and it surprised the hell out of her.

She was glad Logan was here.

He squeezed her hand and let go, and she looked back to find him lowering himself back into the chair. His blue eyes met hers, soft and sympathetic.

Sympathy wasn't something she typically appreciated. She'd experienced her fair share of medical issues after the car accident, and people's *I'm sorrys* and *get better soons* had become redundant and hollow.

Words didn't change anything. Words couldn't make her heal faster or return what she'd lost.

Her scholarship.

Her independence, even if that loss had been temporary. It had been long enough.

The life she'd always envisioned, with a man who loved her and a house full of children.

All of that had changed in an instant, and the only thing she could do was pivot and move forward in another direction. Set new goals and forge a new path, even if it was different than she'd ever imagined. It was easier said than done, and few people truly understood the impact that accident had had on her.

Strangely, though, what Logan offered her in this moment didn't feel like pity. It was reassuring. And soothing. Something in his eyes told her he'd been here before and his sympathy was from a place of understanding and shared experience.

This wasn't the first time she'd had that feeling, that there was more to him than he let people see.

What kinds of things did he keep hidden?

She sat beside him, resisting the urge to lay her head on his shoulder. She was suddenly exhausted, even though a quick glance at the wall told her it was barely eleven o'clock.

"Tell me something." She kept her eyes on her feet and the old tennis shoes she'd slipped on in such a hurry. She hadn't even put on socks.

He turned his head to look at her. "Like what?"

"Anything. Just talk to me. Keep my mind from going down the dark path it keeps trying to sprint toward."

"It might be nothing," he pointed out. "A virus that just needs to run its course."

His voice lacked conviction, but she didn't object to his attempt to keep things positive.

"I know." She sighed. "Still, I'm not a patient person, and I hate the waiting. I'm asking you to distract me."

He didn't say anything for a few seconds, and when she

glanced over at him expectantly, a wry grin passed his lips. "I'm thinking."

"Think faster," she said, the familiar spark of ire she often had around Logan a welcome feeling.

He chuckled. "Do you know how I met your brother?"

"No." Andrew had talked about his friend Logan for a couple of years, and she'd just assumed they met in college. "Wasn't it at KU?"

Logan shook his head. "We were there at the same time but didn't know each other. It was actually his first year of law school. One Sunday, I was watching football in my condo and heard the guy who'd just moved in next door yelling at the television every time something happened in the game. I realized he was watching the same thing, and I figured it was as good a time as any to meet my new neighbor. I went over to invite him to watch the game, but when I saw his TV was three times the size of mine, I offered to trade a few beers to watch it on his screen."

Jeni grinned. "Football and beer. The ultimate bromance meet-cute."

"It was sort of ours too, you know. You and I drank beer and talked sports the first day we met."

She snorted. "Amongst other things."

He cocked an eyebrow and just smiled, a sort of secretive expression on his face. "Anyway, it became a regular thing for Andrew and me to watch football together. We did that for almost two years, even when I bought a house and moved."

"You already bought a house?" She'd probably be renting for at least another five or ten years before she had enough money for a down payment. "Aren't you my age?"

"I'm twenty-seven," he said.

"Impressive," she said and meant it.

His gaze drifted away, and he shrugged. "I'm not saying it's paid off already. But it was important to me to put down permanent roots and have a stable place to live. A home that's mine."

Jeni could understand that, but she didn't quite feel the same. She liked Kansas City so far, but moving here had been more about leaving Nebraska than finding a place to settle down. The ability to pick up and move if she needed to, or even if she just wanted to, was almost as important. She wanted space of her own but figured she could find it anywhere and relished the freedom to make that call for herself.

"So, where'd you learn to cook?" Logan asked. "The food tonight was awesome."

Tonight? Had it really just been a few hours ago that they were in her living room, eating and watching the games? It felt like days ago.

"My mom," she said. "She's like the Pioneer Woman. Hangs out in the kitchen and makes these big meals while my dad works the farm. I didn't pay much attention when I was younger, but as I got older, I started helping out and trying to learn a few things." After the accident, she'd nearly gone crazy being stuck at her parent's house and had been desperate for things to keep her busy. Helping with meals had been one way to escape.

Her mind immediately shifted to those challenging years and how, if that had been her only escape, maybe things would have turned out differently.

She could have finished her degree earlier and been further along in her career. Maybe she wouldn't have such a bad taste in her mouth when it came to men and relationships. Perhaps she'd be a little more open-minded and less closed off.

It hadn't happened that way though. She'd allowed someone—her ex-husband—to lure her in another direction, and it had felt like the right decision at the time. She'd eventually seen the error of her ways but not until she'd wasted several years of her life.

But if there was one thing she'd learned from the past, it was to never make the same mistake again. Repeating that decision was something she was determined not to do.

No matter what.

CHAPTER SIX

Jeni had gone somewhere in her head, and Logan took the opportunity to study her. Her hair was still pulled high atop her head, and he marveled at how soft it looked. In a move that was quickly becoming familiar, she reached up to readjust her glasses. She had on the same Broncos jersey as earlier, but instead of jeans, she now wore black yoga pants.

Had she been changing for bed when he called her? Did she sleep in a T-shirt or maybe something that revealed a little more skin? Maybe she didn't wear anyth—

Whoa. He slammed the brakes on that train of thought.

He cleared his throat and shifted in his chair.

"Anyway." She brought his attention back to the present conversation. "I enjoy cooking, but it feels like a waste when it's just me. That's why I go all out when I know someone else is coming over, like today."

"I, for one, am glad. You can cook for me anytime." He loved his mom more than anything, but she was a terrible cook. A meal from her was almost guaranteed to be takeout or something from a box. He'd never complained though—she did the best she could, and he never went hungry.

Jeni arched an eyebrow and looked at him, a question in her gaze.

He met her gaze head on. "I mean it. Against my better judgment, I find I enjoy your company. Most of the time. We should hang out more."

She narrowed her eyes.

He laughed. "What? Why do you look so skeptical?"

"I'm not the easiest person to get along with. I know that." She frowned a little, a sort of confusion clouding her features. "I'm just trying to figure out what you're after."

"Friendship? Laughter? Witty banter?" He nudged her elbow with his. "Arguing can be fun when it's done right."

Her features relaxed, and a small smile tipped her lips. Logan's stomach clenched, and he curled his fingers into a fist. Damn, he was attracted to her. Every time she smiled—which wasn't often —that attraction pushed front and center in his brain.

And elsewhere.

"That's true," she said quietly. "Maybe you get me, Logan Davis. There aren't many people out there who do."

That thought was strangely satisfying, and a warmth settled beneath his ribs. He relaxed his shoulders a little, and his upper arm rested against hers. She didn't move away. In fact, it almost felt as if she leaned a little closer.

"Miss Bishop?" A nurse peered into the waiting room. "They're all finished with the biopsy. You can come back to the room now if you'd like."

Jeni was on her feet immediately. "Thank you."

Logan stood and followed her to Andrew's room. Andrew was sitting up in the bed, looking exactly the same as when they left.

Jeni went straight to the bedside. "Are you okay? How did it go?"

"Fine. They stuck a big ass needle in my back but numbed me up first." Andrew regarded Logan, who hovered in the doorway.

"Don't feel like you have to stay, man." He tossed a glance at his sister. "You too. We won't know anything tonight."

Jeni shook her head and sat down on the couch, making a show of getting comfortable.

The couch was the only seating in the room, and even though Andrew was a close friend, Logan didn't want to impose. "Yeah, I'll get going." He ran a hand through his hair. "Okay if I come back tomorrow?"

"Sure," Andrew said. "You can bring me a smoothie from Whole Foods."

Logan grinned. "That, I can do." He turned to Jeni. "Let me know if you need anything too."

"I will." She met his gaze, her expression soft and appreciative. A far cry from the way she'd greeted him on her doorstep that morning.

Oddly, he found he liked both sides of her.

Jeni Bishop was a puzzle, one he definitely wanted to figure out.

Logan had trouble sleeping that night. When a text message lit up his phone at one a.m., he realized he wasn't the only one.

Jeni: You up?
Logan: Yeah. Why are you?
Jeni: It's impossible to sleep in a hospital room. The machines, the nurses, the lights. My thoughts.
Logan: Same on the thoughts. Andrew asleep?
Jeni: He's out cold.
Logan: Good. He probably needs the rest.
Logan: Are you okay?

He considered asking if she wanted him to come back up

there and keep her company, but that might be taking things a little too far.

Jeni: Yeah. My mind is wandering and I thought you could distract me again.
Logan: I'll never deny a woman asking me to distract her at 1am.

When she didn't respond after a few minutes, he sent a follow-up message.

Logan: Sorry. That was supposed to make you smile.
Jeni: It did. I was trying to come up with a snarky reply, but I'm not in top form tonight.
Logan: I admire your sass, but let's just keep it simple tonight.
Logan: If you could be an animal, what would you be?
Jeni: That's random.
Logan: You don't get to dictate how I distract you, even though I'm sure you want to.
Jeni: So bad.

He laughed in the darkness of his bedroom.

Logan: I was asked that in an interview once. So?
Jeni: I'll say a horse.
Logan: Why?
Jeni: I've always loved horses. We had several on the farm growing up. They're graceful but powerful. Intelligent. They have speed and endurance and are loyal companions.

He could see several of those characteristics in her. Graceful, powerful, intelligent. He might add a few of his own—beautiful, sophisticated, free.

And stubborn.

Logan: Good answer. You got the job.
Jeni: What did you say?
Logan: Dolphin. Might sound weird but made sense for the job to name an animal that's known for communication skills. I also like that they seem to want to enjoy life and have fun too.
Jeni: I like that. I could use more fun in my life.
Logan: Why do you say that?
Jeni: It's been a while since I've let myself relax and have fun. School and before that…other things.
Jeni: I'm just so used to being focused on what needs to be done, I haven't looked up in a while.
Logan: I can help with that.
Jeni: Propositioning me again?
Logan: No but only because you're my best friend's sister. If I didn't have that hanging over my head, I can't promise I wouldn't go there.
Jeni: I'm gonna choose to take that as a compliment.
Logan: Good.
Jeni: I'm also gonna choose not to tell Andrew you said that.

He grinned.

Logan: Also good.
Logan: I just meant I know fun stuff to do around Kansas City. We could go to the Blue Room and listen to jazz music. Drink beer at the Power & Light district. Ride around on the street cars and people watch. Tailgate at a Chiefs game.
Jeni: Two things. One: you seem to think you'll be coming

along in my quest for fun. Two: you had me until the tailgating.

Logan: One: my ideas=I'm coming. Two: you don't know tailgating unless you've done it in the Arrowhead parking lot with 75,000 people grilling the world's best BBQ.

Jeni: Are you saying their pulled pork is better than mine?

Logan: I plead the fifth.

Jeni: Wise. We've already discussed my competitive streak.

Logan: Yeah, let's talk about that. Where'd that come from?

Jeni: Obvious ploy to change the subject, but I'll let it slide.

Jeni: I think it started with sports? My family is serious about football. I started playing softball and I was good at it. It felt good to win. Even though I don't play much anymore, it sort of bleeds into every part of my life.

Logan: Ambition's a good thing. Many people don't have enough of it.

Jeni: What's your thing?

Logan: What do you mean?

Jeni: If I'm competitive, what are you?

Logan dropped his head back against the headboard, thinking. How *would* he describe himself? He strived to be honorable. Generous. Industrious. But he was a work in progress and wasn't confident he always lived up to them. So, he went with something simple.

Logan: I'd say adaptable.

Jeni: Hmm. Explain.

Logan: Damn, you're bossy.

Jeni: Fine. Explain, please.

He grinned at his phone. Again. He tried to answer truthfully without inviting more questions.

Logan: I moved around a lot as a kid. I guess I sorta got used to figuring things out no matter where I was or what situation I was in. I'm pretty good at thinking on my feet and making thing work.

Jeni: Your boss must love you.

Logan: Everyone loves me.

Jeni: Maybe confident should have been your word.

Logan: Adored?

Jeni: Tipping the needle toward arrogant.

Logan: Treasured?

Jeni: Definitely arrogant.

Logan: Okay, okay. Almost everyone loves me. Everyone except Jeni Bishop.

Jeni: I'm a hard sell, it's true.

Logan: I'll change your mind eventually.

Jeni: You're welcome to try.

Logan cocked his head and lifted his eyes to the dark room beyond. He could almost hear the challenge in her message. *You're welcome to try.*

It was late, and he was spent, emotionally and physically, which probably explained the thought that ran through his head in that moment. Thankfully, he had the restraint not to say it to her, but that didn't stop him from thinking it.

Watch out, Jeni Bishop. I just might.

CHAPTER SEVEN

H odgkin *Lymphoma.*
Hodgkin fucking Lymphoma.

On Sunday, Jeni had never even heard of it. By Tuesday, she was practically an expert.

Often occurs in patients in their twenties. Has been linked with the Epstein-Barr virus that causes mono. Common symptoms are anemia, cyclic fevers, drenching night sweats. Treated with chemo and radiation. Typically has a good prognosis.

That last part she clung to as if her life depended on it.

Andrew needed one more procedure called a PET scan that would hopefully confirm the doctor's suspicion that his disease wasn't extensive.

"When's Mom getting here?" Andrew asked for the fifth time.

Jeni checked her phone. "She said they're just passing St. Joseph. They're an hour out." She sat in a chair beside Andrew's bed, her sock-covered feet propped on the mattress.

Andrew scrubbed a hand down his face. "All of them?"

"Do you even need to ask?"

"I keep hoping one of them bailed. Maybe Valerie didn't want to leave the kids?"

"Her in-laws are helping while she's gone."

"Rhonda?"

"Rhonda's the least of our problems, and you know it."

Andrew made a noise that kind of sounded like a growl or exasperated grunt of some sort.

"Mom also said the Suburban is giving them some trouble. Maybe we'll get lucky and it will break down."

"Unlikely."

Jeni dropped her head back. "Aw man, I'm gonna have to put them up at my house, aren't I?"

"Family doesn't stay in a hotel," Andrew said, mimicking their mother's voice perfectly.

She groaned. Even if Andrew wasn't sick, she was the only one with an extra bedroom.

The door to Andrew's room opened, and a nurse entered. Her cheeks were flushed, and she had a ridiculous smile on her face, like she'd just heard something outrageously funny. From her seat near the window, Jeni frowned, confused—until Logan followed close on the nurse's heels. His expression, on the other hand, was smug and confident.

Irritation sparked. This was the second time she'd come across Logan flirting with the nurses over the past two days. He'd spent several hours here yesterday after work and at one point offered to go to the cafeteria to get everyone coffee. He'd taken forever, and Jeni finally left Andrew's room to look for him. She found him—their coffee getting cold nearby—at the nursing station, laughing and chatting with the women sitting there.

Two days ago, Jeni had actually thought she had a partner in this—someone to help her be Andrew's caregiver. Not that she'd ever use that term in front of Andrew. His immediate reply would no doubt be that he didn't need anyone to take care of him. But she'd depended heavily on other people after her accident, and as much as she hated to admit it, she'd needed the help. Andrew was going to need it too.

Logan's help the night Andrew had come to the ER, and then his silent support for her in the waiting room and late-night text conversation, had lit a small flame of appreciation and hope inside her that she might be able to rely on him. She'd actually started to like the guy.

But that was before he started hitting on every woman in the whole damn hospital. If he was hanging around just to get laid, he could move on down the road. She'd find a way to handle everything, even if it meant asking her mother or one of her sisters to stay.

The nurse turned her attention to Andrew and started chatting immediately, her voice annoyingly high-pitched and chipper. Jeni couldn't even imagine the sounds this woman would make if Logan worked his magic on her in the bedroom.

Thinking about Logan in that setting made her stomach flip, and she rubbed her eyes, trying to wipe the image.

Logan came to stand next to her and leaned his upper back against the wall. He tilted his head down at her and winked.

Jeni narrowed her eyes, and he grinned.

"Are you in any pain?" the nurse asked.

"No," Andrew said.

"Nauseous?"

"No."

"Good. The radiology technician should be up to take you for a PET scan soon."

"How long does that take?" Jeni asked.

"About two hours." The nurse recorded Andrew's vital signs in the computer mounted against the wall, asked him if he needed anything, and left. Not before flashing Logan a smile first though.

Naturally.

What was it about this guy that made him so irresistible? Jeni didn't get it.

Okay fine, she did. But she wished she didn't.

Also, he never flirted with her like that.

Whoa, where did that come from? She didn't want Logan to flirt with her. Did she?

It had been more than two years since the divorce, and so far, she'd had no problem sticking to her new plan to stay away from anything relationship-related. No one had even begun to tempt her otherwise.

Until now, it seemed. Which only pissed her off.

Andrew turned his head looked at her. "Guess you'll be on your own to intercept the crew when they arrive."

Jeni squared her shoulders. "Don't worry, I got this."

"I can help," Logan offered. "I'm looking forward to meeting your family."

She frowned and cast him a skeptical eye. "You can leave when they take Andrew for the scan."

Logan's smile faded, and for a brief moment, she felt a tinge of guilt.

Andrew looked at Logan. "Can you give us a minute?"

Logan nodded, a small pinch between his eyebrows, and left.

"Why are you being so rude?" Andrew slid a hand through his brown hair.

Jeni balked. "I'm not. This is a family thing. He doesn't need to keep hanging around, flirting with the nurses and distracting them from your care. It would be best if he just gave us some space right now."

"Us or *you*? I don't need space. He's good company, and it's nice to have him here. He's been through this with someone close to him, and he knows what to expect. I don't know how long this road is going to be, but either way, Logan's going to be in the car. You need to get on board with that, and the sooner the better. Your attitude isn't helping."

She pushed past her immediate desire to defend herself. "Who did he go through this with?"

"Someone in his family. What does it matter?" Andrew asked.

Jeni sighed and rubbed her temples with both hands.

"What is it with you? Everyone loves Logan."

"Women especially."

Andrew cocked his head to the side. "Are you jealous?"

Her laugh nearly choked her. "No."

One eyebrow rose, and Andrew spoke slowly. "You sure?"

No. But she'd die before admitting it. "Andrew, there are only two things I'm thinking about right now. You and what I'm gonna do with Mom and the others when they get here. No room for jealousy in there at the moment."

"If you say so. Look, just try to be civil, okay? I need both of you right now, whether you like it or not. Can you please try? For me?"

Jeni looked at her brother. At the circles under his eyes and the washed-out pallor of his skin. The hospital bed where he reclined, lined in white sheets and a light blue blanket and monitors covering the wall behind his head.

Her heart clenched, and tears pricked in her eyes.

When had she become so selfish? This was her brother, her confidant, her lifelong defender. He was sick and facing something potentially life threatening. When their roles were reversed and she was the one in the hospital bed, he'd done anything she ever asked of him. Without question.

Plus, she wasn't sure what her issue was with Logan. Her feelings seemed to extend to both ends of the spectrum, hot one minute and cold the next. Andrew didn't need to be dragged into her irrational mind. She didn't even understand it.

She leaned forward and took one of his hands in hers. "Of course. I'm sorry. I'm just scared. I'm scared for you, and I'm being a bitch. Of course, I can be civil. Logan and I will be here for you. Together."

"It's cold in here."

"Jeni, do you have softer towels?"

"I should have brought Bear. I miss him already."

The Bishop women had descended upon Jeni's usually quiet home after a few hours at the hospital and a stop at a car repair shop. Evidently the family SUV hadn't fared well on the drive, and now the four of them would be sharing Jeni's Hyundai Sonata until they could figure out what was wrong and fix the Suburban.

Rhonda, the oldest and most practical of the group, promised Andrew she'd use Jeni's car and be back with dinner for him. He agreed but vehemently declined letting anyone stay the night at the hospital. Jeni had been there the last two nights, and he said he'd be fine on his own for tonight.

"Jeni, where are you sleeping?" Rhonda came out of the guest room where she'd dropped her suitcase. Of all the siblings, she most resembled their dad, with brown hair so dark it almost looked black.

"In my bed?"

"Mom and I are sharing it," Valerie said.

Looked like Jeni was on the couch.

Rhonda passed by where Jeni stood listlessly in the hallway and entered the kitchen. "Wow, those walls are *yellow*. Where's the Dr. Pepper?"

"I don't have any," Jeni said.

"*What?*" Rhonda reappeared in the doorway.

"I don't drink it."

Rhonda looked at her blankly, like she'd just said something incomprehensible, such as *I don't have running water.*

Jeni turned her back on Rhonda and entered the living room, where Valerie had begun unpacking a small bag, shoving Jeni's books aside to place several notebooks and a computer on the coffee table. "What's your Wi-Fi password?"

"I don't know, some weird combination. It's on the back of the router," Jeni said.

"Thanks. What's for dinner?"

Rhonda spoke up before Jeni could respond. "I'm taking Andrew Chinese food tonight."

"Are you sure he should be eating that?" their mom asked from her position in the recliner.

"Why wouldn't he?"

"All those preservatives and cancer-causing chemicals. It just seems counter-intuitive."

"A little late to be worried about that," Jeni said. All three women gasped and stared at her, and Jeni shrugged. Andrew would have said the exact same thing.

"What about pizza?" Rhonda asked.

"Andrew and I had that last night," Jeni said.

Rhonda heaved a sigh. "Mom, what are you making? Maybe I'll just take a plate to him."

Their mother stood and disappeared into the kitchen, and several cabinet doors creaked open. "Jeni, honey," she called out. "Where's the pantry?"

"I don't have one."

"Where do you keep the food?"

Jeni poked her head in. "Right there, where you're looking."

"This is it?" her mother squawked. "How do you live?"

"It's just me. I don't need much."

When Jeni said the words *just me*, her mother opened her mouth like she might comment but thankfully chose to shut it. "I'll have to go to the store."

Jeni shrugged. "Fine."

"We don't have a car," Valerie said.

"You can take mine," Jeni said.

"Okay," her mom agreed. "Just let me go start the diffuser in my room so it's ready by the time I go to bed."

Jeni groaned inwardly. Her mother had recently gotten into

essential oils and used various scents to fill every room of the house, depending on the mood she wanted to achieve.

Ylang-ylang in the bedroom for relaxation and sleep.

Lavender in the living room for balance and calm.

Peppermint in the home office for mental clarity.

Jeni's nose was like a bloodhound's, and the slightest aroma was like a potent blast to her senses. The last time she'd been to her parent's house, she'd had a headache for three days straight.

Rhonda sat on the couch and turned on the television. "Do you have Netflix?"

"No."

"Seriously?"

"If I'm watching TV, it's for sports," Jeni said.

Rhonda hit the Guide button and flipped through until she found a *Real Housewives* from somewhere. Oh hell. Four women on the television and three live ones in her house? With nowhere to escape?

"Jeni, honey, can we turn the air down? It's freezing back here," her mother called.

"What's your internet speed?" Valerie asked. "It's slow as molasses."

Jeni couldn't take another second.

"I've gotta go," she blurted out.

Valerie and Rhonda both looked at her.

"What?"

"Where?"

"Ah…" Jeni's mind raced to find a good reason to leave the house and said the first thing that came to mind. "I have a date."

"A date?" her mother's voice screeched from down the hall.

"Yeah."

"You're going on a date tonight? With us here and Andrew in the hospital?" Valerie frowned. "Surely this guy would understand if you asked for a raincheck."

In for a penny, in for a pound. "Andrew insisted I go," Jeni said, the lie slipping from her tongue surprisingly easily. "He knew how excited I was about it and said he'd be really disappointed if I cancelled on his account."

Rhonda nodded sagely. "That sounds like our Andrew."

"Yeah. So I'd better get going." Jeni looked around for her purse.

Her mother returned. "Is that what you're wearing?"

Jeni looked down at her jeans and long-sleeved T-shirt. "Oh. I guess not."

She went to her room and grabbed the first date-acceptable top she could find, holding her breath to avoid inhaling the scent of the oil diffuser. She slipped into the bathroom and changed her shirt, smoothed her hair into a cleaner ponytail, and applied mascara.

She returned to the living room and picked up her keys. "I'll be back later."

"Hold on. You can't take your car," Rhonda said. "Mom needs it to go grocery shopping, and I need to take Andrew dinner later."

Shit.

"This guy wasn't going to pick you up?" Valerie asked.

"I…he…we were just going to meet there." Jeni scrambled as she spoke. What was she supposed to do now? She was desperate to get out of here and could only think of one person to ask for help. "I'll just text him and see if he can swing by on his way."

Jeni's hand paused over the screen of her phone. Was she really going to do this?

A desperate housewife began crying, and Rhonda cackled. Jeni's fingers began moving of their own volition.

Jeni: You busy tonight? I need your help.

CHAPTER EIGHT

J eni jumped into Logan's truck like a pack of dogs chased after her.

"Where's the fire?" he asked with a laugh.

"Can you just drive?" she asked, buckling her seatbelt.

His eyebrows lifted, but he did as asked. A light scent of vanilla drifted across the cab, and he inhaled deeply. She looked nice, but he kept that thought to himself.

When they were out of the neighborhood, she breathed a sigh of relief. "I'm sorry. I just...I had to get away from my mom and sisters. They were driving me crazy. There's something wrong with the SUV they brought, and my mom needs mine to go to the store."

Logan blinked. "That's your emergency? I'm rescuing you from your sweet and caring family?"

"They are not sweet."

"I thought they were great."

"You were with them for an hour."

He shrugged. "I liked them. Especially your mom."

Jeni mumbled something unintelligible and leaned her head against the seat. It was silent for a moment, and she closed her eyes, like she was savoring something. The look on her face had Logan shifting in his seat.

He focused to keep his eyes on the road. "What did you tell them?"

"That I had a date."

Logan's jaw dropped, and he laughed.

Her head twisted to look at him. "Why is that funny? You think I couldn't get a date with you?"

"The opposite actually. What was it you said? You're a hard sell? I think I'm the last person you'd ever want to go out with."

"Be that as it may, I don't know any other men in this town, so I had no choice."

"I'm flattered. Why didn't you just call an Uber?"

Jeni stilled. "Damn," she muttered under her breath.

They came to a red light and stopped. Logan peeked over at her, and she regarded him from behind her glasses.

"I didn't really think this through," she said. "Any ideas for what we should do?"

He stretched his right arm out and rested it on the back of her seat, grinning. "I could take you to my place."

"Hard pass."

He'd said it to annoy her, but for some reason he felt a little offended. "Fine. You pick then."

"Somewhere bright and well populated."

"Jeni. I know this isn't a real date. I'm not gonna put the moves on you."

"Your propensity to flirt with anything that has breasts says otherwise."

Any man who knew anything about women knew jealousy was a good sign. He lifted an eyebrow and smirked at her. "I think you're worried about your ability to stop yourself from putting some moves on *me*."

"Keep dreaming, Squinty."

"We're still doing that?"

"Just shut up and drive."

Once again, Logan complied. For some reason, he did that often around Jeni—let her boss him around. "You're kind of a bully, you know that?"

She looked affronted. "Am not. I was friends with everyone growing up. Popular kids, nerds, athletes, anyone and everyone."

"Didn't you go to a tiny school?"

"It wasn't that small."

"How many people were in your graduating class?"

"Forty-three."

Logan choked back a laugh. "I graduated with eight hundred."

"Holy crap. Did you know them all?"

"Not even close. Some of them had been in the district since kindergarten, and I moved there when I was thirteen. Seventh grade wasn't a good time to jump into a new school."

"Ugh, I believe that. Middle school is rough on everyone."

Most would agree with her. But for Logan, the elementary years were the worst of his life and not because of the school he went to.

"It's a little early for dinner, but I know a great place just down the street that has vegetarian options. Tacos and beer?"

"Tacos and beer is my love language," she replied.

He tucked that bit of information away. "Duly noted."

She pulled her bottom lip between her teeth like she was trying not to smile.

Fifteen minutes later, they were settled at a high-top table at Mateo's, beers in hand and a plate of chips and salsa between them.

"Tell me more about Jeni Bishop," Logan prompted, pushing the slice of lime into his bottle of Corona.

Jeni mimicked his movement, and both drinks fizzed as the fruit settled to the bottom. "Like what?"

"Anything. Something I don't know."

"This is gonna run both ways, right? I'm not going to talk about myself all evening."

He shrugged. "Depends on what you want to know."

Jeni arched a brow. "If I'm opening up, you have to, too."

His gaze drifted to a television above her head. "My early childhood is off the table. Other than that, I'm an open book. Mostly."

"You do realize now all I want to ask about is your early childhood, don't you?"

Logan clenched his jaw in an effort to keep his expression neutral but firm. "Sorry. I'm sure you have some things you don't want to talk about."

"Not really. I mean, I've got some issues, sure. But I don't mind talking about them."

His eyes locked on hers as she took a swig of her beer. "Even your marriage?"

She swallowed hard. "How do you know about that?"

"Andrew mentioned it. Seemed like he's been worried about you since your divorce."

"He and I worry about each other too much. Twin connection and all that, I guess."

"How long ago was it?"

"The divorce? Two and a half years. When I was twenty-four. We got married young, at nineteen. I wasn't in a great place mentally and thought I was in love. He thought he could save me from myself. We were both wrong."

"Why would he think you needed saving?"

Her eyes dropped to the table for a few seconds. "Remember the car accident I told you about when I changed career paths? It turned my world upside down. I lost my scholarship to play softball at Oklahoma. I had several surgeries, had difficulty getting around, and was dependent on other people for a while. It was a really hard time for me."

"That's understandable," Logan said quietly.

"Jackson was a good friend from high school, and he started coming around more after the accident. He'd pick me up from the farm and take me into town. He helped me breathe a little. I hated being stuck at home with my parents. Andrew left for college, and I was the sole focus of my mother. She suffocated me, and the only thing I looked forward to was the days Jackson would show up and take me away.

"I told him as much, and we both thought I needed him. When enrollment came around for the next semester at Nebraska, I still couldn't drive, so I thought I'd have to wait another six months to get away and start college. But he proposed and told me we could move to Lincoln for school. He promised to help me get to campus when I was ready. I was blinded by eagerness to get away and mistook that and feelings of affection as true love."

Logan scratched his thumb across the words inscribed on his beer bottle. "Circumstances can lead us to make decisions we wouldn't otherwise make, that's for sure." He knew that better than anyone. "But it sounds like Jackson was a good guy and helped you during a rough period of your life."

Jeni hesitated. "He took good care of me at first. But that fell away when it became less convenient for him." Her expression shuttered, and she lifted her gold-brown eyes to his. "Enough about that. What about you? Ever been in love?"

"Nah."

"I figured."

What was that supposed to mean? "Why do you say that?"

"Can I be honest?" she asked.

"Aren't you always?"

She flinched but met his gaze straight on. "I don't want this to come out wrong, but you seem like a major player."

Logan stiffened. "When did Judgmental Jeni show up?"

"Do you deny that you sleep around?"

He looked away for a moment. "I don't know. I have no idea what your definition of *sleeping around* is. I enjoy meeting women and talking to them. And if it goes in that direction, I usually don't stop it. It's never my goal just to hook up with a woman just for the sake of getting laid, if that's what you're suggesting. But even if it was, if both parties consent and know what the end goal is, what's the problem?"

She didn't answer his question and instead asked one of her own. "If that's not your goal, what is?"

That was easy. "I like being that close to another person. The focus, the intensity. The connection." That's what he sought anyway. He wasn't going to admit he rarely found it.

"And is it really the sex that does that for you?"

"Can't get any closer to a person than that."

Jeni lifted her beer to her lips and took a slow drink. "Actually, I'd argue it's not the sex that does it. That connection comes from something else, somewhere beneath our skin and bones."

Logan paused and absorbed her words. *It's not the sex that does it, the connection comes from something else.*

Huh.

"But I could be way off base," she continued. "I haven't even found that, and I was married. What do I know?" She laughed lightly. "I actually see your point, truth be told." She looked a little surprised at herself. "I guess there's nothing wrong with two adults enjoying themselves."

Logan looked at her with eyebrows raised.

She rolled her eyes. "What? Don't look so shocked. I might be quick to judge, but I'll also admit when I'm wrong."

"That's an admirable trait." He was starting to think she might have several of those. "Not many people can say that, including me. That's why it's a good thing I'm rarely wrong."

She snorted good-naturedly, and he chuckled.

A commercial about the Chiefs flashed across the television nearby, and a thought occurred to him. "I almost forgot. I got two tickets to the Chiefs-Broncos game for you."

Her face lit up. "You did? Thanks!"

"Happy to do it."

"Can you come too? Sit with me?"

Logan was pleased at the request. "I can't. I have to work during the game. Bring whoever you want. I don't suppose I can persuade you not to wear a Broncos shirt?"

"Hell no. I'll be decked out in blue and orange."

"I figured as much." He chuckled. "Have fun, drink beer, and eat as much junk as you want."

They eventually decided to order more than chips for dinner, and as they ate, their conversation covered a multitude of topics —music, books, hobbies. Favorite foods, movies they'd recently seen. Actors and actresses they found attractive. Seeming to come to an unspoken agreement to get along, they avoided talking about football and family, with the exception of Andrew. They each had entertaining stories that included him in some way or another, and it kind of felt like they'd broken through a barrier, forming a real friendship.

At the end of the meal, they landed on the subject of Andrew's diagnosis, and as they finished their drinks, the air surrounding them turned somber.

"What if it's bad, Logan?" Jeni wiped her hands on a napkin and folded them in her lap. She pushed her beer bottle to the side, her gold eyes fearful.

Logan thought again how beautiful she was but tried to focus on the subject at hand.

He set his jaw and intentionally spoke in a steady, calm tone, despite the worry weighing on his own chest. "If it's bad, we'll face it head on. We'll fight just as hard as if it's the best stage it can be, okay? Andrew's strong. So am I, and so are you. I've only known you for a few months, and I already know that for a fact. Between the three of us, plus the best oncologists in the state, he'll beat it."

Jeni swallowed and nodded, though the worry lines on her

forehead didn't abate. Logan almost reached across the table to cover her hand with his.

Almost.

"You're right," she said. "Thank you. For saying that and for hanging out with me tonight."

They stood to leave, and as they walked to the door, an attractive redhead smiled at him. He gave her a friendly smile in return then opened the door for Jeni and gestured for her to precede him.

"You never have trouble with women, do you?" she asked when they reached his truck. She didn't say it rudely, just as a curious statement of fact. Or question, rather.

Logan gripped the back of his neck. "I don't know how to respond to that."

"That's answer enough," she said with a light laugh.

His lips tipped up in a small smile, his vision filled with her symmetrical features, gold-brown eyes, and long, silky hair. "I bet you don't have trouble either."

She snorted. "Right."

"I'm serious." His tone confirmed his words. "You're beautiful. If you'd take down the *Fuck Off* sign you wear around your neck, there'd be a line of men waiting to ask you out."

"To date me or sleep with me?"

"Either. Both."

Jeni dropped her gaze to the ground, her cheeks reddening. She looked strangely vulnerable in that moment, and he didn't like it.

Without thinking, Logan put a finger under her chin and tilted her head up, his eyes searching her face. "You know that's true, right?"

She shrugged.

Did she really not know how tempting she was? "When's the last time you went out with someone?"

"When I was married."

75

Might be too nosy but… "Slept with one?"

"Same."

Logan's jaw dropped. "You said you got divorced two-and-a-half years ago."

She stiffened. "Don't say it like that. It's not *that* big a deal."

"I beg to differ."

"Yeah, I got that. I know it's at the front of a lot of people's minds but not mine. The first time, I waited until I was married to have sex. And it just wasn't what I thought it would be. It never was."

"He didn't do it right."

Jeni snorted. "Let me guess. You'd show me how it's supposed to be done, right?"

"Definitely not."

She balked.

"I have no interest in having sex with you."

Her incensed expression told him his comment came out differently than he intended.

She spoke before he could try again. "Why not?" she demanded, eyes flashing.

Dammit. "I didn't mean—"

"I'm not your type?"

"No, that's not it. I just…I hadn't thought about you like that."

"Am I the *only* woman you haven't thought about like that?"

Logan rubbed a hand across his mouth. He didn't think anything he could say would be the right thing. "I don't usually go after women who aren't interested. It's pretty clear you don't wan—"

Then, the last thing he'd have ever expected happened. Before he could finish his sentence, Jeni slipped her hand around his head and pressed her lips to his.

Logan froze. Time stopped.

Jeni was kissing him. *Really* kissing him.

What.

The.

Hell?

His body reflexively kissed her back while his mind sprinted to catch up. His lips yielded to hers, pressing forward and retreating, and his feet stayed planted rather than backing away while he processed.

But when the surprise wore off and he was fully in the moment, he realized how nice it was. He'd kind of thought a kiss with Jeni would be one of those aggressive, teeth-clashing, tongue-warring kisses, where clothes were being pulled and bodies pushed up against any solid surface. Passionate and force-ful, like the woman herself.

Yeah, he'd lied. He'd thought about it before. Once or four times.

It wasn't like that though. She'd come at him hard but loos-ened up when he didn't resist. Her lips were soft and pliant, and her hands gently moving in his hair felt fucking amazing. His hands slid around her waist, and she sighed into his mouth.

He opened his eyes to look at her while he kissed her, some-thing he rarely did. Her glasses were high on her nose, and her eyes remained closed, with dark lashes resting against her sparsely freckled cheek. Her expression was soft and serene, a far cry from her usual demeanor. Something clenched in Logan's chest, and his breath caught in his throat like his air supply had been cut off. He slid his hands up along her back and cupped her face in his palms, his thumbs tracing her delicate cheekbones.

His eyelids drifted shut, and his tongue slid out for a taste. It wasn't even intentional on his part. It just felt like the natural progression of a kiss. Of *this* kiss.

And damn, did he want to taste her.

When she touched his tongue with her own, the intensity went up a notch. She moved closer, her body flush against his, from their chests down to their thighs, not an inch of space between them. His back was against the hard metal of the truck. Heat spread through his body, and blood pulsed in his ears.

Logan had been around. He'd kissed a lot of women.

A *lot*.

But never in his entire life had a woman's kiss made him feel like this.

CHAPTER NINE

Logan lifted his head, his lips an inch away from hers. A strangled sound escaped his throat, and it sounded like it might have been a question. Jeni couldn't be sure.

How many beers had she had? Three? She couldn't remember. All she knew was this kiss made her feel something she'd never felt before.

They stood there, separated by a mere inch, with halted breath and a spark hovering between them.

Why had she done that?

Oh, right. Because he'd said he didn't want her and then used the excuse she wasn't interested in him.

Which was true. Sort of. She was attracted to him, which wasn't the same thing. Regardless, what he'd said pissed her off, so she'd acted on impulse.

And she wanted to do it again.

His lids were still low, his eyes on her mouth. She leaned forward again, pushing up on her toes and seeking contact. Just before their lips touched, he sucked in a breath, as if realizing what had just happened and would happen again.

He gently put his hands on her upper arms to still her movement.

"I, uh…" He cleared his throat and blinked several times. His gaze moved around her face, like he was drinking her in, before his eyes met hers. "I…no, I can't."

"You can't kiss me?" She resisted the urge to back down. His lips had felt too good.

Logan closed his eyes. "You're Andrew's sister. It doesn't feel right to do that."

A small piece of her confidence slipped away. "I've seen you flirt with a dozen women."

"That's different."

"How?"

"None of them were the sister of my best friend."

Her jaw went tight, and she stepped back, leaving a cold sensation along the front of her body. Disappointment settled heavy on her chest. "Got it."

He gripped the back of his neck, and a frown descended. "I can't think of you that way. Out of respect for your brother—"

"Logan," she cut in. "I just kissed you. I don't want to talk about my brother." Rejection washed through her, and she eyed the door behind him meaningfully. "If you don't mind?"

"You didn't let me finish. More importantly, I'm trying to respect you too."

"Okay." She avoided eye contact, trying to hide her embarrassment, and put her hand on the door handle next to his elbow.

With a sigh, he moved to the side and allowed her to get inside.

The drive back to her house was silent and awkward. Logan made a few attempts to start conversation, but she wasn't in the mood. She gave him single-word answers, and he eventually gave up. He pulled into her driveway, and she went for the door handle.

Logan's hand shot out to cover hers. "Wait."

She craned her head around to look at him. "What?"

"Don't be upset with me."

"I'm not." She was upset with herself.

"I'm glad you texted me tonight."

Her eyes met his.

"I mean it," he added.

She dropped her gaze and sighed. Before the sting of rejection, she'd had a great evening with him. She pulled out of his grasp, opened the door, and climbed out. She offered him a small smile before she closed the door.

"Me too."

~

"What *is* that?"

"Is it what I think it is?"

"Oh, sweet mercy." Jeni's mother's eyes went wide. "Someone is, um...oh my."

Jeni shoveled eggs into her mouth, wishing she could slide under the table. Her mother must have opened the window near the kitchen table, letting in more than the sound of birds chirping. "It's my neighbor. She likes to sleep with the window open."

"That doesn't sound like sleeping," Rhonda quipped. "If it is, I'll take some of whatever sleeping pill she's got."

"Rhonda!" their mother gasped.

"What?"

Jeni stood and walked to the window. "I'll just close this."

When she resumed her seat, the breakfast table was suddenly awkwardly silent, and her mother seemed unable to make eye contact.

"What time's the appointment?" Jeni asked. It was at nine, but she needed to say *something* and wanted to move on from the subject of her neighbor.

Cassidy.

Usually, the woman brought Jeni nothing more than irritation. Today, she was reminded of the morning she'd first seen Logan, and her thoughts filled with him—his lips in particular. More than a week had passed since their kiss, but it felt like yesterday. She remembered how it felt to be in his arms that night, his open mouth hot against hers. She wasn't sure what shocked her most, the fact that she'd kissed him in the first place or how much she'd enjoyed it.

Ever since that night, she'd felt an unfamiliar sense of awareness and curiosity, and she had no idea where to go from here. She'd been operating under the assumption that avoiding relationships meant she probably wouldn't be having sex either. She'd never had a one-night stand and wasn't currently interested in going that route.

But what if there was a third option?

"Nine." Rhonda interrupted her thoughts.

Jeni cleared her throat, grabbed her plate, and stood. "We'd better get moving."

Forty-five minutes later, the four of them sat in the waiting room of the oncologist's office. Andrew had met them there and sat beside her, his knee bouncing.

Jeni's phone dinged, and she fished it from her purse.

Logan: You've been avoiding me.
Jeni: Have not.
Logan: Liar.
Jeni: …
Logan: I had a good time last week.
Jeni: Me too. You know, before you shot me down.
Logan: If it helps, stopping that kiss might be the hardest thing I've ever done.
Jeni: It helps a little.
Logan: I've thought about you a lot.
Jeni: Really?

Logan: Yeah. More than I probably should.

Her fingers paused over the screen. What was she supposed to do with *that?*

"Who are you texting?"

She jumped at the sound of Andrew's voice, quickly flipping her phone over. Her brother raised an eyebrow.

"No one."

"Jeni." He was attempting to use a firm tone with her, and she almost laughed. "Is it a guy?"

"Shh," she growled, glancing at her family sitting opposite them. "They'll hear you."

The waiting room was large, and thankfully none of them seemed to be paying attention. Rhonda was on her phone, and Valerie and her mother were animatedly conversing about something that Jeni would assuredly not be interested in.

It would be bad enough if they thought Jeni was talking to any guy. If they knew it had been Logan? God help her. It had been barely more than a week since they first met him at the hospital, and he'd been around on a few additional occasions with Andrew since then. Logan was right—she'd avoided him each time, finding something else to do when he was there. Her mom and sisters couldn't get enough of him, apparently having consumed whatever Kool-Aid he doled out to women. They didn't even care that he worked for the Chiefs.

Well, Rhonda kind of did. She was the most hardcore of them all. And if Jeni's dad were here instead of keeping their farm running, he'd have sided with Jeni and Rhonda on that. She was sure of it.

"Maybe if they do, you can distract them while I slip through that door unnoticed." Andrew tilted his head to the door leading to the exam rooms. "Pretty sure I don't need four of you with me."

"I'm not giving up my spot, and I can guarantee not one of

those women will either. This is your first appointment with an oncologist. We're with you in this, Andrew." Jeni put a hand on his forearm, taking the rare opportunity to tell him how much she cared. "We love you more than life itself."

"I know." He gave her a half-smile and patted her hand with his. "If only you'd love me from a distance."

Jeni yanked her hand away and elbowed him in the ribs. "When I was the one in your shoes, there was no getting rid of you."

Andrew leaned back against the chair and closed his eyes. "I was your saving grace."

"That's true."

Still resting on the wood, his head tilted in her direction, and one eye opened. "Until I wasn't. I'm sorry I left you there."

"You went to college. It wasn't like you had a choice."

"I could have waited a year. Took classes online like you did. If I had, maybe you wouldn't have—"

Jeni geared up to interrupt him, but a man in scrubs opening the door did it for her.

"Andrew Bishop?" the man called.

Five Bishops stood and followed the man into an exam room entirely too small for all of them. Jeni and their mother claimed chairs next to Andrew, while Rhonda and Valerie stood along the wall.

Dr. Patel, a thin, beautiful, dark-haired woman with a kind smile and intelligent eyes, entered soon after. If she was annoyed with how cramped the room was while she examined Andrew and spoke to him about his treatment plan, it didn't show.

Jeni took notes while Dr. Patel outlined her recommended treatment—four months of chemotherapy. She said Andrew didn't need radiation and reiterated the high possibility of cure for his early stage disease. She gave them ample time to ask questions and then explained that a pharmacist would come in to discuss the side effects of chemotherapy.

A short time later, a knock sounded at the door, and a red-headed woman entered. She looked young to be a pharmacist, but Jeni was still asked for her ID at bars so she didn't have room to talk.

Then, the strangest thing happened.

The woman stopped short when her eyes alighted on Andrew. He sat up straight, his gaze fixed intently on her. Jeni looked between the two of them, feeling the urge to reach up and snap a finger between them.

Interesting.

Andrew broke the silence. "Hi."

His voice seemed to break the pharmacist out of her trance, and she sat on a stool, introducing herself as Lauren. "You must be Andrew?"

"That's me." He introduced the rest of the family.

Lauren spent the next half-hour explaining what he could expect from the chemotherapy. Jeni didn't miss the way Lauren's cheeks flushed every time she glanced in his direction.

Again, interesting.

When Lauren finished and asked their family if they had any questions, everyone jumped right in. They asked several, from when he could expect his hair to fall out to whether he had to wear a mask in public, but it all went to hell when their mother asked if it was safe for him to have sex while he was on chemo.

Jeni covered her mouth to hide her laugh. Andrew's face was suddenly a shade of dark red. He made several attempts to move the conversation along, but their mother wouldn't be deterred, insisting it was important to him to know.

"Caroline and I broke up, okay?" he finally announced, tone laced with frustration.

An echo of gasps reverberated throughout the small room, and Jeni's head snapped up. Now that she thought about it, he hadn't mentioned Caroline since his diagnosis. She was pleased by the news, but she'd be damned if she would allow a woman to get away with dumping her brother because he'd gotten sick.

"If she dumped you because of this, I'm gonna punch her in the ovaries," she said through clenched teeth.

"Can we talk about this later?" Andrew bit out.

Jeni and the rest of the family grudgingly kept quiet while Lauren finished up, and they left the oncologist's office. Jeni somehow wormed her way into Andrew's car, sending the other three back to her house in hers.

"Is Mom's car almost fixed?" he asked as he approached the parking garage exit.

"Supposed to be ready tomorrow."

"Thank God."

"You know they won't leave until after you start chemo."

"I know. I'll take the first appointment they offer me." He rolled down his window to hand the parking attendant his validated ticket and thanked her when the gate lifted.

Jeni waited several minutes to give him the opportunity to bring up Caroline, but he didn't. "So, what happened?"

Andrew sighed. "We broke up."

"I got that part. When?"

"Does it matter?"

She ground her teeth. "I'm gonna key her car."

He laughed. "No, you won't. It was a mutual decision. We weren't right for each other, and you know it."

"Well. I'm glad you finally came to your senses." She glanced over at him. "But I'm sorry, all the same. Break-ups suck, no matter what."

"They do," he agreed but didn't look too torn up about it. "Do you ever miss Jackson?"

She put her elbow on the narrow ledge by the window and rested her palm against her hair. "I don't miss *him*. I kind of miss the companionship sometimes."

"I know you were texting a guy earlier. Are you considering going out with someone again?"

"I told you before. I'm never dating again."

He looked at her with wide eyes. "I didn't think you were serious."

"As a heart attack."

"Jeni, you're twenty-six. You can't throw in the towel after one bad relationship."

"It wasn't just a relationship. It was a failed marriage. One that crashed and burned in such spectacular fashion that I'll never do it again." She looked out the window as she spoke. "What's the point?"

"I just worry you'll wake up at fifty and regret never trying again."

Jeni turned her head and gave her brother a sad smile. "I won't."

The only thing she regretted was getting married in the first place.

CHAPTER TEN

After his text exchange with Jeni, Logan tried to throw himself into work to calm his wandering thoughts. He'd received a text from Andrew that morning, saying his lymphoma was stage two and "greater than 80% cure rate" but that he'd need chemotherapy. Logan was relieved the prognosis was good, but the downside was that the good news meant the other concern weighing on his mind moved to the forefront.

Jeni.

She plagued his thoughts all day. He tried to focus on diagnostic reports from the social media platforms the past week, but he kept going back to her and the night they had dinner together.

Logan had really enjoyed himself. She was witty and interesting, and he'd actually started to enjoy her jabs about the Chiefs. When his team ended up Super Bowl champions this season, which appeared to be a real possibility, he'd enjoy rubbing that in her face even more. He admired her dedication to her job and couldn't think of a better person to stand up for children who needed someone on their side.

He thought about all the other things he'd learned about her too. At Mateo's, they'd discovered several things they had in common—both loved action movies. Favorite cuisine was Mexican. Both had a desire to travel. Best of all, he'd finally met a woman who shared his interest in home brewing.

And then, of course, there was that powerful thing called attraction.

Damn, but he was drawn to her. He'd had to physically restrain himself more than once to keep from touching her. The first time he had the urge was back when they had lunch at the ramen place and she'd told him about her accident. Her pull on him had only increased with time.

And that kiss. Shit. He couldn't remember the last time he'd experienced a kiss like that. He'd felt something deep inside during those few minutes, something electric and soothing yet almost painful, all at the same time. It had been more than simply a physical response, of that much he was certain.

What did that mean? Did he want to date her?

He considered her a friend of sorts, and the thought of doing something to ruin that rubbed him the wrong way. He'd seen enough of people's backs as they walked away from him to last a lifetime and didn't like the idea of Jeni joining the crowd.

But she'd said she was starting to like him and, even following the awkwardness after the kiss, admitted she was glad she'd texted him. What if she saw something in him? What if she was different from the others?

By the time he got home that evening, his thoughts were all over the place. But one thing was sure: he wanted to see her again and soon.

He considered several options, but nothing felt right. Ask her to dinner? Too date-ish. Just drop by to say hi? Too stalker-ish. Then he realized he hadn't given her the Chiefs tickets yet, and the game was that weekend.

A grin spread across his face as he sent her a text.

Logan: Can I bring the game tickets over tonight?

Jeni: Actually, do you mind if I come get them? I'm dying for an excuse to get out of here.
Logan: Fine with me.
Jeni: Send me your address, and I'll be there at seven.

The knock sounded at his door ten minutes before seven.

"Sorry," she said the second he opened the door. "I couldn't wait any longer to get out of there."

"Why do they annoy you so much?" he asked as she walked past him. He'd tidied up a little when he'd found out she'd be coming over, though there wasn't much to clean. Hopefully she wouldn't notice how empty his house was.

"For the same reason it's annoying to have a cricket right outside your bedroom window. They *never stop.*" Jeni stopped in the middle of his living room and turned in a circle. "Haven't you lived here a while?"

"Yeah." His house was set up similarly to hers—living space and a small office nook just off the entry, leading to the kitchen. A short hallway with two bedrooms and a bathroom. That was it. Twelve-hundred square feet of living space that he couldn't bring himself to decorate.

She looked at him in confusion. "It's so…bare."

He wasn't offended. She didn't say it rudely, and besides, she was right. "Yeah. Do you want to sit down? Can I get you something to drink?"

"Okay," she said with a shrug. "I'd love a beer."

Logan grabbed two bottles from the fridge, opened them, and carried them back to the living room. Jeni had made herself comfortable in the middle of his couch, looking entirely too appealing in some sort of yoga pants that hugged her legs and a hooded Nebraska sweatshirt. Women in loungewear was a particular weakness of his. He'd take a woman in a soft T-shirt over a lowcut dress any day.

Not that he'd mind seeing Jeni in a dress though.

No. Stop it. He handed her the beer and regarded his seating options. She was on the couch, which meant he should probably sit in the armchair.

He sat down next to her.

She didn't seem to mind and slipped off her shoes and pulled her legs underneath her, her thigh brushing against his leg. He took a deep breath, inhaling the aroma of hops from the beer and vanilla from her skin.

"How was your day?" he asked.

"Fine. I'm happy Andrew's oncologist appointment went well today. I assume he told you?"

Logan nodded.

She took a drink and looked down at her hands. "There was a difficult case I had to deal with at work today. That was hard."

"Do you want to talk about it?"

She looked up at him, her eyes darting back and forth intently between his. "Not really, no."

He understood and didn't push it. They talked easily about nothing in particular while they drank their beers. After a half-hour had passed and she set her empty bottle on the coffee table, he put his half-finished drink down as well.

Just as he was about to stand and get the tickets for her, she put a hand on his arm.

"Logan." Her voice was quiet, and when he looked over at her, her cheeks had turned pink.

"Yeah?"

"Can I—um, can I see something?"

He frowned. "What do you mean?"

Jeni opened her mouth then closed it again. She looked at him wordlessly, a small frown between her brows.

Then her eyes dropped to his mouth.

He realized her intention two seconds before she slid her hand around the back of his neck and pressed her lips to his.

His conscience rose up, beseeching him. *Pull away. Stop this.*

And then, *not yet.* He'd let himself enjoy her lips just for a little while first. He'd been thinking about their soft, full texture since the last time he was here, reliving the perfect way they'd fit together.

Just for a few seconds...

This kiss was gentle and tentative but every bit as powerful. In no time, his heart thundered, and he wrapped an arm around her waist, pulling her closer. A little moan came from her throat, and he groaned in response, fire licking through his nerve endings. He deepened the kiss, fresh memories washing over him at the feel of her tongue brushing his.

Suddenly she pulled back, breathing rapidly. She blinked a few times, and he resisted the urge to pull her onto his lap.

"Yeah," she said on an exhale. "That's what I was afraid of."

He pulled his hand from her body. "Huh?"

Jeni looked around the room, squinting a little, as if thinking about something. He wasn't sure she'd even heard his confused question. When her eyes focused on his face again, her expression cleared. She nodded, almost as if to herself, and put her hands on her thighs. "I want to talk to you about something. About you and me."

His gut clenched, and he cleared his throat. How could he be both dreading and longing to hear what she meant by that? "Me and you?"

"Yeah. Well, maybe me first, then you and me."

Logan stared at her. Where the hell could she be going with this? He was riveted and terrified.

Her eyes locked on his, and her voice was steady, the slight flush creeping up her neck the only indication she might be a little out of her element. "You know the basics—that I was married, Jackson is the only man I've slept with, and it was never what I would describe as earth-shattering. I just accepted the fact that I'd probably built up a fantasy in my head of what sex was supposed to be like. I decided maybe I'm just not a very, um, amorous person."

She looked down at her hands.

Logan formally declared Jackson a world-class idiot.

"I'll never get married again, so I haven't really wanted to date. Because what's the point? People date for one of two things: sex or love. I figured if I don't want love and don't enjoy sex, why do it? Plus, I was working on my Master's degree, so I was busy with school. But since I moved here, a few things have happened. One, I live next door to a woman who clearly enjoys sex. If there was any doubt in your mind, I'm pretty sure she's not faking anything with those noises."

Logan felt a mixture of pride and embarrassment, and his face warmed.

"It annoys the hell out of me when I'm trying to drink my morning coffee, but it's also made me second-guess myself. What if it's possible that I could have an experience like that and the reason I never did before is because Jackson and I just weren't good *together*? When we were talking last week, you said 'he didn't do it right.' And both times we've kissed, I've felt more than I did after five years with him. What if you were right? What if he and I never cared enough to make the experience something worth mentioning? What if it *wasn't* all my fault?"

She must have missed the paralyzed expression on his face because she held up a finger while she grabbed his bottle and took long drink of beer. Her motion for him to stay silent was completely unnecessary—he wasn't sure he could form a word if he tried.

"I'm just going to come out with it. I want to propose you and I become friends with benefits."

"Friends—" Logan's voice cracked, and he swallowed before trying again. "Friends with benefits."

"I don't want a relationship, but I'm curious about what I'm missing when it comes to sex. You're obviously good at it, and I get the feeling you don't want a relationship either. You know my history and that I'm not a virgin but am…inexperienced. But ever since we kissed, I just can't stop wondering if I'm capable of having good sex. Great sex, even."

Logan's eyes were wide, and he reminded himself to blink. He leaned forward, elbows on his knees, and pressed his fingertips to his temples. His body was taut as a live wire.

"Jeni." His voice came out strangled.

Her hand gently touched his back, and he nearly jumped away from her for fear he was about to jump *on* her. "Logan."

His heart raced, and he thought it might burst right out of his ribcage. Before he did something stupid, like agree to her insane proposal, he stood up and paced on the other side of the coffee table.

"I need…I can't think." His hands slid around to the back of his neck, where he gripped hard.

Not an option. She's Andrew's sister.

Jeni stood and walked around the table to stand before him, and his arms dropped to his sides. Her expression was a mixture of pleading and vulnerable, and that in itself nearly made him grab her by the waist and pull her close.

A woman like her shouldn't be so unsure, about her body or what she wanted. He loved when women knew what they wanted and weren't afraid to ask for it. Confidence and equality in the bedroom were key to making the experience enjoyable for both parties. Selfishness and insecurity were ingredients for disaster and usually left one, or both, people unsatisfied.

Logan silently cursed her ex-husband for whatever he did to make her feel this way or whatever he didn't do to help her overcome it.

"Don't think, Logan." Her arms went around his neck, her

hands curling into his hair. He didn't miss the slight tremble in her fingers.

All the thoughts flew from his head, and as if disembodied, he watched his hands slide around her waist and spread across her lower back.

"You're shaking," he whispered.

Her golden eyes didn't leave his, not for a second, the certainty in her expression at odds with the words she spoke. "I'm nervous."

She pressed her lips to his jaw, and a heavy breath escaped his lips.

"Jeni." His resolve was crumbling by the second.

"I'm nervous, but I want this." Her lips met his skin again, closer to his mouth. "I want this."

Oh hell.

So did he. He didn't remember the last time he'd been this turned on.

He kept one hand on her back and slowly slid the other up her spine, coming to a stop at the back of her neck. His thumb caressed the soft skin just beneath her hairline, and she leaned into the touch, her eyes drifting closed.

Logan lowered his head and brushed his lips across hers. Soft and deliberate, like the kiss they shared before.

She arched into him, her breasts pressing against him, driving him crazy. He threaded his fingers into her hair, gently gripping the back of her head as he deepened the kiss. When her tongue entered his mouth and a shock ran through his body, he knew.

He was going to let this happen.

They moved down the hallway to his bedroom, trying to walk and kiss at the same time, hands grasping and lips searching. They stopped at the foot of the bed, and he reached back to yank his shirt over his head. Jeni gripped the hem of her own with both hands and pulled it off. Her hair drifted back down to spill over her shoulders and breasts, contained in a simple black bra.

Logan's heart picked up speed as he moved his eyes from her chest to her face. She had pulled her bottom lip between her teeth, her eyes wide but trusting. She reached for him again, tracing her hands from his pectorals down to his stomach. His abs clenched as her fingers traced each ridge.

"Wow," she breathed, and the heated look in her eyes did something to him.

He spun her around so her back was to him and brushed her hair to the side, exposing her right shoulder. Slowly, he ran his hands up her ribs, stopping with his fingers just below her breasts, his thumbs stroking small circles on her back.

Logan took a deep breath, willing himself to keep it together. Usually, he prided himself on patience and intentionality, but in this moment, he was damn near to throwing her on the bed and fulfilling the primal need rising inside him.

He was near the limit of his own control, which caught him off guard.

He never lost control during sex. He was always watching, feeling, adjusting. Paying close attention to his partner with the goal of taking them to the edge of sanity. He loved watching a woman lose control, but never did so himself.

Focus, man.

Logan buried his face in her neck, dropping kisses along the curve of her shoulder and inhaling her scent deeply. She leaned forward slightly, putting both hands on the bed like she needed something for balance.

He followed the movement, feet planted wide behind her, curving his body over hers. His hands slid down her arms, leaving goosebumps in their wake, eventually meeting her hands on the mattress. He curved his fingers around hers and moved his lips from her shoulder to the curve of her jaw and cheek. She turned her head to meet his lips, and they kissed deeply for several moments, her back against his chest, barely stopping for air.

Logan straightened and dipped his thumbs into the waistband of her yoga pants, slowly dragging them down. He slid his hands back up, taking his time, feeling every muscle and curve along the way. Her legs were incredible.

Jeni turned back around to face him, and he gently urged her onto the bed. She scooted back until she was in the middle, one leg bent at the knee and her upper body propped up by her elbows.

She was beautiful.

He removed his jeans, and her eyes scanned the length of his body, the hungry look in her eyes making his mouth go dry. When he joined her on the bed, her hands went to his boxer-briefs.

He stilled her movement and shook his head. There weren't many things about him women wanted to stick around for, but this was definitely one of them.

"We're not there yet," he said in a low voice. "Not even close."

A small smile formed on her lips and she met his gaze with a look of such trust and anticipation that Logan's heart stopped for a moment.

What the hell?

He looked away from her face. *Stay on task.*

As he spent long minutes exploring and worshiping her body, Logan struggled to keep it together. He didn't know if it was the unconventional request that brought them here or if it was something about the woman herself. But when their bodies finally joined and she gripped his back with desperation, her breath and sweet moans in his ear, he did know one thing.

He'd never had an intimate experience quite like this one.

Not even close.

CHAPTER ELEVEN

Seriously, is that what I've been missing?

Jeni tried and failed to calm her racing heart and catch her breath. She wanted to wipe a bead of sweat away from her hairline, but her arms weren't working just now.

She could barely move, and it had nothing to do with the solid man currently on top of her. Well, maybe that had something to do with it, but she had no intention of asking him to move. Surprisingly, she liked the heaviness of his weight pressing down on her.

No, her current boneless state stemmed from somewhere else entirely. Her mind skipped back to a few minutes prior, when Logan buried his face against her neck with a low groan, his voice thick and rough as he told her how good she felt.

Right back at ya, buddy, she'd wanted to say.

It hadn't exactly come out like that though. It had been more of a moan/scream/completely unfeminine growl of some sort. A noise she had no idea she was capable of making and one she might have been embarrassed about if it hadn't been so well received by the man making her feel so unbelievably good.

"Tell me," he'd rasped, gripping her hip in his large hand. "Tell me what you want."

Her heart jumped, and her stomach coiled again just thinking about it. Her fingers tightened on the hard ridge of his shoulder, and he shifted to the side.

"Sorry, I'm crushing you." His voice was deep and his words almost slurred, like he was drunk.

She shook her head, still not sure she could find her voice. *Please don't move. I like it.*

"Damn, Jeni." His head lifted, and their eyes met. His wavy blond hair stuck out in all directions, his breath still coming quickly.

She braced herself for the embarrassment she was sure would flood her at any moment.

But then he dipped his head and touched his lips to hers, and the sweetness of it calmed her nerves.

There was a brief moment right after she'd asked Logan to sleep with her where she suddenly feared she might regret this. She'd quickly told her conscience to shut up, and she pressed on and hoped she wouldn't regret *that*.

Now? That fear was long gone. She'd remember what just happened for as long as she lived.

"Thank you," she said quietly.

He lifted a brow and one corner of his mouth curved up in a crooked smile. "Um, you're welcome?"

"I mean it. That was…" She was at a loss for words and finally settled on, "Eye-opening."

Logan tilted his head to the side. "That's one I haven't heard before."

"That's something I've never felt before."

"You never…" He trailed off.

"Apparently not." Not like that anyway. "But I don't just mean that. I see what you mean about the connection."

There had been a moment when his face was right above hers

and his hand cupped her jaw, his thumb brushing her lower lip. Their eyes met, and instead of closing her eyes or looking away like she always had with Jackson, she'd held his gaze. It had felt like his blue eyes could see directly into her soul.

"Does it always feel like that for you?" she asked.

He stilled and dropped his gaze. "No," he said as he pulled away. "It doesn't always feel like that."

Logan sat on the edge of the bed with his back to her, rubbing a hand down his face. She couldn't tell if he said it in a good or bad way, and a feeling of awkwardness creeped in. He sat there, not speaking, for several minutes. Jeni didn't know what to do. Should she leave now? They weren't in a relationship, so she shouldn't stay over, right?

His continued silence was answer enough.

Not to mention the questions it would invite from her mom and sisters if she stayed out all night. Still, she couldn't help feeling a little disappointed as she slid out of bed to locate her clothes.

Logan stood to get dressed too, and they moved around each other for the various garments strewn about. She bumped into him when she leaned down for her pants, and he jumped back. Neither said a word, and the air thickened with discomfort.

He grabbed the tickets and handed them to her before they walked to the front door. When he stopped to face her before opening it, she thought he might kiss her, or at least hug her.

Instead, he said, "An hour ago, if someone asked me what I'd be doing tonight, never in a million years would I have said this."

He was within reach but didn't touch her. She stared at his chest, unable to look at him as she said honest words. "An hour ago, I was hoping for it."

"Jeni," he said quietly. "Look at me."

She did.

"Are you okay?" His eyes searched hers.

Jeni smiled. "I'm great."

He nodded. "Good." He opened the door and stepped back. A muscle flickered in his jaw, and he seemed to be considering what to say. "So, I'll see you later?"

That's it? Jeni swallowed. "Yeah. See ya."

She walked to her car, the light from his doorway shining on the lawn. When she started the engine and backed out of the driveway, he finally closed the door.

Jeni suddenly felt bereft, and it confused her. This was exactly what she wanted, right? She'd wanted sex, and Logan gave it to her. And it was everything she knew she was missing.

The problem was—once wouldn't be enough.

Logan hijacked almost every single thought in Jeni's mind for two days straight. She finally felt a reprieve on Sunday when she found herself at Arrowhead Stadium surrounded by seventy-five thousand Chiefs fans. The crowd thundered around her, and as soon as the kicker's foot hit the ball at kickoff, she was all in. In no time she was on her feet and focused on nothing but the field, excitement pumping through her veins.

"*Come on*, ref! Where are you looking? He's all over our guy!" Jeni turned to Rhonda, who had come in Andrew's stead after he'd said he wasn't feeling well. Naturally, Valerie and their mom had high-tailed it to his condo, and he was well cared for. "Did you see that?"

Rhonda was equally red-faced. "Oh, I saw it. What I didn't see"—she faced the field— "was *a flag!*" She sat down and cross her arms.

They called a TV timeout, so Jeni sat down as well. "Remind me never to see a game in enemy territory again."

"You're full of shit. You love this, and you know it."

Rhonda was right. Jeni loved coming to live football games. It was so much more fun than watching on television, even if it was from the other guy's stadium. Jeni was pleasantly surprised to find a couple seated behind them in Broncos shirts, and though it was just halfway through the first quarter, the four were friends already.

"Gotta pee." Rhonda stood and inched out of the row. They were only three from the end, which was nice. The seats were incredible, right on the fifty-yard line and ten rows up from the sideline. Jeni wondered how Logan scored such awesome seats. Were they his? Or did he just get the hook up because he was an employee?

Jeni frowned. She'd successfully avoided thinking about him since the game started. Which had only been fifteen minutes, but she counted that progress.

She hadn't heard from him once in the two days since they'd had sex. She had no clue how these things normally worked and told herself it was probably normal. Even so, those days of silence had her second-guessing how good it had been for him. There was no downplaying the fact that Logan was mind-blowing in bed. He'd rocked her world, and at the time, she'd have sworn he had a good time too.

But it didn't take much for a guy to enjoy sex, did it? Had their night been a one-time thing? Had he already been with another woman since, someone who knew what she was doing?

She pushed Logan out of her head and looked around for a distraction during the timeout. The couple sitting by the aisle were nice but serious Chiefs fans and season ticket holders. Other than the couple behind Jeni, everyone around her seemed to be regular attendees who all knew each other. The two seats on her other side had been vacant since she and Rhonda arrived, and Jeni used the seat next to her as a purse holder.

Several minutes later, two older women came toward her, and they were headed for those two chairs. They were probably in their seventies and decked out in Chiefs gear. It would have been obnoxious on guy but on little old ladies?

"You two look awesome," Jeni said with a grin, removing her purse from the seat beside her.

The first woman eyed Jeni's Broncos jersey as she passed. "You look terrible."

"Orange isn't your color, dear," the other said, looking like she was fighting a grin.

Jeni burst out laughing. "Might want to check the scoreboard before you start trash-talking."

The first lady waved a hand in dismissal. "It's only the first quarter. Our guys know to start slow and finish big. Works in football and in the bedroom."

Jeni's eyes went wide.

The second lady rolled her eyes and patted Jeni on the arm. "Ignore her. Don't worry, she'll tone it down if you have a kiddo with you. Are you a foster parent?"

"Um, no." What an odd question. She intended to be someday, but with the recent move and job change, she wasn't quite ready yet.

Both ladies looked at her with confusion, and Jeni felt like she was supposed to say more.

"I do work for the child welfare office though," was all she came up with. Why were they looking at her like that?

Something about that helped because they both smiled and nodded.

"Oh, I see," the first lady said.

Before Jeni could say anything else, Rhonda returned, eyeing the new ladies with amusement. "That's going to be us someday."

Jeni laughed. "Damn straight."

Her phone vibrated in her pocket.

Logan: Find the seats okay?

A thread of warmth seeped into her skin at his name on her screen.

Jeni: Yes, they're awesome. Thanks again.
Logan: Good. Have fun.
Jeni: Are you here?
Logan: Yeah.
Jeni: Where?
Logan: It's a secret.

Jeni pursed her lips and jumped in surprise when Rhonda yelled something next to her.

Jeni: Gotta go, my Broncos need me.
Logan: You're right, they do. Gonna step in as quarterback?
Jeni: I was a star pitcher in my day. I could throw a football.
Logan: It's harder than it looks.
Jeni: That's what she said.
Jeni: Also, you're going down.
Logan: We'll see about that.

CHAPTER TWELVE

Final score:
    Logan - 1
Jeni - 0

Or Chiefs 24, Broncos 14. However one said it, the outcome was the same.

Logan would never let Jeni live it down. At the end of the fourth quarter when there was no way the Broncos could come back, he'd run to the closest shop in the lower level of the stadium and bought a women's Chiefs T-shirt. At the register, he picked up a small Chiefs helmet too, about the size of a golf ball.

He'd hardly been able to think of anything but her since that night. He'd gone through it over and over in his head, trying to figure out exactly what happened. To him, to her, to them.

He hadn't fucked her.

He hadn't made love to her.

What they'd done landed somewhere in the middle. The best way he could think to describe it was…intimate.

Intensely intimate.

Whatever it was, it had been different. He'd felt a pressure in his chest, a thickness in his throat, and a foreign sense of wholeness as she lay beneath him, looking up into his eyes. It terrified him, but he couldn't figure out why. Wasn't a connection like that what he'd been looking for all this time, what he wanted?

He'd never felt with another woman the way he had with Jeni. Was it because he knew her beforehand? That they were sort of friends first? Was it because she was Andrew's sister and she was like forbidden fruit?

He didn't know. He just wanted to be back at Mateo's with her, talking and laughing over tacos and beer. And he wanted her in his bed again.

In that order, which was the part that was messed up. For him anyway.

His phone vibrated in his pocket and his heart leapt with anticipation that it was Jeni. She was probably texting with a list of excuses of why the Chiefs didn't deserve to win. He'd give her the questionable pass interference call in the third quarter, but otherwise it had been a fair game.

Logan looked at the screen, disappointed for a split second when he saw it wasn't her. It was about her though, and he smiled. He loved the seventy-something-year-old sisters who shared the seats next to his.

Sally: Cute girl in your seat today.
Logan: Don't get too excited. She's just a friend.
Sally: Margaret talked shit to her the entire game. Your girlfriend gave it right back. She's a feisty one.
Logan: Not my girlfriend. And I don't think you're supposed to say 'talked shit' at your age.
Sally: I can say anything I want at my age. Has your mom met your girl?
Logan: We're done here.
Sally: Say hello to your mother for us.
Logan: I will. You can expect regular visitors in the seats next week.

Sally: OK. Don't forget to invite us to the wedding.
Logan: Bye Sally.

The Monday after a game was always busy at the office. Logan didn't have time to be distracted, so it was particularly irritating that he thought about Jeni at least once every ten minutes.

Jeni's frown.

Jeni's smile.

Jeni naked.

That one was his favorite, but not ideal to picture while discussing marketing strategy with Mr. Knipplemeier, his fifty-year-old boss.

There was no question he'd still have work to do when he got home tonight. He put his elbow on his desk and rubbed his forehead. Out of the corner of his eye, he noticed his phone screen light up.

Andrew: Lunch?

Damn, it was awkward to get a text from Andrew when he'd just been thinking about Jeni's soft, smooth skin.

Jeni: Can't today. I have a home visit at noon.

Logan perked up when he saw her name. He hadn't realized this was a group text. Then he read what she'd said. *Home visit.* Memories flashed through his mind at the words, and he quickly shook his head to clear them.

Logan: I'm swamped today too. Tomorrow?
Andrew: I can do that.
Jeni: I'll let you know.

Logan sat there for a moment then switched to a private text with Jeni. He'd had a lot of sleepless nights lately and done a lot of thinking. He didn't have it all figured out, but he did have some things to talk to her about, and maybe seeing her in person would bring him some clarity.

Logan: Avoiding me?
Jeni: I kind of thought it was the other way around.
Logan: I'm sorry I haven't called. Can you stop by tonight?
I have something for you, and I want to talk to you.
Jeni: What time?
Logan: Sometime after 6.
Jeni: I'll come after dinner.

Logan couldn't help the smile that spread across his face. Now that he knew he was seeing her tonight, he was able to focus a little better for the rest of the day. He arrived home a little before six and immediately changed into jeans and his favorite gray T-shirt. He warmed up leftover chicken and ate in front of the television, trying to calm his nerves with a mindless sitcom.

It didn't work, so he went through what he wanted to say to her. No matter how he put the words together, it sounded ridiculous. There was no way she'd go for it.

No one else ever has.

He sighed and clenched his fists, determined to try anyway. Nothing ventured, nothing gained, right? He wasn't one hundred percent sure why he wanted to go for it either, but as he'd lay in bed the night before, thinking and unable to sleep, his plan had seemed like a good idea.

When someone wanted a different outcome, they should change their approach, right?

Seven o'clock rolled around, and along with it, the Monday Night Football game. The Patriots were playing, and they were a fun team to watch no matter what. After he made his proposition, would Jeni stay and watch it with him?

When she knocked on the door, the nerves in his stomach increased tenfold. He opened the door wide and stood aside. "Hey."

"Hey yourself." She smiled as she walked past, leaving a trail of vanilla in her wake. "Is the game on?"

By the time he could respond, she was already in front of the television. She settled on the couch, eyes on the screen.

Logan smirked and closed the door before walking back to the living room. "Want a beer?"

She grinned. "Always."

He went to the kitchen to grab her one and brought it to her. She was wearing yoga pants again, dammit. And her hair was down, like a golden-brown waterfall across her back. If he pulled her onto his lap it would be all over his chest—

Logan mentally reset himself and sat in the chair beside the couch, ignoring the raised eyebrow she shot his way. He needed to keep his distance if he was going to get this out.

The game was on a commercial break, and he had her attention. It was now or never.

"Jeni," he began, but the words got stuck in his throat. How was he supposed to say this?

She waited a moment, and when he couldn't seem to keep going, she said, "You said you had something for me?"

"Oh, yeah." Thankful for the opportunity to delay the conversation he'd planned, he jumped up and retrieved the bag from his bedroom. He handed it to her and sat back down.

She pulled out the Chiefs T-shirt and tiny helmet then shoved them both back into the bag, dropping it at her feet. "I hate you," she said, lips fighting a smile.

Logan jerked his head back theatrically. "Is that how you thank someone for a gift?"

"A gift like that? Yes."

"I just thought you might want to cross over. See what it's like to root for a winning team."

"We'll see you in the playoffs." She glared at him, and his grin widened. It was sexy as hell when her eyes flashed like that.

Damn, she was incredible. A tiny voice in the back of his mind asked what on earth she could possibly see in him, but he forced it down. "I look forward to it."

She huffed out a breath and leaned back. At least she hadn't stormed out the door.

The game came back on, and they watched in silence for a while, except for the occasional comment about a play or referee call. He peeled at the label of his beer bottle, and when the next commercial began, he couldn't hold it in any longer.

"I…I have something to say," Logan announced. What the hell was wrong with him? Was that a necessary preamble?

Jeni's brow furrowed, but she simply waited for him to keep going.

"I want to date you, Jeni," he blurted, just as surprised by saying the words out loud as she appeared to be hearing them.

Her frown deepened. "What did you just say?"

"I want to date you."

"Were you listening the other night? I said I don't want a relationship."

He nodded. "I heard you. But I've done a lot of thinking since then. About what you said that night and the night we ate at Mateo's when we talked about my, um…sexual past in particular. I'm not embarrassed or ashamed, but I did start to reflect on it. And I think you made a good point when you said real connection comes from a place deeper than the physical."

She bit the corner of her lip, and his eyes dropped there, desire filling him.

Ignore it. Keep going.

He took in a shaky breath and stood up, needing to move. "I don't seek out physical-only relationships, but it seems to be where I usually end up. Maybe I haven't had a long-term relationship because I have unrealistic expectations about sex too, just in a different way. Every time I've gone there with a woman, things end pretty quickly because one of us feels like something's missing. I suddenly realized that maybe it's because of me and what I was hoping sex would bring to the relationship. I thought I was connecting with those women, but the only place I got to know them was in the bedroom." He put his hands in his front pockets. "So, I want to try something different. I want a relationship that starts without sex as the primary element."

Jeni looked stunned. She pointed to her chest. "And you want that with me?"

"Yes. When I was with you, it was different. Nothing missing. It was damn near perfect. I don't want to mess that up like I have with everyone else."

She stared at him for a second, and then her countenance completely changed. She threw her hands in the air. "What's wrong with you?"

A lot of things, probably. "Nothing."

"I told you I wanted a fling. A no-strings attached, just sex, no-relationship-expectations-type thing."

"And I want the complete opposite."

"That's ridiculous. A real relationship would never work with us."

"Why not?"

"Have you ever even had one?"

"Not really, no."

Her eyes went wide.

"Don't look so surprised. I've been honest with you."

Jeni pursed her lips. "Well, I have, and it didn't work out so well."

"That doesn't matter to me."

Her tone softened. "You could have any woman you want."

"As luck would have it, I want you."

She shook her head. "I don't think you do. I think we were good together and you're confusing the desire to sleep together again with that for a relationship."

"I don't want to sleep with you again."

Jeni laughed once. "You're lying."

"I know." And how. "And old Logan would give in to that, hoping sex would eventually turn into something more. I don't know why I haven't seen it before, but now that I look back, it's never worked out that way. So, I want to try something new, in the hopes the outcome is different." It could be the way he'd always gone about things or it could be *him*, and he was hoping for the former. Especially now that he'd met Jeni. He raked a hand through his hair. "With you, I don't want to sacrifice what I want most for what I want right now."

Jeni processed that for a moment. She tilted her head to one side. "What does that mean? What do you want most?"

It was a good question. Logan's thoughts felt a little cloudy, like he'd just woken up from a deep sleep and was trying to orient himself.

"I'm not sure I know." A small frown formed between his brows. "I just have a feeling. And until I know for sure what it means, I'm not sleeping with you." He walked around the table and sat beside her. He lifted one hand and brushed her hair away from her face.

Jeni jerked back, her expression shuttering. "Sorry, no deal. I thought we were set on being friends with benefits. If you're throwing dating into it, I can't agree to that."

Logan lowered his hand. "Then I guess we're at an impasse."

She shot to her feet. "No, we're not. I don't accept that. Someone wins, and the other loses. I don't do ties."

He shrugged. "Go on a date with me then."

"No. That means you win."

"You didn't specify who won, just that someone had to."

She pressed a hand to her chest. "Obviously it has to be me. Now take me to your room, and let's get started."

"I'll consider your proposition if you put on the Chiefs shirt."

Jeni snorted. "Never."

"Sex with me isn't worth that? I'm a little offended."

"If you knew me, you wouldn't be."

"Knowing you is exactly what I'm trying to do."

She made some sort of noise in the back of her throat, and the memory of her moans of pleasure slammed into him. Maybe they could do it just one more time…

Her angry voice pulled him out of the haze of desire. "Fine. You want a competition? Sex versus dating? You've got yourself a competition." She grabbed her phone and keys and stormed to the door. "Brace yourself, Logan Davis. You're going down."

CHAPTER THIRTEEN

The following night, Jeni received her third invitation of the day.

Logan: What are you doing tonight?
Jeni: My mom's making enchiladas. It's the one thing worth hanging around for.
Logan: I guess asking you to dinner is out.
Jeni: My answer would be no. Just like it was when you asked me to breakfast. And at lunch.
Logan: Friends eat together all the time.
Jeni: Would you let me pay?
Logan: No.
Jeni: = date. No.
Logan: Is Andrew there?
Jeni: No, he needed to study.
Logan: Fine. Guess I'll find someone else to go out with.
Jeni: Of the female variety?
Logan: Maybe. Jealous?
Jeni: Not in the least.
Logan: I'd rather it be you.

Jeni: Have fun.

Jeni settled back into the armchair and turned her attention to the reality show Rhonda was watching. She had to admit, she'd begun to see why these shows were so addictive. It was like a bad habit she desperately wanted to avoid, but she got sucked in against her will. Tonight in particular, she was glad for the distraction.

Did she want to spend time with Logan? Yes.

Was she jealous that he might go out with another woman tonight? Also yes.

Enough to go back on the promise she'd made herself almost three years ago? Unfortunately, no.

Ten minutes later, the doorbell rang, and Jeni jumped up to get it, assuming it was another Amazon Prime package being delivered for Valerie.

It wasn't.

"Logan?"

He stood there smiling, hands in his pockets, looking irritatingly sexy in well-worn jeans and a black fleece pullover. His blond hair was wind-blown, and the dimple in his cheek teased her like someone handing out samples at the supermarket. *Just one little taste*. What a bunch of bull. They know you're gonna buy the whole damn box.

"Hey. I just wanted to stop by and see if anyone checked on Andrew today—what smells so good?" He took a step forward and snuck his head inside the door.

"Logan! Is that you?" Valerie called from the couch.

"Logan's here?" Jeni's mother yelled from the kitchen. She appeared in the living room, one hand holding a spatula and the other encased in an oven mitt. "Jeni, invite the poor man inside! I'm making enchiladas, would you like some?"

"I'm starving. That sounds incredible, Mrs. Bishop." He slipped inside.

Jeni closed the door, quickly catching up to him. "Stopping by to ask about Andrew?" she asked, voice laced with sarcasm.

He ignored her as he headed for the kitchen. "Need help with anything, Mrs. Bishop?"

"Please, call me Susan."

Jeni slumped down into her chair. *Just stopping by, my ass.* He would have just called Andrew himself if he wanted to check on him. She trained her eyes on the television, determined to ignore Logan's presence.

It wasn't long before the five of them were seated around the table in her yellow kitchen, Logan to her left with a smile brighter than the walls. He'd taken off his fleece, and his corded forearm lightly dusted with hair caught her eye. His chair was closer to hers than necessary, and she scooted in the opposite direction.

She could still smell him though. That nice, masculine scent she wished she didn't find so pleasant.

Her mother set a plate of delicious-looking enchiladas down. "These are cheese and spinach." She turned to Logan. "The rest are chicken. You're not a vegetarian too, are you?"

"No, ma'am," Logan said. "I'll eat just about anything."

Jeni's mom nodded with a smile of approval and set the large dish of enchiladas in the center of the table. "Dig in."

"I still remember the day you decided you weren't going to eat meat anymore," Valerie said to Jeni.

Jeni's mother laughed. "Me too. What were you, seven?"

"Six." Jeni waited for everyone to dish out helpings of the meal before she began eating.

"That's right. You marched in from the field one evening, stood on a chair, and made your declaration. I was sure you wouldn't last a day."

"You've been a vegetarian since you were *six*?" Logan asked.

"Yep."

"What made you want to do it?" he asked.

"She broke one of the basic rules of being a farmer," Rhonda said. "She saw our animals as pets."

Jeni picked up her fork. "We had this cow named Daisy, and I loved her. I was brushing her in the barn that day, and Andrew decided that was the moment to enlighten me about where steak and ground beef came from. I'd never really made that connection before—that these living, breathing animals were the same thing I was chewing at the dinner table. He didn't stop there either. Told me about chicken and bacon and anything else he could think of, though how he knew all this was beyond me. We were the same age."

"He spent more time with Dad than you did. That's how." Valerie sat on Logan's other side and leaned closer to him. "Our dad doesn't know the meaning of sugar-coating."

Logan cut his eyes to Jeni's and said in a low tone, "Now I know where you get it."

"It wasn't just that she stopped eating meat either," Rhonda continued. "She became a full-blown animal activist for years."

"Can we not talk about this?" Jeni took a bite of the cheesy tortilla, savoring the creamy flavors. She'd tried going vegan for a while but…cheese.

"Please, keep going." Logan's eyes were cheerful, and he took a drink of water.

Jeni shot him a scowl, and he grinned.

"When she was in seventh grade, she joined some sort of online group for PETA. One of their projects was to send letters of encouragement to activists who had been arrested for the cause—"

"Like breaking into a lab and releasing hundreds of test mice," Jeni put in. She smiled at the memory, despite the fact she hated being the center of conversation.

"One day our dad found a dozen letters going out from our mailbox addressed from Jeni to a bunch of inmates in the state prison system," Valerie said. "I don't think I've ever seen him so mad."

"Not even the time Andrew snuck out and took Dad's old Corvette out for a joy ride in the middle of the night and wrecked it?" Jeni asked, hoping to divert attention from her.

"Not even then."

"It was close." Her mom put her fingers to her temple. "You and Andrew are the reason I went gray."

"Andrew hasn't told me that one. This is great," Logan said between bites. "I need to have dinner with you ladies more often. What else do I need to know about these two?"

"Absolutely not." Jeni put her fork down. "Let's not talk about me anymo—"

"Did you know she used to be obsessed with Twilight?"

"I sure didn't," Logan said, eyes twinkling.

"Every girl my age had a thing for Twilight," Jeni grumbled.

"But did they all write fan fiction about it?" Rhonda asked.

Jeni stared at her, willing her older sister to read her mind. She felt a sense of relief when Rhonda gave her a small nod and focused on her dinner.

Unfortunately, Valerie didn't catch on. "Oh my gosh, I completely forgot about that! You shut yourself in your room for *weeks* to write that story. You only came out to eat and play softball then went right back to it."

Logan raised a hand. "Sorry, but what is fan fiction?"

"It's…" Valerie stopped and squinted one eye.

Rhonda shrugged.

"I'm not going to pretend I ever had any idea what that was about," her mother said.

Jeni sighed. "Fan fiction is when people write their own stories using characters from another book or TV show."

"Do you still have it? Can I read it?"

Jeni's face heated. "Definitely not."

"I can send it to you," Valerie offered.

"You will do no such thing," Jeni said firmly.

"We'll talk later," Logan said to Valerie.

"I should have stuck to softball." Jeni had the urge to bang her forehead against the table.

"You've mentioned that a few times before," Logan said. "Do you still play?"

Jeni perked up. "Yes. I'd love to find a rec league around here, actually." She'd started looking into it, but Andrew's diagnosis and her family's arrival had distracted her. "Do you know of any? After the accident, I'm not as good as I once was, but I hold my own."

Logan leaned back in his chair. "I play in a coed league. You could play in the spring for sure. The fall season's already under-way, but we're always looking for fill-ins. You'd be welcome to come, and if we're short, we'd love to have you."

"Really?" Excitement filled her at the prospect of playing again. It had been almost a year since she'd had the time and a team to play with. "That would be awesome."

"So long as they don't have games in the morning," her mother said before raising her fork to her mouth.

Valerie laughed, and Rhonda nodded.

Logan twisted his lips to the side. "What's that about?"

"Jeni's not a morning person," Valerie answered for her.

"At all." This from Rhonda. "Don't talk to her for at least two hours after she wakes up, or you'll regret it."

Jeni turned her head and found Logan looking at her, his blue gaze roaming her face.

Was he thinking about the day they met? Judging by his contemplative expression he was thinking about *something*. She wished she could ask him, but she didn't dare. Not in present company.

"Note taken," Logan said quietly. He broke eye contact and cut another piece of enchilada. "Susan, this is one of the best meals I've ever had."

Jeni's mom smiled sheepishly. "Thank you. You're welcome for dinner anytime."

"How long will you be in town?" Logan asked.

"We plan to stay until after Andrew's first chemotherapy treatment. Valerie needs to go home soon after that, regardless. She's got two young kids, you know. Rhonda is able to work remotely, and I'll stay as long as I'm needed."

Jeni bit back a snort. Jeni and Andrew and their mother had different definitions of what it meant to be needed.

"He's lucky to have all of you." The sincerity in Logan's voice was unmistakable.

"Tell us about your family," Valerie prompted. "You're from Kansas City, right?"

The muscles in Logan's forearm flexed, like he'd tensed up. "Yes, I was born in Kansas City. Lived here my whole life except for the four years in Lawrence at KU and one year in San Francisco for an internship. It's hard to imagine living anywhere else."

"What do your parents do?" Jeni's mom asked.

He cleared his throat. "My mom's a teacher. And my dad was an accountant."

It wasn't the first time Jeni had caught him referring to his dad in the past tense. He hadn't readily offered much about his family, and she'd refrained from commenting. Not everyone was as open as she tended to be, and while she was curious, she figured he had reasons to keep that information to himself.

"Is he retired?" Valerie asked, and Jeni mentally slapped her.

"Um, no." He shifted in his seat. "He passed away. When I was in college."

Valerie grimaced. "I'm so sorry."

All the women around the table regarded him with sympathy, and Jeni had the urge to touch him. If he died when Logan was in college, it had been several years, but still, from the few times he'd mentioned his dad, she'd gotten the impression they were close.

Jeni's mom broke the silence. "Well, the next time you come for dinner, bring your mother too. The more the merrier."

Logan smiled. "Thank you. I think she'd like that." He adopted a grave expression. "But you should know she's a loyal Chiefs fan. My dad had season tickets, and before I came along and started stealing her seat, she used to go to all the games. She'll probably wear red just to be contrary."

Rhonda leaned forward to put her elbow on the table and said nothing. Her competitive nature rivaled Jeni's, and she'd probably make sure she was wearing a Broncos jersey the next time Logan came over.

"Red's fine. We'll pretend she's a Huskers fan," Valerie said.

Logan laughed.

The conversation flowed easily through the rest of the meal, though somehow it kept coming back to Jeni in some form or another. An embarrassing moment or an achievement of hers or something she and Andrew had gotten into. She was apt to blame Logan, as it seemed he kept steering things in that direction.

She leaned toward the latter and thought back to their conversation at his house last night, when they'd come to a standstill in their relationship. She hadn't come up with a plan of attack yet but figured seducing a man wasn't so difficult and had assumed she'd slide into a pretty easy win.

Jeni knew better than to underestimate the competition, but she hadn't expected him to show up and charm his way into her house and use her family to further his agenda.

He wasn't playing fair.

If he thought he'd get away with it, he had another thing coming.

CHAPTER FOURTEEN

Logan was in over his head.

He sat on his couch, head in his hands. Last night he'd spent the evening at Jeni's with the entire female side of her family. Even though they weren't dating, he'd kind of felt like he was a new boyfriend she'd brought home for dinner.

The fact that she hadn't invited him was beside the point.

The point was he'd liked the feeling. A lot.

He'd thought about her all damn day, to the point he'd had difficulty concentrating at work. Again. His desire to spend time with her only grew, and this was problematic for several reasons.

First, she didn't feel the same way.

Second, he hadn't mentioned this to Andrew, whose good opinion was important to him.

Third, he wanted to approach this—whatever 'this' was—from a different angle than ever before. He wanted it to stick, but he had no clue how to do that. All he knew was he wanted to do the opposite of every relationship before he'd met Jeni. Because all of those relationships ended. Most barely even started, and it chipped a piece of his heart away every time someone walked away from him. Contrary to how it looked on the outside, he wanted a relationship that would last forever. He was just shit at going about it.

He frowned when a knock sounded at his door. Standing, he made his way across the room, wishing he had a peephole. It was almost ten o'clock.

Logan opened the door a fraction but swung it open fully when he saw who stood on his porch. "Jeni, what the hell are you doing?"

She shoved a bouquet of flowers in his hands. "I don't want these."

He clutched them to his chest, inhaling the sweet smell. "Why not?"

"Don't send me flowers. I'm not your girlfriend."

Damn, he wanted to kiss her. "Okay."

"It's cold. Can I come in?"

He stepped aside, and she passed by, an unfamiliar scent following her. He set the flowers on a nearby table. "Are you wearing perfume?"

"Maybe."

Why would she think she needed it? He liked the way she usually smelled.

Logan closed the door and narrowed his eyes. She wore a long, black, wool coat, and his eyes continued to track downward. Her lower calves and ankles were bare, a pair of tennis shoes on her feet. She put a toe to the heel of each shoe and pushed them off.

His pulse quickened, and he immediately shook his head. "Jeni—"

Her hands went to the buttons on the coat, and she spoke over him as she worked each one through. "Did you enjoy yourself last night? Asking my family all sorts of questions about me?" Her fingers slowed a fraction, but kept moving. A sliver of tanned flesh appeared at her collarbone, and Logan's mouth went dry. "Some people would call that cheating, Logan. I'm disappointed in you. But not so disappointed that I won't stoop to your level. Two can play at this game."

The coat dropped to the floor.

Logan's eyes swept down her body, his jaw following suit. He dropped his chin to his chest and twisted around, his forearm hitting the back of the door and his head landing just below it. "Fuck. Jeni, I ask you again, what the hell are you doing?"

Her body heat closed in from behind. "What does it look like?"

"What are you even wearing?" he croaked out.

"A bikini. I don't own any lingerie."

"It's nice."

"I know. Turn around, Logan."

"I can't."

"You can."

"I won't."

"You know you want to."

"Damn straight I do."

She ducked underneath where he hunched over, and he jerked his head back as she straightened. She now stood before him, wearing hardly anything, with his hands on either side of her head, braced against the door.

Logan focused on taking deep, measured breaths. *In through your nose, out through your mouth.* His eyes dropped to her breasts. A strangled noise escaped his throat. His blood was racing through his veins, his heart pounding harder than he thought possible. Not to mention the rest of his body.

He forced his eyes to her face and frowned. Something was different.

"Where are your glasses?"

She shrugged. "I thought it would be sexier if I wasn't wearing them."

Logan latched onto the change in subject like a drowning man to a lifeline. *Glasses. Glasses. Think about glasses.* "That's ridiculous. I love them."

"Really?" She dipped her head and slid out of his near embrace. He immediately wished he hadn't watched her go because she bent over to slide a hand into the coat pocket, giving him a glorious view of her scantily clad buttocks and muscled thighs. She straightened and faced him again with one hand on her hip, glasses back in place.

"Holy hell, woman. Are you trying to kill me?"

"No. I'm trying to seduce you."

Logan rubbed the heel of his hand against his forehead. He'd never wanted a woman so much in his life.

Why was he doing this to himself, again?

Because you want more than just her body, and if you give in now, that might be all you'll ever get. He had to repeat that to himself a few times because his brain wasn't doing much thinking just now.

He sighed deeply and took two steps forward, kneeling down to gather her coat.

Jeni pursed her lips and glared at him as he slung it over her shoulders. "I never took you for a prude, Logan."

"It's a first. Trust me."

She huffed out a breath. "I knew I should have just been naked under here."

Logan's eyes nearly rolled back into his head. He cleared his throat, holding the coat together at her stomach. "Jeni. Stop this."

"You first."

He shook his head. "I want to be with you, Jeni. I want to spend time with you and get to know you. I'm determined to go about it differently this time. No matter how badly I want to carry you to my bed right now." And just because he'd never want her to feel unattractive or rejected, he added, "And I want that pretty damn bad."

Jeni slipped her arms through the sleeves, a win for his sanity. She lifted her chin. "I hate you."

"No, you don't."

"No, I don't."

He raked a hand through his hair. "Want to stay and hang out for a bit? You came all the way here."

Her fingers paused in the process of pushing a button through. "It's late."

"Were you planning on sleeping when you came over?"

She smirked. "No."

"Stephen Colbert's about to come on." He hoped she'd talk to him instead of watch TV, but he'd take her beside him either way. "Friends watch late night talk shows together."

She hesitated, and he was sure she'd refuse him. But then she shrugged. "Okay."

Thank God she didn't see the ear-splitting grin he aimed at her back.

"So, what's with the Hawaii sticker on your truck?"

Logan glanced over at her, sitting on the couch beside him. She'd changed into one of his T-shirts, and he liked seeing her in it entirely too much. "Came with the truck. I bought it used and never took it off."

"Oh." She turned her attention to the television, where the host interviewed some famous actress.

"Did you know Colbert's been married twenty-five years? Says it was love at first sight." It was a risky thing to say but he went with it.

Jeni rolled her eyes. "What a load of bull."

"Which part? Being married that long or love at first sight?"

"Both."

"You sure are jaded, aren't you?"

"I'm twenty-six and divorced."

"You can't let one event reconfigure your entire life."

"Sure, I can. People do it all the time. Because of my accident, I chose a completely different career path. The job offer with the Chiefs changed yours. I'd bet when Andrew's finished with this whole cancer thing, he'll say the process permanently altered his life in some way or another."

"Those are different."

"How?"

He paused. "I don't know."

She looked pleased with herself. "Can I ask you a personal question?"

"You can ask anything you want." He just might choose not to answer. He crossed one ankle over his opposite knee.

She tucked her hair behind her ear, her gaze steady on his. "How did you lose your dad?"

"Aneurysm," he said, rubbing at his ear. It had been a long time since he'd told anyone about it, but with her attention on him like a warm ray of sunshine somehow soothing the pain of the memory, he kept going. "It was sudden. I still remember exactly where I was when my mom called. I was at a bar with some friends. Straight up dropped the beer bottle in my hand, and it shattered all over the floor. My buddies laughed at me like I'd just had too much, and I just turned and walked out. It was one in the morning and I was a good two miles from home, but I walked the entire way."

"That's terrible. I'm sorry."

"Me too. I didn't have enough time with him."

"You were in your twenties?"

"Twenty-one." He almost added that he hadn't met his dad until he was thirteen and had only had eight years to get to know him.

To learn from him.

But the words got stuck in his throat. He never talked about his life before coming to live with his parents. Tried not to think about it either. But that was harder to do.

"This is going to sound so nosy, but I thought maybe he had cancer. Andrew mentioned you'd been through that with someone."

Andrew needed to keep his mouth shut. Logan didn't want to talk about himself. He wanted to learn more about her. "That was my mom. She was diagnosed with breast cancer two years after my dad died."

Her gaze softened. "You took care of her?"

"Yeah." He gripped the ankle propped on his leg. "She didn't really have anyone else around to help."

"How's she doing now?"

"She's good. She's in remission, and we're just waiting for that magic five-year mark."

Jeni smiled. "I'm glad to hear that."

Logan steered the conversation away from his family. "How was work today?"

Jeni crossed her legs in front of her. "Fine. Busy."

"Sometimes I don't mind busy days at the office. Even though I like my job, it's nice when the day goes quick."

"I get that." She absently gazed at the television. "It feels like a lot of kids are entering the system lately. We desperately need more foster families."

Logan studied the freckles on her cheek. "I've always been curious about being a foster parent."

Jeni's head jerked toward him. "Really?"

"Yeah. I'm not sure I could do it as a single guy though."

"It's a common misconception that single men can't become foster parents. You just have to pass muster like anyone else, same as married couples."

"I know they'd let me," he clarified. "I just meant I think it would be hard for me to provide the kind of home a child would need right now. I couldn't foster a newborn because I have to go to work. And with my schedule, I'd have trouble getting older kids to and from daycare or school consistently. I have to work odd hours sometimes depending on when the Chiefs play or when there's a publicity event."

"There are always reasons not to do it." Her tone was gentle, not accusatory. "It's a serious commitment. It's good you're looking at it from several angles. Too often we get people who register and only last a few months."

Logan shook his head a little. "When I do it, I won't half-ass it. If I have a child in my home, I want to be there for them."

Jeni's golden eyes swept over his face, her expression softening as she listened.

"It just seemed like something I'd do with my wife someday," he continued. "When we could take on the responsibility together."

Her countenance changed in an instant. "If fostering required marriage, I'd be screwed," she said flatly. "I've always wanted kids, so I plan to do it someday too. Hopefully I'll eventually move up to an administrative position where I'm not at risk of being on call as much. But no matter my job, I'll be on my own and need to figure out how to make it work."

She really hated the idea of marriage with a passion, didn't she?

That didn't bode well for him and his newfound approach to relationships.

Or relationship—singular. He only had an interest in one, and he didn't want something so casual it was easy to walk away. He'd dealt with that almost from the moment he was born, and he was finally drawing a line in the sand.

She glanced at the clock and stood. "I'd better go. It's almost midnight." She tugged at the hem of the T-shirt she wore. It fell to the tops of her thighs. "Should I—"

"Keep it," Logan said quickly. He didn't know if he could handle it if she took it off in front of him. Her coat was draped over the back of the chair, and he handed it to her with a grin. "It feels weird to say I'm glad you came over. You know, since you were trying to seduce me against my will."

"I'm gonna win this game we're playing, Squinty." She put the coat on, and they walked to the door together.

He stopped short of opening the door, turning to face her instead. She stood close, and he could smell whatever perfume she'd put on. He didn't mind it, he just liked the way she usually smelled better.

She lifted her eyes to his, the thick frames of her glasses making her beautiful eyes seem even larger.

"It's not a game to me," he said in a low voice. Pursuing her was one of the most serious things he'd ever done.

Her gaze dropped to his chest, like the statement made her uncomfortable. He put his fingers underneath her chin to tilt her face up. To see those one-of-a-kind eyes again. She didn't resist the movement but closed her eyes, her eyebrows coming together in a slight frown. Her hand came up to grip his forearm, but she didn't pull his hand away like he thought she would.

Logan inched forward as if pulled by an invisible force, studying her lashes, her freckles, and perfect full lips. His heart rose to his throat as he dipped his head lower—

"What are you doing?"

He stopped but didn't pull back. "I was going to kiss you."

Her eyes opened. "Friends don't kiss."

Her breasts brushed against his chest with each breath, and he took solace in knowing she wasn't unaffected. He pressed his forehead against hers. "I don't want to just be your friend, Jeni."

She sighed heavily. "I know." She looked like she might say something else, but then she took a step back, opened the door, and walked out.

Logan closed the door and sank against it.

Jeni Bishop was going to kill him.

CHAPTER FIFTEEN

"I have bad news."

Words no one wanted to hear from their boss.

Jeni sat at the large table in the conference room with the other social and case workers.

Sandra's lips, usually turned up in a smile, flattened into a grim line. "I received news of impending budget cuts to our department. I don't know exactly what it means yet, but I just want everyone to be prepared."

"Prepared for what?" one of the seasoned case workers asked. "Are jobs being cut?"

"I'm not sure yet," Sandra said. "I don't even know which programs are losing funds. It might not affect the foster service line. And if it does, I don't know how significant the deficit will be. It could be we just can't use the nice printer paper anymore and have to buy generic coffee for the breakroom. Or it could mean I lose FTEs. I wish I knew. But if the latter is even a possibility, I wanted to get it out there so no one's blindsided."

Jeni clasped her hands together in her lap. She was the newest employee. If someone had to go, it would be her.

What would she do? Yes, one of the perks of being unattached meant she could go anywhere for a job if she needed to. It was one of the reasons she intended to remain that way. But she'd finally gotten settled in Kansas City and was gaining her bearings in her position. She'd worked hard to establish rapport with the foster families assigned to her and was slowly but surely getting to know the children under her supervision. She'd work hard no matter where she went, but Andrew's diagnosis made staying in town more important than she'd anticipated. She needed to be here with him. His first chemo treatment was tomorrow, in fact.

She could find another social worker position if she got laid off, but it wouldn't be the same. CPS was the best opportunity to make a difference in the foster care system, and she'd been confident getting her foot in the door here early would pay off in the long run. She hoped she'd work her way up, maybe even fill Sandra's shoes one day. The Kansas City metro needed more foster families too, and she had ideas for community events to increase awareness and provide information to the public. Ideas that would appeal to the demographic here—which meant barbecue would definitely be involved. Maybe she could even ask Logan about some sort of coordination with the Chiefs as a service event for the team that would also bring the publicity to benefit the agency.

Speaking of...a gorgeous, smiling man with wavy blond hair and blue eyes flitted through her thoughts, which was ridiculous. Logan's presence in Kansas City had no connection whatsoever to her desire to stay.

When those around her began to stand and filter out of the conference room, Jeni came back to the present. She hadn't even listened to the rest of the staff meeting.

She and Sandra were the last ones to leave.

"Should I be worried?" Jeni asked bluntly.

"I don't know." Sandra put a hand on Jeni's shoulder. "I hope not. You're doing a great job. If it were up to me, there's no way I'd let you go. It's too early to worry though, okay? I'm just hearing rumblings of financial upheaval from some of the legislators I know. Nothing has come directly from the Governor's office."

Jeni heard the unspoken word that followed.

Yet.

"One down, seven to go." Jeni reached over to squeeze Andrew's shoulder. "Wasn't so bad, was it?"

Andrew sat in the passenger seat, looking out the window. He looked the exact same as he had yesterday. Last week. Last year. That made it easy to make light of the fact he'd just received a shit-ton of chemotherapy.

How long until the side effects started? How long would it take for the chemo to change him?

Whenever it was, Jeni would be there.

He shot her a side-eye. "It's been ten minutes since I finished. It's a little early to draw conclusions."

"At least we didn't embarrass you too bad." She glanced in the rearview mirror where their mother, Rhonda, and Valerie followed in the repaired Suburban. They'd flocked around him the entire treatment. Even if he pretended to be annoyed by it, Jeni knew Andrew appreciated their show of support. At least a little.

"Easy for you to say," he muttered.

Jeni gave a sly grin. "What's up with you and Lauren?"

The cute pharmacist they'd met during his first oncologist visit just happened to pass by during his infusion. It hadn't seemed to have been by accident.

"I don't know what you're talking about."

"You were flirting hard."

"Was not."

"I don't think she minded."

His neck colored, and her grin widened. She barely knew Lauren but already liked her better than his ex.

"Are they following us to the condo?" Andrew asked, his eyes on the side mirror.

"Yep."

"They don't expect to come in, do they?"

"Yep."

"No."

"Mom wants to make you chicken soup. She's got everything she needs in a cooler in the back. Rhonda brought *Parks and Rec.* Valerie...well, she'll tuck a blanket around you. Get you water. Or something."

He groaned.

"Andrew, so help me God, just be strong and handle the chemo like a champ, and soon they'll leave us alone." More than anything, she needed him to do well because he was her twin brother and she loved him. But cracking jokes about the rest of their family was what they did, and keeping it light was what they both needed right now.

Cancer was serious. Chemo was serious. Jeni would follow suit when necessary, but right now, she wanted Andrew smiling.

He smirked. *Success.* "I'm texting Logan."

Jeni perked up at that. "What? Why?"

"I'm seeing what he's up to tonight. Maybe he'll be an excuse for me to escape if they won't let me breathe."

"You can't go *out.* You just got chemo."

"I feel fine."

"It's been fifteen minutes!"

Andrew shrugged, tapping at his phone screen with his thumbs. "I'll play it by ear. I'm just gathering my options."

His phone dinged with a text message.

"What did he say?" Jeni asked without thinking. She cringed internally. Was it obvious she wanted to know if Logan had plans tonight? If he did, with who? Did he have a date? She shouldn't care about any of that, but the questions ran through her head all the same.

Andrew didn't seem to think anything of it. "He's going to McNellie's tonight."

"With who?" Good grief, she had to get a hold of herself.

This time Andrew gave her a strange look. "He didn't say. Why?"

"No reason," she said in what she hoped was a nonchalant tone. "Do you really think you should go to a bar right after your first treatment?"

"I don't want my diagnosis to turn my life upside down. I still want to have fun and do things like normal." He ran a hand through his hair. How long would he be able to do that before it fell out? "I won't drink."

"At least let Mom make you soup first. She's talked about it for days."

"Fine."

"And tell us all thank you and how much you love us and that you're glad we're here to take care of you."

Jeni expected a snarky reply, but Andrew put a hand on her shoulder just as she pulled into the parking lot of his condo building. She put the car in park and looked at him.

"I love you, sister," he said with sincerity. "I'm glad you're here."

She blinked, her eyes filling with tears. "I—"

"I'm not done. Thank you for everything. Especially for taking Mom and Rhonda and Val to your house and giving me space to deal with this. I don't know what I would have done without you."

She swiped a finger under her eye and sighed. "Fine. You can go out with Logan tonight."

"Yes!" Andrew pumped a fist and jumped out of the car, leaving her sitting there, shaking her head.

"Sneaky bastard," she muttered. "I just got played."

Seemed her brother and Logan had more in common than she thought.

∽

Logan: What are you doing?
Jeni: Thinking about tacos.
Logan: That's weird.
Jeni: A commercial for Mateo's just came on TV. Now I want some.
Logan: Let's go. I'll meet you there.
Jeni: I already ate.
Logan: Come to McNellie's later?
Jeni: No.
Logan: It wouldn't be a date. Your brother's coming.
Jeni: You'd still take advantage of the opportunity somehow, I'm sure.
Logan: Just come. It will be fun.
Jeni: There will be plenty of other women there. Have fun with them.
Logan: Seriously?
Jeni: Seriously.
Logan: Fine.

An hour later, once Jeni, her mom, and sisters had arrived back at her house, Jeni's phone lit up.

Logan: I just got a woman's number. Happy?

No.

Jeni: I don't have feelings about it one way or another.
Logan: Liar

She so was.

Jeni: Is Andrew doing okay?
Logan: So far so good.
Jeni: Take care of him please.
Logan: I will. You don't have to ask.

She knew that. It was something she really liked about Logan —what a good friend he was to Andrew. There were a lot of things she liked about him actually, now that she'd learned more about him.

But no matter how much she liked him or how attracted she was to him, nothing could happen between them.

She'd learned several things from her marriage to Jackson, but two were the most life altering. One: commitment to another person meant putting her goals to the side. Both people can't get what they want all the time, and chances were her dreams would be the ones to go down the drain. As far as Jackson was concerned, Jeni was expected to conform and submit to his life decisions and do it with a smile on her face.

Two: she wasn't the kind of marriage material most men wanted. Sure, some might find her attractive or interesting at first, like Logan apparently did, but the likelihood of making someone happy long term was low. There were things she couldn't offer, and even if it came across as selfish, in reality she was trying to protect both parties from inevitable future disappointment.

She'd realized these things far too late, but either way, she'd never tie herself to another man again.

A loud knock came from the front door. Jeni shifted to get off the couch, but Rhonda was closer and made it to the door first.

"Did someone order food?" Rhonda asked.

"No," Jeni said.

Valerie's eyes never left the TV. "Not me."

Their mom had already gone to bed.

Jeni tilted her head a little and came to stand next to Rhonda.

A young man stood on the doorstep, a worried look on his face. "Damn, did I get the address wrong? I've got a Postmates order for a Jeni Bishop."

Rhonda looked at Jeni quizzically.

"That's me," Jeni said. "But I didn't order anything. What is it?"

"It's from Mateo's. Is there someone who might have sent it to you?"

Jeni pursed her lips to fight a smile. "Um. Yeah, there is. I'll take it. Thank you very much."

The delivery guy handed over the paper bag and left. Rhonda had returned to her spot in the living room, and both she and Valerie eyed Jeni when she sat back down. Jeni put the bag on the coffee table and pulled out several wrapped items.

"Anyone want a taco?"

CHAPTER SIXTEEN

"What are you smiling at?" Andrew asked.

Logan glanced up from the Postmates delivery confirmation on his phone. He wished he could see the look on Jeni's face right now.

"Nothing important." Logan sat back and perused the room. Jeni was right—there were a lot of women here. He'd scored one phone number, but dickhead Andrew had swiped it for himself, claiming he knew the girl.

Whatever. Not only was Andrew a friend Logan cared about, but the dude had cancer. Logan would give him the shirt off his back if he thought Andrew needed it.

Logan wasn't really interested in any of the women around him anyway. He'd approached the girls earlier for three reasons. One, they'd both smiled at him, and one beckoned him over for a chat. He felt like an asshole walking away without showing some interest, and they were perfectly nice. Two, he thought it might irritate Jeni. Three, Andrew had no idea anything was going on between him and Jeni—*Logan* didn't even know what was going on between him and Jeni—and Logan figured he needed to keep up his usual habits when he was out.

"Still doing good?" Logan asked, sipping his beer.

Andrew narrowed his eyes. "Fine. Just like I was the first four times you asked so cut it out. I get enough of that from my family."

Logan gritted his teeth. "Sorry, man."

"How was work this week?"

"Busy. I'm sure you've noticed the Chiefs are doing well this season."

Andrew's lip curled, and he muttered something into his water glass.

Logan chuckled. "Anyway, took me two days to engage with audience comments on the Twitter and Facebook posts I put out during the game. And I've got an upcoming marketing campaign to publicize the team's involvement with a middle school sports program."

"How's the other thing?"

"Fostering Sweet Dreams?"

"Yeah."

"Man, it's awesome. Word finally got out about us, and the donations are rolling in. I got nine beds and two large monetary donations this week. I don't want to complain, but it's going so well I might need to find someone else to head things up soon. I'm spending a lot of my free time organizing pick-ups and drop offs, and with my job responsibilities, it's a little much."

"Damn, nice job. How long has it been since you started it?"

"Uh, almost three years now, I guess."

"That's great. It's a cool thing you're doing. Have you run into Jeni at any of the events? I figured you two would cross paths at some point through foster care stuff."

"Not yet." It seemed Jeni still had no idea how involved he was, and he was fine with that. He didn't want to invite questions. "But I'm sure it won't be long."

∽

Jeni: Thanks for the tacos, I guess.

Logan: We really need to work on how to thank someone for a gift.

He settled against his couch, smiling. He could picture her perfectly, glaring at her phone.

Jeni: I didn't ask for them.

Logan: = gift.

Jeni: How do they make their tortillas so good?

Logan: Hell if I know. But they are. Any left over for me?

Jeni: Nope. Rhonda and Valerie had some too.

Logan: Damn. My plan was to have an excuse to stop by tomorrow.

Jeni: Guess you'll have to think of something else.

Logan: Yeah?

Jeni: Sure. I won't be here.

Logan: Working?

Jeni: No, I'm driving to Lawrence for the day to see a friend.

Logan: That's too bad. We have a softball game tomorrow night, and I thought you might want to play.

Jeni: No! Seriously?

Logan: Yep.

Jeni: I want to play so bad. But I can't cancel on my friend last minute. It's almost November so I assume the season's almost over?

Logan: We have two more next week. A few of the earlier games were rained out so we tacked on one more week at the end. One on Tuesday night and the Championship tournament on Saturday.

Jeni: Count me in if there's an open spot.

Logan: I'll check and let you know.

Jeni: Thanks.

Jeni: I guess. :)

~

Four days later, Logan knocked on Jeni's front door. Shawna, one of the three women required to play coed softball, had sprained her ankle playing soccer with her son yesterday. It wasn't a grievous injury so Logan wasn't an asshole for being a little pleased about it, right? Shawna was out for the last two games, which meant Jeni had an open invitation.

Better still, she agreed to let him pick her up.

Jeni opened the door. "Hey."

"Hey."

Shit, she looked sexy with her hair pulled in a high ponytail and legs clad in tight-fitting pants. He'd always been drawn to athletic women.

He handed her the team shirt he'd brought.

She took it but didn't move. "I'll just change in the car."

"What?" Logan croaked.

"What? I'm wearing a sports bra under here," she said, tugging at the hem of her Nebraska T-shirt.

Logan was about to protest further when Rhonda approached, followed by Valerie and Jeni's mom.

"You're so sweet to take Jeni to play softball," her mom cooed.

"She misses it," Rhonda said.

"She had a full scholarship to play at Oklahoma, you know," Valerie added. "You should let her pitch and watch the strikes pile up."

"Jeni was the star of our little farming town," her mom said with a sad cluck of her tongue. "Did she tell you about what happened?"

"Hello?" Jeni waved a hand in the middle of the little circle of people. "I'm right here."

Her mother and Valerie looked at her like they'd just realized she was standing there. Rhonda rolled her eyes and winked at Logan, and he grinned.

Rhonda might be his favorite.

After Jeni, of course.

"Well you don't exactly talk much, honey," her mother said. "I just thought Logan should know—"

"Are you ready?" Jeni interrupted with a hand on Logan's forearm. He wished he wasn't wearing an Under Armour shirt underneath his jersey so he could feel her fingers against his skin.

"Sure. Yeah, we'd better head out so we aren't late." He smiled at the other women. "I'll have her home at a decent hour, I promise."

Everyone laughed. Except Jeni.

"Why did you say that?" she said as they climbed into his truck. "This isn't a date."

"Calm down, I know." He started the ignition and backed out of her driveway. "Women are usually excited to spend time with me, you know."

"I'm sure they are."

He narrowed his eyes.

"I'm serious." She turned the full force of those golden eyes on him, and it took his breath away. He focused on the road as she continued. "I've had the full Logan Davis experience. I can't blame them for coming back for more."

Was she suggesting his talents in the bedroom were all he had to offer? He supposed his track record with women pointed to that.

With Jeni, he wanted much more.

"Hell, I tried to come back for more," she added. With impeccable timing that was no doubt intentional, she unbuckled her seatbelt and pulled her T-shirt off over her head.

Logan tried and failed to keep his eyes on the road. Her body was spectacular, even in a sports bra and belted softball pants. Her stomach was flat and smooth, and his eye caught on the small smattering of freckles across her collarbone. He shifted in his seat, attempting to maintain control of the truck and his body.

"You know what you have to do for more." His voice sounded rough to his own ears.

"I can't date you, Logan." She put the jersey on and lifted her hips to tuck it in.

Logan nearly groaned aloud. "Can't, or won't?"

"Both. It's nothing personal. I don't plan on dating anybody. Been there, done that, wasn't worth it."

"Was Jackson the only guy you ever seriously dated?"

"I mean, I had boyfriends in high school, but do those count?"

He shrugged.

Jeni answered her own question. "I'd consider him the only serious one."

"And you ditched him because he was bad in bed?"

She whipped her head around, an incredulous expression on her face.

Logan blinked. "That's the only thing you've told me so far. He got you out of the house after your accident and took care of you while you healed. He was a selfish asshole in bed. I'm out of information."

Jeni kept her face turned toward him for a moment, possibly debating whether she wanted to tell him more. They had a few minutes before they arrived at the softball field, and he hoped for as much as she'd give him. He wanted to know everything about her, especially things that affected her decision to date him.

Finally, she sighed. "I think I mentioned that when we got married, we moved to Lincoln and went to the University of Nebraska for college. He knew I wanted to be a social worker and work with kids, so I needed a Master's degree. During our last year of undergrad, Jackson's dad died suddenly of a heart attack. He wanted to move home to his family's farm to help run things, but he said it would only be temporary until they sold the place. Family's important, and I didn't mind taking a semester or two off.

"Once we got there though, he didn't want to leave. The farm was hours from a major town, and me continuing school was impossible. I kept asking when we would get back to our life, and one day he sat me down and said he planned to keep running the farm. He liked doing it, and it was our new life, whether I liked it or not. He said he had a responsibility to his family and I needed to support him in that and basically expected me to conform to the farm wife. Cook, keep the house clean, wash his clothes. I'd watched my mother do that my whole life, and it was never something I wanted for myself. I tried to do it for a while, just to give it a chance. I hated it. I was miserable, and I hoped Jackson would notice and we could figure out something that worked for both of us."

Logan liked Jackson less and less the more he heard. "I'm guessing that never happened?"

"Nope. No one lived nearby, so I had no friends. Jackson was always out working, so I was alone all the time. It was miserable and lonely. Worse even than the days after my accident, the situation Jackson swore he was saving me from."

Anger spread through him, hot and intense. "I can't believe he didn't give you any say in the matter."

Jeni sighed. "I hated the idea of divorce, especially at such a young age. But his refusal to compromise on anything I wanted, and the fact that I c—" She stopped short, her lips clamping shut. "I just decided I wasn't doing it anymore."

Stopping at a red light, Logan turned his gaze on her for a moment. What had she stopped herself from saying?

"The divorce was relatively simple. He wasn't happy being married to me by that point either, so he didn't resist."

Not happy with Jeni? Fucking idiot.

"After that, I moved to Omaha and finished my Master's degree. Got the job here in Kansas City, and the rest is history."

Logan absorbed the information. She spoke again after a few moments.

"You're quiet."

"I'm processing."

"Oh."

"I'm glad you didn't stay in a situation where you were unhappy. It sounds to me like you did the right thing."

She nodded. "I think so too."

"But…"

"But?"

"I think it could be different with someone else."

"When people get married, someone has to sacrifice something. It's inevitable. One gets a promotion in another town, and the other one has to quit so they can move. One loses their job, and the other has to pick up a second one to make ends meet. They get married over a mutual love of travel, have one bad flight, and one of them is too scared to fly again. The examples are endless. I just don't see how it's possible to pursue my dreams if I'm tied to another person. I've had to give up everything I wanted once before, and I'm not doing it again."

Commitment came with a certain degree of sacrifice, it was true. The concept didn't scare him, but then again, he'd lived most of his life on the other end of the spectrum with little to no commitment to anything or anyone. She'd had a completely different experience.

But that was his point, wasn't it? It could be *different* with him.

"What are these dreams that would be impossible to achieve if you were with me?"

She was quiet for a long moment. "It's not being with *you*. It's being with anyone. Dreams evolve over time. I'm pretty happy with where I'm at right now, but that could change in an instant. The same's true for you. Surely you have things you want out of life, right? Things you've always wished and hoped for and others that hit you out of nowhere, shocking the hell out of you because you hadn't even known it was something you wanted?"

"Yeah. That last one especially. Her name's Jeni."

Her eyes went soft, and she brushed his arm with her fingers. "You're really sweet, Logan. But I doubt my ability to make you happy—like, the real, bone-deep happiness you deserve." She took her hand away and pressed it against her heart. "I'm messy in here. Everywhere, actually. I know it sounds like my decisions about dating are all about me. But the more I get to know you and realize how much I like you, the more confident I am it's not just about me. There would come a day you'd want to move on, and I'm trying to protect both of us from something I know won't last."

"You can't know that."

"I do though."

They pulled into the sports complex, and Logan parked at the end of the row. He turned off the ignition and leaned his head back on the headrest, looking at her beautiful, stubborn face. He wanted to touch her. Shake her and kiss her and hold her, all at the same time.

Instead, he simply said, "Thank you for telling me what happened."

She pinched her lips together and narrowed her eyes. "That's it?"

"What do you mean?"

"You're not going to try to convince me I'm being unreasonable?"

"You went through a lot, and it's not unreasonable to be hesitant. But to refuse to consider another relationship? Ever? That's probably unreasonable. And I'm definitely going to try and change your mind. Just not today."

Jeni snorted. "You've got your work cut out for you."

He grinned. "Go big or go home. That's what I always say."

She reached back to tighten her ponytail and grabbed her bag. "We're going big tonight."

"I can't wait to see what you've got."

Jeni quirked a grin and opened her door. "That's what she said."

They met at the front of his truck, and he shook his head. "Why do you have the perverted mind of a fifteen-year-old boy?"

"I don't. I have the mind of Michael Scott."

"Fan of *The Office*, eh?"

"Love it."

"It's too awkward for me," Logan admitted. "I can't handle it."

She laughed. "If you don't like awkward, you definitely can't handle that show."

They approached the complex, and Logan led them to the assigned field. His teammates' curious eyes settled on Jeni. He didn't mind those, but the full body sweep from a few of the guys made his muscles tense up.

He introduced her as a friend, and a few minutes later, the game began.

If Logan thought he knew how sexy Jeni was before, he'd been sorely mistaken. Jeni on the softball field was mesmerizing. The intensity in her face while on the pitcher's mound, the confident smile when she struck someone out, and the frustration when a pinch runner needed to be sent in when she hit first base. Her car accident had mostly affected the lower half of her body, and she'd admitted she was too slow for a competitive game like this.

It was the final inning of the game, and Logan had just made a run for home, giving them an additional point that put them on top. He jogged to the dugout, breathing hard, and slapped his hand against Jeni's as she passed him on her way to bat.

"Nice job," Curt said from his spot on the bench. The guy was good at softball, but Logan had never cared much for his personality. "Nice addition to the team you brought today. Where've you kept her hidden away? She's damn good. We could've used her early on in the season."

"She just moved here a few months ago."

"You fucking her?"

Logan choked on his sport's drink. "The hell? We're not friends, Curt. Don't ever ask me a question like that again."

He ignored Logan's response and tipped his head in Jeni's direction. "Mind if I do?"

Logan's fingers curled into a tight fist, and his jaw went taut. He forced himself to take a breath so he didn't lay Curt out on the dirt. He'd love nothing more than to smash his fist in the guy's pretty face, but they were in the middle of a game and they were on the same team. And Logan didn't have a claim on Jeni, nor did he think she needed him to protect her.

In fact, he was confident Jeni would set Curt down quite nicely. "I'd like to see you try."

Curt threw his head back and laughed. "She shoot you down?"

Logan kept his mouth shut and stripped off his batting gloves, tossing them on the bench. He turned his back on Curt and watched Jeni step up to the plate. He kept his eyes on her hands so he wouldn't look at her ass while she waited for the pitch. She gave a perfect swing and hit a line drive straight past the second baseman, giving her enough time to jog to first base.

"Nice!" Logan called.

The answering smile she shot in his direction went straight to his heart. He grinned back at her, gripping the chain links between his fingers.

He was in trouble. Big trouble.

CHAPTER SEVENTEEN

J eni had almost forgotten how great this felt.

Pushing her body.

Being part of a team.

Having fun and winning.

She stripped the helmet from her head and walked toward the dugout, prepared to wrap Logan in a bear hug for bringing her here tonight. And it wasn't just an excuse to touch him, though she'd be lying if she said she wasn't looking for one.

But the second she passed the gate, a dark-haired man stepped into her line of view.

"Great job out there," he said with a cocky smirk.

What was his name? She couldn't remember. She'd felt his eyes on her all night though and not in a respectable way. "Thanks."

She stepped to the side to get around him, but he moved with her.

"Want to grab a drink after the game?"

Jeni sighed. "What was your name again?" She thought she heard a chuckle come from Logan's direction, but the ballpark was loud and she couldn't be sure.

The guy's grin tightened a little. "Curt."

"Right, Curt. I appreciate the offer, but I'll pass."

"You sure?" He angled his head a little and winked at her. "I think we'd have a good time."

Jeni looked at him hard in the eye. "I'm sure."

Curt shrugged. "Suit yourself. I'll be here if you change your mind."

She wouldn't. Edging past him, she couldn't stop the smile from spreading on her face when she saw Logan. "Hey."

He tilted his head up in greeting, matching her smile. "That was disappointing."

She stiffened. "The hit?"

Logan huffed out a breath. "No. That was awesome. I meant you rejecting Curt. I thought you'd put a little more spark into it."

So he had been listening. "Did you know he was going to ask me out?"

"Not before three minutes ago. But I'm not surprised. Every single guy on the team wants to. The women and married guys too, probably."

She rolled her eyes and hoped the warming of her cheeks wasn't noticeable.

"Whatever." She almost argued that the two other women on the team definitely weren't watching her but didn't want to bring his attention to them. Both had flirted with Logan as soon as he and Jeni arrived, and even though she had no reason for it, their attention on him irritated her.

She felt his gaze on her as she leaned against the chain-link fence.

"This suits you," he said.

Jeni looked at him, her ponytail swinging over her shoulder. "What do you mean?"

"Being here. Playing. All of it. I can see how much you love it."

She really did. "After the accident, I didn't know if I'd walk again, let alone play softball. And then when I was married, I didn't have the option, even if I could have, physically." She swallowed. "I played a little while I was getting my Master's, and it was the first time I realized I was really free. To do things I enjoyed and on my own terms. To be happy again."

His blue eyes held steady. "Happy Jeni is beautiful," he said quietly.

She quirked a brow at him, trying to ignore the flutter in her stomach.

"Grouchy Jeni is too." He leaned in close. "Flirtatious Jeni, worried-about-her-brother Jeni, and tipsy Jeni. All beautiful. But so far, happy is my favorite."

Her smile couldn't be stopped. "Mine too."

A few minutes later, the third player on their team struck out, ending the game. They won by two runs, and Jeni took pride in the fact that she helped make it happen.

"You in for Saturday?" Logan asked as they walked back to his truck.

"Definitely."

His phone rang as soon as he started the ignition. "Hey, Mom. What? No, I had a game tonight, remember? I thought we moved it to tomorrow."

Jeni glanced over at him.

He rubbed a hand down his face. "I'm sorry. We just finished, and I'd come over but I have someone with m—"

Jeni put a hand on his arm. "What is it?" she mouthed.

"Mom, hang on a sec." He pulled the phone down and covered the speaker with his other hand. "I was supposed to eat dinner with my mom tonight. I asked her last week if we could move it back a day because of the rescheduled game. I guess she forgot. She made dinner and was wondering where I was."

Jeni thought for a moment. There was an obvious choice here, and she surprised herself a little by saying, "She went through all that trouble. Let's go, if she wouldn't mind you bringing me."

He raised his brows. "Really?"

She shrugged. "Sure. I'm starving."

He frowned a little and slowly put the phone back to his ear, his eyes on Jeni. "Mom? Is there enough for three?"

Ingrid Davis was a delight. Jeni didn't think she'd ever hit it off with another person so quickly.

"Are insta-friendships a thing?" she asked when Logan's mom stepped away to refill Jeni's water glass.

"Apparently," he replied, his eyes happy and bright.

They'd finished dinner, and Ingrid had a Marie Callendar's apple pie in the oven. Jeni was impatiently waiting for the ding of the timer. Because she loved apple pie, not because she wasn't having a blast.

The three of them had sparred about NFL football. Talked about Ingrid's job as a teacher. Discussed Jeni's decision to be vegetarian, especially after an awkward exchange where she declined the main dish which contained ground beef, hence her eagerness for dessert. Ingrid even discussed her breast cancer diagnosis and treatment, which was tremendously helpful. Hearing what it was like from the patient's perspective would hopefully help Jeni relate to Andrew better in the months to come.

Ingrid returned with Jeni's glass, and Jeni realized how little she and Logan looked alike. Ingrid was tiny—barely over five feet, she would guess—with jet black hair and brown eyes. A stark contrast to Logan's six-foot frame, blond hair and blue eyes. She made a mental note to look around for family photos and get a glimpse of what his dad had looked like.

"Thank you," Jeni said.

"You're welcome." Ingrid sat down across from Jeni and Logan. "I don't think I've asked—what do you do for a living, Jeni?"

"I'm a social worker. I specialize in child welfare and work at CPS, mainly with the foster care system."

Ingrid's mouth dropped open. "Really?" She swung her gaze to Logan. "What a small world."

Confused, Jeni looked from Ingrid to Logan and back again. "I'm sorry, I don't follow."

"Surely Logan's told yo—"

"I haven't, Mom," Logan interrupted quietly.

"Oh." Ingrid sat back against her chair. "Not even about Fostering Sweet Dreams?"

Jeni perked up at the mention of the nonprofit her boss worked so closely with and did such wonderful things for the foster care community. "What about FSD?"

"Well, that's Logan's organization, dear."

It was a good thing Jeni wasn't holding her glass, because it would have slipped from her hand and shattered all over the floor. "It's what?"

Logan's blue eyes regarded her, unwavering, his expression unreadable. "I founded FSD three years ago."

Jeni's mind went blank for a moment, like her brain stopped functioning. She thought she had Logan pegged but suddenly felt like she knew nothing about this man next to her.

"I, um…I had no idea. That's incredible," she said slowly.

"Logan's always had a heart for foster children," his mother said, oblivious to Jeni's near-paralysis or the way Jeni and Logan were staring at each other like they were having a blinking contest. "He gives away nearly all of his Chiefs season tickets to foster families and has given over two hundred children a place to sleep through his foundation."

Jeni's heartbeat quickened, and a lump formed in her throat. Warmth bloomed deep inside her, slowly seeping through every cell in her body. "I don't understand." Was that her voice that sounded all breathy and weird? "Why…how did you get into that?"

"It's kind of a long story," Logan said. "We can talk about it some other time."

Jeni didn't push, and Ingrid went on to reveal that she and her husband had been foster parents early on in their marriage. That was probably what sparked Logan's interest.

Logan suddenly pushed his chair back, the legs scraping against the tile. "I'll be right back."

Jeni watched him leave the room. Ingrid kept talking, and somehow Jeni made appropriate responses despite her whirling thoughts.

After a few minutes the oven timer dinged, and Ingrid went to the kitchen, leaving Jeni alone at the table.

She rubbed her eyes then jumped up and left the room.

CHAPTER EIGHTEEN

Logan stared at his reflection in the bathroom mirror. He didn't know what just happened in there, but something passed between him and Jeni. His mother and her big mouth.

Eh, whatever. He would have told Jeni himself at some point.

All he knew was after tonight, he didn't know how to stay away from her. After watching her kick ass on the softball field, happily eat his mother's canned peas and crescent rolls from a cardboard tube while gushing over how delicious it was, and feeling whatever electric current transferred between their bodies just now—he was screwed.

Royally.

He turned the cold water on and splashed his face. Swiping the towel hanging on the wall, he dried his skin and put both hands on the counter.

The bathroom door opened, and Jeni burst in, closing the door behind her.

Logan straightened.

"Jeni? What are you—" His question was cut off as her hands gripped his shirt and she spun him around, his back hitting the door with a thud. His hands reached out for purchase, one landing on her upper arm while the other gripped her waist.

"Why do you have to be so wonderful?" she said, her tone accusatory.

"I'm not." He flexed his fingers against her. It felt so good to touch her like this.

Her eyes were on his for a second before they dropped to his lips, and she kissed him. Hard, open-mouthed, and hot. The temperature in the tiny room shot up by ten degrees instantly, and Logan groaned as her tongue entered his mouth.

Desire filled him, and he spread his hands across her back, pulling her flush with his body. The door handle dug into his lower back, but he didn't care. Her scent in his nostrils, her tongue in his mouth, her hands in his hair—all those things were worth it. One of her hands moved to wrap around the back of his neck, and she put pressure there.

"Jeni," he laughed into her mouth. "I can't get any closer."

She lifted her eyes to his, and they were like gold fire. "Try."

Logan took a sharp intake of air, and it still wasn't enough. Heat engulfed him, and he couldn't breathe.

He leaned over her and gripped her upper thighs in his palms, lifted her as he pivoted, and gently lowered her onto the counter. He slid one hand to the back of her ass, and the other moved up to slide through her hair and cup the back of her head. He held her head in place as he leaned over her, tugging her lower body toward his, pressing into her.

"*Oh*," she whispered, her voice throaty and filled with wanting. He'd never heard anything so sexy in his entire life. Her legs came around his waist, wrapping around him like a vise. Her muscular thighs squeezed hard, and he loved it. He pulled her lower lip between his teeth, gently nipping at her. Each little noise she made was an aphrodisiac, lighting his ardor and spurring him on even more.

He didn't know how to stop.

He didn't want to stop.

Hell, he had to stop.

He tore his lips from hers, and she fisted her hand in his shirt, bringing him right back. He went willingly for several glorious minutes. At one point, she leaned her head back against the mirror, maybe to take a breather, and he followed her, helpless not to. She didn't seem to mind, and her arms wound around his neck.

A knock sounded at the door. "Whenever you two are finished in there, pie's ready."

Logan lurched back, and Jeni's hand flew up to cover her mouth. They stared at each other, wide-eyed and breathing hard, then burst out laughing.

"I feel like I'm sixteen and just got caught sneaking a girl through my window."

"Holy hell, I'm mortified. I don't know what came over me. I just...it's like I lost my head for a minute."

Logan brushed a few wisps of hair back from her forehead. "I hope you never find it again."

She leaned into his palm then suddenly gasped and twisted around to look in the mirror. "Oh my gosh, I look like complete shit. I can't believe I came in here and jumped you when I'm all dirty and have helmet hair."

With his hands on her shoulders, Logan turned her to face him again. "You couldn't look like shit even if you rolled around in it. You're the sexiest woman I've ever seen."

He pressed his soft lips against hers, his heart pounding.

How did she smell so good after the game they'd just played?

Logan pulled his head back, and they looked at each other for a moment. She suddenly looked shy, and a protectiveness he didn't know he had flared inside him.

He helped her down from the counter. "We should probably get back out there."

"I don't know if I can," Jeni said. "What kind of first impression am I giving your mother?"

"Don't know, don't care." Logan adjusted his pants. "Besides, I'm the one who can't leave yet," he said with a wry grin. "You gotta go first."

"What? No."

"But there's pie," he reminded her.

If Logan had the choice to stay here and keep kissing Jeni or have freshly baked apple pie, he'd choose the former, hands down. He wasn't sure she'd say the same as she licked her lower lip, her eyes going bright.

"I do love pie," she said.

He almost pulled her against him for one more kiss.

Instead, he opened the door for her. "I'll be out in a minute."

Logan remained in the bathroom for a few minutes to let his mind and body cool down. It wasn't easy, since he kept replaying what just happened over and over in his head. Had Jeni really just burst in and initiated a hot make-out session in his mother's powder bath?

Hell yes, she had. He'd wanted his mouth on hers ever since he had her in his bed. Before that, even. Touching her was just as powerful this time as it had been then, and he was more convinced than ever there was something different about her.

About them, together.

Jeni wasn't some one-night stand. He couldn't be her friend with benefits. He wanted to know all of her, inside and out. He wanted to know her mind, her body, and her heart.

And after what just happened, he had hope she might feel the same.

Logan finally rejoined Jeni and his mother. They were halfway through their pieces of apple pie and his mom was happily chatting away. She winked at Logan when he walked in, and he grinned and shook his head.

Jeni sat stiffly in her chair, a polite smile on her face as she listened. Her demeanor was the polar opposite of the laughing vixen from ten minutes prior, but she probably felt awkward after what just happened. She kept her distance from him through dessert and saying goodbye to his mom, and he couldn't fault her for that. She wasn't his girlfriend—yet—and he couldn't imagine her mother being on the other side of a door, knowing Logan's hands were all over her daughter.

But when they were back in his truck, he started to worry. She stayed strangely quiet as he weaved out of the neighborhood. When he reached for her hand, she pulled away.

He frowned. "What's wrong?"

Jeni glanced over at him then focused her gaze on the dashboard in front of her. "I shouldn't have kissed you like that. It was a mistake."

"What are you talking about?"

She rubbed her forehead with the heel of her hand. "I meant what I said earlier. I really like you, Logan. Each new thing I learn about you only makes me like you more. But I kind of got carried away, and I'm sorry because I know you probably thought that meant I was open to starting something real. Like a relationship."

He sure as hell had thought that. And he'd swear in that moment she had too. What happened between then and now to change her mind?

"Don't do that," he said as gently as possible despite the knots forming in his stomach. "Don't put a stop to this before it's even begun. I'm not like your ex-husband, Jeni. Give me a chance to show you that. I'd never try to control you or stop you from doing what makes you happy."

She'd started to shake her head before he even finished his sentence. "I can't. I'm sorry, but I just can't. If you want, I'm still down for a no-strings-attache—"

"No." His voice came out harsher than he intended, and she seemed to shrink into her seat. "That's not what I want from you."

Jeni peeked over at him. "Not even a little bit?"

"Don't make a joke. It's pretty obvious what my body wants when you're nearby, but I want more. I've made myself clear on that point."

"So have I."

Logan slowed the truck to a stop at a red light. He turned his head to look at her, frustrated at how beautiful she looked even when she was pissing him off beyond reason. "You won't even let me try? Prove I might be the kind of man you need?"

"The problem is with me, Logan. My issues not only make me averse to that level of commitment, but they also make me a shitty partner and that's not fair. It's not about proving yourself. You're perfect just the way you are."

He wasn't though. He wasn't perfect. Deep down she probably knew it too but was trying to cover with this "it's not you it's me" bullshit. Why had he thought he might convince her to be the first one to stick around?

The light turned green, and he hit the gas hard, the truck lurching forward.

"I understand," he said.

Her fingers brushed his bicep, and he stilled. She quickly retracted her hand. "It's not you I don't want. Tell me you understand that."

Logan met her eyes for as long as he could before needing to look at the road again. "I understand."

"You're a wonderful man on the inside and are so insanely hot on the outside sometimes it hurts to look at you. Someday you'll make another woman very happy."

She was trying to be kind, but her words only served to further his frustration. For the first time in his life, he'd found someone he wanted to open up to. He wasn't ready to yet, but she already knew more about him than anyone else had, and it felt like he'd gotten closer with her than anyone else. It was just his luck that some motherfucker got to her before he did—before he could treat her like she deserved—and ruined her belief in marriage. Relationships in general, it seemed.

Someday you'll make another woman very happy.

Doubtful because even though he'd only met her four months ago, everything in him told him he'd never want another woman.

He only wanted her.

CHAPTER NINETEEN

Jeni didn't make it inside her house until an hour after Logan dropped her off. As soon as she hit the front porch, she waved him off and sat on her wooden porch swing. Thank God her neighbor was quiet. Jeni didn't think she could handle that tonight.

For the first time, jealousy surged through her at the memory of Cassidy and Logan's morning tryst. What would he do if Cassidy called him now? Would he go out with her? Sleep with her? Would Jeni hear the sounds of another woman experiencing the intense, focused attention of Logan Davis?

The thought made her stomach turn.

But so did the words his mother spoke tonight, moments before Logan returned from the bathroom where Jeni had the best kiss of her life.

"It does my heart good to see Logan so happy. I haven't seen this kind of joy in him in a long time."

Jeni had sputtered something in response, though she couldn't remember what. It must have been good enough because Ingrid had gone on.

"My late husband was the best role model Logan could have

ever asked for. I have no doubt in my mind Logan's destined to be a family man, even if his current lifestyle doesn't attest to it." She smiled wryly, and Jeni wondered how much Ingrid really knew of her son's exploits. "He's just trying to get things figured out. I know he would have stayed in San Francisco for a job at Twitter if it weren't for me. Social media communication is what he loves, but when I was diagnosed, he turned their offer down and moved back home. He had to take a job he didn't care for and only recently got an opportunity at the Chiefs. He's back in a field he's passionate about but is starting at the bottom because he lost so much time."

That had surprised Jeni—only because it was new information, not because it didn't fit the man she was starting to see beneath the ladies' man exterior.

It was Ingrid's words about seeing Logan happy and his destiny as a family man—which surely meant married and with children—that knocked the wind out of Jeni and elicited a stab of pain in her chest. She would never be able to make Logan happy in the long run. It would be unfair to let things move forward.

If only Ingrid had said those things before Jeni followed Logan to the bathroom, maybe she could have stopped herself. Talked some reason into her wayward heart.

Maybe she wouldn't have though. She'd wanted to do that ever since their almost kiss the night of her failed seduction attempt.

Either way, once they were alone in the dark cab of his pickup truck, she had to shut it down. He'd seemed okay with things lately, almost like he enjoyed their weird, non-dating friendship. She'd been hopeful their conversation wouldn't bother him too much and that they could just go back to the way they were.

But that moment when he looked at her in the truck, his blue eyes almost gray in the darkness, she knew she was mistaken.

The front door swung open.

"Shit!" Jeni's hand flew to her chest.

Rhonda rolled her eyes. "Relax, it's only me." She closed the door behind her and joined Jeni on the swing, glancing at her watch. "This isn't a respectable hour."

"I've been out here a while," Jeni said. "We went to his mom's house for a bit after the game."

"Really?" Rhonda raised a dark brow. "What's going on between you two?"

"Nothing."

"Really?" Rhonda asked again.

Jeni glared at her sister. "I'm not in the mood."

"You can't blame me for asking. You two have hung out a lot lately, and I know he's the one who picked you up for a date"— she used air quotes around the word—"the other night. You haven't dated anyone since your divorce."

"Maybe I have and just didn't tell you."

"Have you?"

"No."

Rhonda sighed. "Look, it's fine if you don't want to talk about it. But he dropped you off an hour and ten minutes ago, and you've been moping out here ever since."

"How do you know that?"

"I know everything. Are you okay? Did he do something to hurt you?"

"No, nothing like that. Logan's a great guy. One of the best I've ever met, actually. On par with Andrew."

"That's a high bar. So, what's the problem?"

Jeni's toe pushed them into a slow swinging motion. She focused on the rhythmic movement for a moment. "Can I ask you something?"

"I'm trying to get up in your business, but I guess so."

Jeni huffed out a single laugh then went serious again. "Why haven't you ever gotten married?"

"Haven't met anyone I wanted to marry. Now, back to you. Why are you moping?"

"I have. I thought I wanted to marry Jackson, and look where that got me. Now I'm messed up and broken. Ruined for all relationships forevermore."

"Are you saying this because you want to marry Logan and don't know what to do?"

"No. But he's the first guy I've wanted *more* with since Jackson. And I want to be with him, but I just don't see the point. I try to be smart with my decisions and not make the same mistake twice."

"Maybe marriage wasn't the mistake. Maybe it was *who* you married."

Jeni shrugged. "Maybe."

She said it more for Rhonda's benefit. Her sister was just trying to help. But the problem hadn't only been Jackson. It was her too. She knew, deep down, that it wouldn't work with anyone else.

Especially a man like Logan.

∼

Jeni: Am I still invited to play tonight?
Logan: We could use you. First game's at 6:30 and if we win we'll have one more. See you there.

He wasn't willing to give her a ride this time. She guessed that was fair.

Jeni locked her phone and tossed it on the couch beside her. Her mom and sisters had gone back to Nebraska two days ago, and the house was quiet. Even though she was relieved to have her solitude back, she'd kind of gotten used to having them, and her mother's cooking, around.

With her family gone, nothing to do, and no friends to hang out with, she suddenly felt lonely. She needed to make some other friends in Kansas City, but there weren't any other young, single women at CPS. Sandra was in her sixties, and the others were middle-aged at best.

Jeni thought of Lauren, the pharmacist who'd met with their family during Andrew's first oncologist visit. She was about Jeni's age and seemed nice. Lauren had dropped a terrible joke when she stopped by during Andrew's first chemo visit and popped off a few snarky responses to him too. Seemed like Jeni's style.

Andrew's too, if Jeni was judging his reaction to her correctly. He'd watched for Lauren the entirety of his chemo treatment yesterday, Jeni was sure of it. She knew her brother better than anyone else. He was interested. If he started dating Lauren, maybe Jeni could get a friend—or two? Lauren had to know other people around here—out of it too.

There were also two other women on the softball team, who she'd see tonight. They at least had sports in common, and maybe she could try to get to know them a little better.

Except both of them had been pretty flirty with Logan at the game on Tuesday.

On second thought, they didn't really seem like her type.

Jeni arrived at the ballpark at six-twenty. She sat in her car and pulled her hair into a ponytail before she grabbed her glove and got out. Two of the four fields were lit up, and two teams would play a game on each. The winners of those would move on and play head to head for the season championship.

The stands were dotted with people, though not full by any means. Mostly family and friends who wanted an excuse to drink beer and yell obscenities to the other team. Jeni learned on Tuesday this was no family-friendly league. Logan had apologized at one point for his teammate's language, but she wasn't bothered. He should hear the things that came out of her dad's mouth during calf birthing season.

She was just happy to be playing and in a fairly competitive league, at that. The one she'd played in during her Master's was a joke. She'd been forced to take her normal game intensity down about five notches, and even then, she'd become the player the other teams warned each other about.

Jeni approached the dugout where the other team members had gathered. Several were talking amongst themselves, two or three to a group. Logan sat on the bench, wearing a hooded sweatshirt over his jersey. He'd take it off before they played, and she'd only have a few minutes to admire him in her favorite article of clothing on a man. His wavy blond hair was slightly disheveled, like he hadn't taken the time to fix it at all today. His long legs clad in white pants and cleats extended out comfortably in front of him. If it weren't for the way his brow furrowed a little and his arms crossed tightly in front of his chest, he'd have looked like a guy without a care in the world.

Stacy, an adorable blond woman with long legs and a killer smile, sat about a foot and a half away from him. She said something to Logan, and his expression softened along with his deep laugh.

Jeni's heart twisted at the sound. She held her glove by her side in one hand and brought the other across her body.

He looked up and saw her and immediately dropped his gaze. He seemed to think better of it and caught her eye again, lifting his hand in a wave. Stacy hadn't noticed Jeni and leaned across the small space to say something in Logan's ear, touching his forearm.

Jeni had been two seconds away from setting her stuff down at the end of the row, but now took a step forward. "Excuse me."

Stacy looked up. "Oh, hey, Jeni."

Jeni gave her a tight smile and sat down right between them. The spot was barely enough for a person to squeeze into, and her thighs touched theirs on either side.

Stacy let out a small noise of irritation or amusement, Jeni couldn't be sure, and stood. "See y'all out there."

Jeni and Logan sat there alone. They were surrounded by

noise and people, but it felt like they were in their own little world.

Logan remained silent for a moment.

"You can't do that," he finally said. He hadn't moved so much as a centimeter away from her. He smelled wonderful, and Jeni wanted to bury her face in his neck.

"Do what?" she asked.

"Act jealous. You don't get to do that."

"I don't know what you're talking about."

He snorted. Still, he didn't scoot away, and they remained like that, side by side with arms and thighs aligned, until the game began.

They won the first game relatively easily. The second was a struggle.

By the final inning, their team was up by one, and Jeni stood on the pitcher's mound. It was after nine p.m. and probably barely above forty degrees. Her breath puffed out as white mist, but her body was warm and energized.

Two outs, two strikes. A beefy man with thick arms and hard eyes stared her down from home plate, bat clutched between his fingers, no doubt pissed off that he was about to be taken down by a girl.

If she struck this guy out, they'd win the game.

Logan's voice carried from his second-base post behind her. "Come on, Jeni."

She glanced back at him, and the look in his eye as he gazed back at her sent a shiver down her spine. It was the same way he'd looked at her that night she asked him to sleep with her, just before he gave in and kissed her.

Jeni brushed a few stray wisps of hair back with her forearm and turned back to focus on the batter. She gripped the ball in her right hand, tight and steady. She touched the ball to her glove, straightened, and took a deep breath. She swung her arm back and rotated, feeling her body naturally move forward, keeping her arm straight without being stiff. Her down swing was fast, and she snapped the ball free, the power from years of honing the perfect pitch evident in her delivery. The second she released the ball, she knew what would happen.

"Strike three!" the umpire yelled.

Her face split open in a wide smile, and it only took two seconds for her to feel herself lifted from behind, strong arms around her waist.

"Atta girl," Logan said from behind her.

He set her down but kept his arms around her waist, and she turned to face him. Several other players surrounded them now, patting her on the shoulders and back—and one on the ass. She almost whipped around to find the culprit, Curt first on her list, but Logan's fingers tightening around her waist focused her attention on him.

He dipped his head and spoke into her ear, his breath tickling the sensitive skin there. "You're amazing."

She closed her eyes and slid her arms around his shoulders, relishing in the feel of being pressed up against him. This was more than a congratulations for a stupid recreational softball championship, and they both knew it.

But they'd pretend that's all it was.

It was better that way, for both of them.

It was a week and a half later before Jeni saw Logan again. She'd kept her phone nearby at all times, thinking he'd text her at some point, about something. She wracked her brain for excuses to reach out to him but talked herself out of it every time.

This was her decision, and it was the right one.

Didn't make it easy though.

It was the Monday of Thanksgiving week, and Jeni sat at her desk at the office, typing up an update for a case file. She looked up to see Logan approaching her desk, and her heart caught in her throat.

Had he come to see her? Did he miss spending time with her as much as she did him?

"Hey, you," he said, rapping his knuckle on her desk.

"Hey," she said with a small smile. "What are you doing here?"

"I've got a meeting with Sandra in…" He looked at his watch. "Two minutes."

"Oh." Disappointment filled her.

He watched her for a minute, his brows drawing together a little. "It shouldn't take long, maybe half an hour. I planned to hit that deli with the hummus for lunch after. If you're still here when I'm done, maybe you could come?"

Jeni looked down at her hands, passing her index finger over a small freckle on her forearm. She should decline. "Sure."

Logan swallowed and nodded before continuing on his way to Sandra's office. He didn't smile once during their exchange, which made him seem intense and brooding.

And hot.

She definitely should've declined.

In the thirty minutes Logan was in with Sandra, Jeni typed four whole words on her report. She went to the bathroom twice, once for the usual reason and once to make sure her hair looked okay. She doodled an entire family of forest animals on the back of a meeting agenda from earlier that morning.

She jumped when his smooth voice sounded behind her. "Ready?"

No. "Yes." She grabbed her purse, and he gestured for her to precede him.

The deli was two doors down and packed as usual. They took a place in line, and Jeni fidgeted with the strap of her handbag. "How was the meeting?"

"Good. The business about Fostering Sweet Dreams only took ten minutes, but I've learned to schedule for longer when I get with Sandra. She's an old friend, and we always have stuff to talk about."

Sandra was a chatterbox.

"You knew her before you started the nonprofit?" Jeni asked.

"Yeah."

She waited for him to expound on that, but he didn't.

They reached the chilled food display, and just like the last time they'd been in this room, there was only one veggie sub remaining. Jeni glanced at Logan.

He saw it too.

The corner of his mouth twitched, and like lightning, he bolted forward and grabbed it.

Jeni's mouth dropped open.

Logan's blue eyes were bright with mirth, and he released a genuine laugh.

Warmth filled her, and she couldn't help but smile in return. Hell, hearing that sound was worth a sandwich with the city's best hummus. Still, she put her hands on her hips. "Seriously? I'm in line before you."

"But I'm so much faster."

"You're an asshole."

He laughed again, and like an addicted junkie, she was desperate for another one.

"Here." He held the wrapped sub out to her.

She narrowed her eyes. "What's the catch?"

"There isn't one," he said. When she didn't take it, he pulled his arm back toward his body. "I mean, if you don't want it—"

Jeni quickly took it. "I do."

"Thought so." He leaned toward the case and perused the other available options. "I'm feeling a salad today anyway."

"None of the salads have hummus," Jeni pointed out.

He shot her a glare, but the smile on his lips countered the severe look he was going for. "Don't rub it in."

They paid for their meals separately and sat down at a table.

They shared easy conversation through the meal, their flirtatious argument over the sandwich breaking the ice. When they'd finished, they continued to sit across from one another, as if neither wanted to be the one to end their time together. His eyes never darted around the restaurant. He wasn't distracted by the movement of customers around them. Instead, his attention was on her, and her alone.

"Can I ask why you became interested in the foster care community?" Jeni asked.

Logan shifted in his seat and leaned away from her. "My parents were foster parents."

She remembered his mother mentioning that. "Did you have foster siblings, growing up?"

He hesitated and rubbed at the back of his neck. "Sometimes." He dropped his hand to his lap. "So, what are you doing for Thanksgiving? Going to Nebraska?"

Why was he changing the subject? "Do you not like to talk about it?"

"No, I don't." His eyes slid to the table for a moment. "I'm sorry."

Fostering was rewarding and wonderful but could also be difficult and painful, both for the children in foster care and the families taking them in. Jeni wondered what kinds of children his parents had been assigned for Logan to be so closed off about it. She didn't push it. "Okay. I'll be here for Thanksgiving. Andrew's coming over, and we thought we'd order pizza."

"Really? You two can come to my mom's house if you want to. My grandparents are coming over, but it will just be the four of us. There will be plenty of food to go around, I promise." His eyes were back on her, blue and intense. His gaze wasn't one that made her uncomfortable but rather made her feel warm and off-balance.

She took a shaky breath. "Thanks, that's really nice. But at

Andrew's chemo appointment last week I kind of invited someone else to join us."

"That pharmacist? Lauren?"

"Yeah. How did you know?"

"Andrew told me about her. I think he really likes her."

Jeni grinned. "So do I. He was embarrassed when I invited her, but I know he's secretly glad I did. He's never been so hesitant around women before. I don't know what his deal is with this one."

"He told me he feels awkward that she works at the cancer center."

"Oh." Jeni tilted her head. "I guess I can see that. Well, I invited her anyway, and I hope she comes. She's our age, and I'd like to get to know her too. I don't have any friends in town."

His eyes roamed her face. "I'm not your friend?"

Jeni froze then took a drink of water to buy some time. "Sure."

He grunted. "That was convincing."

"I…" she began. She looked around. No one was sitting nearby. "Things got kind of weird, Logan."

For a second, he appeared surprised she'd say it outright. Then his lips seemed to turn down at the corners. "I know."

"I don't know how to fix it."

"I don't think you can." He looked at her intently for a moment, and her skin warmed with each passing second. He dipped his head forward, raking his fingers through his soft-looking hair.

Jeni searched desperately for something to say. She hated the awkward silence between them. It was one hundred times worse than the strained moment at her desk earlier.

Suddenly, he pushed back from the table. "You're right." He sighed. "We're not friends. I want more, and you don't, and that makes it complicated." He stood and came around the table, his solid, warm body invading her space. "I can probably get there someday, to a point where I can just be friends with you. But I know I'm not there today because from the moment I saw you sitting at your desk this morning, I've wanted to pull you into my arms and kiss you like my life depends on it. I want to do it right now."

Jeni couldn't breathe. Her gaze dropped to his full lips, and a spark of longing burst deep in her stomach. She closed her eyes, and her voice shook. "Logan…"

He held up a hand. "Don't." He shook his head. "I'm sorry. I thought I could handle it, but I can't do this. I have to go."

Logan turned and walked away, and Jeni just watched him go. She remained seated for several minutes, fighting the burn beneath her eyelids. When she was confident she wouldn't cry, she finally rose on unsteady legs and walked back to work.

CHAPTER TWENTY

Logan spent the next two months trying to get over Jeni Bishop. One would think it would have been easy, especially because he barely saw or spoke to her and when he did, Andrew was there too.

Also, work was insane and should have provided ample distraction. The Chiefs went all the way to the AFC Championship playoffs, so December and January were nonstop. A missed field goal cost them a spot in the Super Bowl, and Logan was just now getting over his grief. The Broncos were out too, and he wondered how Jeni was holding up.

But most of all, he should have been able to get over her because he never even had her in the first place.

Why, then, was it so damn hard? How could his heart hang on so tightly to something that never belonged to him?

Whatever the reason, he couldn't ignore it when he saw her name flashing on his screen at ten p.m. on a Friday night the first week in February. If this was a booty call, God help him—he'd be in his car and on his way to her house in five seconds flat. He missed her enough to take whatever part of herself she'd offer him.

"Hello?"

"Logan?" Her tone immediately tipped him off that this was serious. She sounded like she'd been crying.

He sat straight up in bed. "Jeni? Are you okay? What's wrong?"

"I'm okay. I just…I need your help."

"Anything. Where are you? What can I do?" He put his phone on speaker and laid it on the bed to put on his jeans.

"I'm at the office. I was on call tonight. The police had to remove a child from his home tonight, and I can't find an available family for him until tomorrow. I've been on the phone for three hours trying to find someone. The only person available is in Texas and won't be back until tomorrow. I don't have anywhere to take him and he's just sitting on the floor underneath my desk, and I can't let him sleep like that. He's four years old, and he can't sleep on this musty, sixty-year-old carpet. I tried to get him to our holding room where we have cots, but he won't budge. I want to at least offer him a bed. Maybe I could slide a single mattress under my desk or something, I think—" Her breath hitched. "He feels safer under there."

"Yes." Her quiet sobs tore him open. "Jeni, it's okay. I've got exactly what you need. I'll be there as fast as I can, okay? I just have to run to the storage facility to get it, but it's close to your office. It will take me twenty minutes, tops. Okay?"

She sniffled. "Okay. Thank you."

"I'll be there soon." He slipped shoes on and grabbed his keys, the phone now pressed tightly to his ear. "And Jeni? Just let him be. If he wants to be under your desk, don't try to bring him out. Let him stay where he's most comfortable."

"All I want to do is hug him and tell him it's going to be okay."

"I know holding him would make you feel better. But you don't know it will be okay. And it's not about what you need right now. It's about what he needs."

She paused, and he listened to her uneven breath through the phone. "You're right."

Logan prayed no cops were out with radars tonight because he pushed his truck well over the speed limit to get to the storage unit he rented. Once inside, he cursed the lack of organization in the space. He had several single mattresses, as they were the most commonly donated, but they were stacked in the back, and it took him a while to shift things around. The space was too small to contain his inventory, but he'd been too busy to do anything about it. He was making do with what he had, but once again he thought about how badly he needed help with the foundation. Someone to keep better track of things, keep it organized, and find a better location for storage.

He focused on the current task and loaded the bed then drove to the CPS offices.

Logan texted Jeni when he pulled up out front. He parked on the main street, not concerned about being in the way at ten-thirty on a Friday night. He was unloading the mattress from the bed of his truck when she unlocked the door. He wanted to drop the bed and pull her close, to feel her arms around him and kiss her hair.

But there was a child inside that needed them more than they needed each other. "There are sheets in the passenger seat," he said. "Can you grab them?"

He followed her through the dimly lit office space until they reached her desk. Not speaking, they made quick work of putting simple white sheets on the bed. He wished he'd had superhero or cartoon character ones instead. Jeni seemed to have composed herself between their earlier phone conversation and now, though her eyes were still red-rimmed.

When they finished covering the mattress, he handed Jeni the stuffed animal he'd grabbed at the last minute. He had a shelf of them at the garage and tried to give one out with each bed the foundation gave away.

Logan had the urge to peek under Jeni's desk and talk to the terrified boy within. But he didn't know what the boy's situation was, and a strange man coming at him likely wouldn't help matters. He also technically shouldn't be here, and Jeni could get in trouble if he tried to involve himself with the child.

She took the bear with a shaking hand. She tried to keep her face stoic, but Logan knew her heart was breaking.

Little did she know, doing this was the only thing that fixed his.

He walked to the edge of the room and leaned his back against the wall to wait while Jeni crouched at her desk, speaking in low tones. He wanted to make sure she didn't need anything else, and he didn't really like the idea of leaving her alone in this office downtown. Maybe he'd sleep in his truck outside, just in case.

He listened to them, mostly Jeni at first, but eventually came the tentative voice of the little boy. He said he had a brown teddy bear at home that looked just like that one. Its name was Brown Bear.

Logan smiled, remembering a toy solider he'd carried in his backpack as a kid. He'd apparently also been into unoriginal names and called it Army Man.

Jeni asked if he wanted to name the new bear, and the little boy immediately said Teddy.

Logan closed his eyes and pressed a fist to his grin.

It was times like this when he knew he'd never stop what he was doing through FSD, no matter how busy or stressed he got. It was too important. The kids were too important.

Twenty minutes later, Jeni approached him. "He's asleep. Thank you," she whispered, her voice breaking.

Fuck it. He pushed off the wall and crushed her to him, one hand on her hair and the other across her back. She came willingly, her arms winding around his waist, hands grasping his shirt and holding him tighter than he'd have thought possible. She pressed her face into his chest, and they breathed deeply together.

They remained there, embracing, for several long moments. Logan dipped his head a little and lightly brushed his lips across her hair, inhaling the scent of her shampoo.

She pulled her head back, and he braced himself for a scolding for kissing her.

"Will you stay with me?" she asked.

"Stay?" He searched her golden-brown eyes.

"At least sit here with me, for a little while?" She pulled out of his embrace, and he immediately felt bereft. She lowered herself to the ground and leaned her back and head against the wall, looking up at him beseechingly.

Like he'd say no to that.

Logan slid down and sat beside her, and she immediately scooted closer, flush against his side.

She rested her head against his shoulder. "Thank you," she said again.

He took her hand, and she held on tight.

"I've missed you," she said so quietly he almost missed it.

Logan held his breath for a beat, and his heart tried to punch out of his chest. "I've missed you too."

They didn't speak for long minutes, and Logan had just decided Jeni fell asleep when she spoke again.

"You were a foster child, weren't you?"

He closed his eyes and released a heavy breath. "Yes."

"Did your parents adopt you from the foster care system?"

Logan always struggled with telling people about this part of his life. But for some reason, in this dark room where people spent their days trying to take care of children who needed safe places to go, it seemed simple to acknowledge her statements. "Yes."

"How old were you?"

"When I went in or when I was adopted?"

"Both. If you don't mind telling me."

"Seven and thirteen."

She squeezed his hand.

"Did Sandra tell you or something?" He wasn't angry, just curious.

"No, why would she?"

"She was my case worker."

"Ohhh," she breathed out. "That's why you two are so close."

"She saved my life."

Jeni turned her head into his neck, like she might kiss his skin. He tensed, bracing himself for the stab of desire it would bring. It was a light brush and the sweetest thing he'd ever felt, soothing him from the outside in.

"She didn't tell me. I've been thinking about you a lot. All the time, if I'm being honest. And earlier, when you were so on point with what that little boy needed, I just knew you were talking from experience."

I've missed you. I've been thinking about you a lot. It felt so good to hear those words, but it hurt at the same time. She sat pressed up against his right side, her head still on his shoulder. He wasn't sure if it was better or worse to not be looking into her eyes as he said this. "Jeni, what are we doing?"

"I don't know."

"Well, whatever it is, it's not working out for me."

Her chuckle vibrated against his shoulder. "It's not working for me either."

"So…"

"Can—could we talk about it later? I'm willing to have the conversation," she said. "But just not right now. Not here. Please."

"Okay."

They were silent for a few minutes.

"What are you doing for the Super Bowl?" he asked.

"I planned on watching it at my house," she said. "Andrew and Lauren are coming over. I finally have another woman to hang out with."

Logan smiled at that. For Jeni's new friendship and because

181

things were finally looking up for Andrew. Not only had he completed his final chemo treatment—earlier today, in fact—but things seemed to be working out with Lauren.

"They're pretty cute," he said.

"They are."

"That could be us, you know."

"Logan."

"Sorry."

"You're welcome to come over. Maybe you could stay after and we can try to figure things out."

"Sounds good," he said, laughing to himself.

Try to figure things out?

Yeah, he was done trying. This time, he would make things happen.

∼

"Andrew and Lauren bailed."

Logan barely contained himself from pumping his fist in the air as he walked into Jeni's house. "What happened?"

She closed the door behind him. "They wanted, and I quote, 'alone time.'" She shuddered. "I can't believe my own brother told me that."

Logan laughed and continued on to the kitchen. He opened the fridge. "I don't blame him."

"Excuse me?" Jeni's shrill voice came from the doorway.

He glanced back at her, surprised by her tone, and found her standing with her hands on her hips.

"Do you think Lauren's cute or something?" she asked.

Ah. Logan popped the tops off two bottles of Guinness and walked over to her. "Nah. Never was attracted to redheads." She took the bottle he offered, freeing up one of his hands. He trailed a finger along her hairline, sweeping her hair back. "I prefer brunettes. Freckled ones. Ideally with glasses."

She appeared mollified, but he continued anyway.

"I said I don't blame him because I know how he feels. I've been dying for alone time with a certain girl too."

Her small hand touched his raised forearm. "You're in luck then."

He leaned in, but she suddenly looked above his head and jerked back.

"Game's about to start."

"You don't even care about the teams who are playing," Logan complained as he followed her into the living room.

"I have to temporarily pick a new team, didn't you hear? Lauren apparently dated the Broncos QB in college. You know, before he was a big deal. And he was a real jerk. Andrew flipped out and made us all swear not to cheer for them as long as Gearhart's on the roster."

Logan hadn't heard, but he knew who she could cheer for. "Chiefs?"

They sat down beside each other on the couch. "Hell, no. While considering my options, the Chiefs and Raiders were the first to go. I went with Green Bay, and they just happen to be playing today."

"Bandwagon fan."

She tipped her bottle to her lips. "It was pretty simple when I thought about it."

"Why's that?"

"Two words: Clay Matthews."

Logan's jaw went tight. "This is probably his last season with the Packers, you know."

She nudged him with her elbow. "He'll be playing today. That's all that matters."

"Fine."

Logan leaned back and directed his attention to the TV just in time for kickoff. Throughout the first half, he went back to the kitchen several times for snacks she'd prepared and for more beer.

And to get ahold of himself.

Jeni was just as fired up about this game as she was the last time he'd been here, and it did something to him.

"He was in!"

"He was not," Logan said calmly. His ass was on the couch while Jeni stood next to him, having jumped up while she screamed.

"Yes, he was."

"His toe was on the line."

She glared at him. "Let's watch the replay, shall we?" She crossed her arms as the slow-motion movement clearly showed that the player had, indeed, failed to get both feet inside the end zone.

"Dammit." She stalked out of the room.

Logan watched her go, a grin on his face.

During the third quarter, it all went to hell.

Jeni shot up and threw a hand in the air. "Intentional grounding!"

He shook his head. "There was a receiver in the area."

"I'm closer to the quarterback than that guy was."

In that moment, something in him clicked. It might have been her passion for the game, the way she smelled each time she brushed against his arm on the couch, or the three beers he'd had. Whatever the case, he stood, and she looked over at him quizzically.

"You are so damn cute," he said, setting his beer on the table. "I adore you."

She frowned. "Don't say that. And stop looking at me like that."

"Like what?"

"Like...like you're..."

He took a step toward her, reaching out with one hand. "A man falling in love?"

Jeni hid her hands behind her back. "Stop being that."

Logan ignored her movement and just put his arms around her. "There's nothing for it. It's happening. I'm falling."

Hard.

CHAPTER TWENTY-ONE

J eni couldn't do anything except stare at him. At his impossibly blue eyes, what looked like a two-day scruff on his jaw, and his perfect lips that were masculine yet soft somehow.

He leaned in and kissed her gently, carefully, like he was afraid she might bolt.

A heavy breath escaped her, and he brushed her lips again, his stubble lightly scratching her chin. She closed her eyes, the fight leaving her body. If she could just shut her mind off for a minute, she'd sink into him. Relish the bliss that was being in this man's arms, even for a little while.

So, that's exactly what she did.

Ever so slowly, she brought one hand up and slid her fingers into his soft, wavy hair. A low groan rumbled from his chest, and it sent sparks popping beneath her skin. She curled her other arm around his shoulder, gripping his neck between her fingers, applying pressure. Just like that day in his mother's bathroom, he wasn't close enough.

Logan rotated so the backs of his knees hit the couch, and he lowered himself down, pulling her onto his lap. Her knees went on either side of his legs, and his large hands wrapped around her thighs, sliding up and down.

The change in position pulled their mouths apart, and he just sat there, his heated gaze a little hazy, like he was waiting for her to make the next move. His hard thighs beneath her and his palms sliding up and down her legs sent her blood simmering. She grabbed his face between her hands and nipped at his lower lip, tracing the seam of his mouth with her tongue. He seemed to lurch upward a little, and they both opened their mouths, the kiss immediately transforming from slow and exploratory to hot and deep in a matter of seconds.

She dug her fingernails lightly into his scalp, and he growled, tilting his head to pull her earlobe between his teeth. She shivered at the touch on her sensitive skin.

"Jeni," he murmured into her ear. "I want you so much."

The words went straight to her heart, attempting to fill some of the cracks and crevices within.

His hands slid to her back, and Jeni rubbed against him, attempting to wrap herself around him as best she could in this position. What was it about Logan that made her behave so wanton and crazed? It had never been like this with Jackson. Not even in the beginning.

"My room." She'd intended a full sentence, but that's all she could get out. His lips on her neck were crossing the wires in her brain.

His hair tickled her ear when he shook his head.

"I don't have sex on the first date," he said into her shoulder.

Somehow, she had the wherewithal to snort.

Logan chuckled. "Anymore."

"I hate you," she said, tilting back a little to give him better access as he kissed his way across her collarbone.

"You don't."

"I don't," she agreed, her voice a little breathy.

With a finger under his chin, she brought his face back up and kissed him once, twice, then scooted back a few inches.

"I don't know what the point of this is." She ran a hand down the soft shirt covering his chest. "I don't know how we can make this work. But I love being with you, and I can't keep my hands off you."

His fingers trailed through her hair as he listened, his gaze steady on hers.

"So, let's talk about it." In a tender gesture, he grabbed her hand and kissed her palm then pressed it against his heart. She felt the steady thump and realized it wasn't racing like hers.

How could he be so sure, so calm? Did this not scare him?

"But if you expect me to think straight, you can't stay there," he said.

"Same." She slid to the left and turned to sit perpendicular, facing him. A shrill whistle reminded her that the game continued in the background.

For the first time in her life, she didn't give a damn about football.

"There has to be some compromise," he said. "I don't want just a physical relationship. I need more. I need you by my side on a random Thursday when I want tacos and a beer at Mateo's. I want to be the one you call when you've had a hard day at work. When we cross paths through FSD, I want to be able to kiss you in front of other people and it not be a big deal."

"I want those things too." Her voice shook with the anxiety she felt with the admission. Despite the nerves, it was true. "But I don't want a permanent commitment. It won't work."

"I'm not asking you to marry me tomorrow," Logan said. "Can't we just have a normal relationship? Go on dates, mess around a lot, and see where it goes?"

"We can. But I need to know you're okay with knowing it won't go beyond that."

"Beyond what, exactly?"

"Casual dating."

"How casual? I'm not okay with you seeing other guys." His expression turned hard, and it sent a thrill through her.

"Oh, hell no, we're not seeing other people. While we're doing this thing anyway."

He relaxed. "So, you say you don't want to get married again, but you're willing to date me for an undetermined amount of time? No end date?"

"That's correct."

"You realize I could easily do that for the rest of my life, right? Date you?" He grabbed her hand and threaded their fingers together. "When we're ninety years old and still dating, it won't be any different than if we'd gotten married."

"There are fewer restrictions this way," she said. "More options and less pressure—for both of us—when life changes. And it will, at some point. I'm not saying I won't choose you when something comes up. I just don't like the fact that marriage takes that choice out of the equation. The same would be true for you if you ever wanted something different."

It sounded terrible when she said it out loud, but she didn't know how else to do it. There needed to be an easy way out when one of them wanted to end things. Even if he didn't know it yet, it would probably be him.

He traced his thumb along the back of her hand. He frowned slightly, his eyes on their entwined fingers. "You already contradict your argument, you know."

She stiffened. "What do you mean?"

"You live for caring for other people, and you'll go out of your way to do it. Look at Andrew and the way you take off work to go to every single chemo and oncologist appointment. And your job. You think you can foster and adopt kids without adjusting your life for them? Hell no. But you'll do it, sometimes gladly and sometimes not, because you love them. It's the same in a relationship."

His thumb kept moving, and she focused on the light touch brushing her skin. Her immediate reaction was to resist. Push against his words and deny them. But if the time apart from Logan had taught her anything, it was that she wanted to be a little more open-minded. Agreeing to date him—sort of—was her first attempt at that.

"You're right," she mumbled, a little hesitantly.

His thumb stopped. "Come again? I don't think I heard you."

Jeni bumped his shoulder with hers. "I mean it. I see your point. But that doesn't erase everything that happened to me or my concerns about future relationships. I still need to do it this way. Slowly and without obligation. For now."

She waited, terrified that he'd say he wasn't okay with doing it this way. She wouldn't blame him, but she desperately hoped he'd agree.

Logan sighed deeply and pressed her knuckles to his lips. "Okay."

"Okay?"

"We'll try it your way." He shot her a slightly annoyed look. "I don't really like it. But at this point, I'll take whatever you give me, Jeni. Even if you're just offering yourself one day at a time. Just promise me that until the day this ends—and I'm not convinced that day will ever come—I have all of you. All your thoughts, your desires, and your fears."

"Fine. But what about these?" She pointed to her lips.

"Definitely your kisses."

Jeni smiled and leaned over to give him one. One turned into two, and two turned into ten, and they spent the rest of the game wrapped up in each other.

It was only when she sat on the couch and Logan was in her kitchen doing her dishes—what man willingly did dishes?—that fear settled back in.

One day at a time.

She could do that. She just had to live in the here and now and not worry about what would happen later.

Despite what Logan thought, that day most certainly would come.

∾

Logan: Hey, where are you?
Jeni: Just leaving work.
Logan: Can you come to McNellie's? I met Andrew here, and he's pretty messed up.

Jeni's heart dropped to her toes. They hadn't told Andrew they were dating yet. He'd finished his four cycles of chemo and had a scan this morning, and Jeni had wanted to make sure everything was fine before dropping the *I'm dating your best friend bomb* on her twin brother.

Jeni: Why? Did you tell him about us? I thought we decided to wait.
Logan: No. His doctor called about his scan already. There's still cancer and he needs more chemo.

Shit.

Logan: I think he needs all the support he can get.
Jeni: On my way.

Fifteen minutes later, Jeni walked into her brother's favorite pub. She spotted them against the wall, sitting at the bar with their backs to her. She'd recognize Logan and her twin anywhere but even more so now. Andrew's bald head was impossible to miss. She'd never forget the day he called to say he'd woken up with half his hair covering his pillow. She'd showed up at his door twenty minutes later, clippers in hand.

Jeni kept her eyes on her brother, knowing if she met Logan's gaze, she wouldn't be able to hide how badly she wanted to touch him.

She slid onto the empty barstool next to Andrew, and he looked over at her with unfocused eyes.

"How many have you had?" she asked bluntly.

Andrew blinked then turned to Logan. "Seriously? You called my sister?"

"No. I texted her."

Jeni poked Andrew's arm with her index finger. "You didn't answer my question."

"It was a stupid question."

"Why didn't you call me?" she asked, trying to mask her hurt that he'd called Logan instead. "You know I'm here to talk."

"I don't want to talk."

"It's better to sit and sulk in silence, drinking away your sorrows?"

"Sure. I feel better."

"You look terrible."

"Thank you, dear sister."

Jeni really wasn't sure what to say here. She and Andrew had been side by side nearly their entire lives, supporting each other. They were siblings, friends, confidants. But they were also a family of hard-working, do-what-you-have-to-do and don't-whine-about-it kind of people. After Jeni's accident, Andrew's constant *you can do this* and *don't stop now*'s got her through it, so she tried the same tactic.

"It's not the end of the world, Andrew," she said. "You'll get through this like you did the others. Now snap out of it."

"No cancer, no opinion."

What the hell could she say to that? She looked to Logan for help.

He held up his hands. "I called you because I couldn't cheer him up," Logan said. "Frankly, you're not helping."

She glared at him and held up her middle finger, and he seemed to fight a smile.

Andrew stared into his beer, not paying them any attention.

Jeni and Logan sat on either side of him for a while, but nothing they said seemed to make a dent in his foul mood. Finally, Jeni decided to call in reinforcements.

Jeni: You busy? It's Andrew.
Lauren: No, what's wrong? Did he hear about the scan already?
Jeni: Yeah. I guess they didn't get it all. We're at McNellie's.

Jeni watched the dots dance along the screen, hoping Lauren would say something comforting, like, *Don't worry, that's normal. We can still cure him.* Or, *He'll be okay, I promise.* Lauren had been a great resource for Andrew and their family through this whole ordeal, and Jeni trusted her knowledge on the subject.

Lauren: Be there soon as I can.

Jeni's stomach dropped, and she turned her phone face down on the bar top. It wasn't long before Lauren's feminine voice sounded from behind them.

"Andrew?"

He flipped around on the stool, and the look on his face the second he saw Lauren pulled at Jeni's heartstrings. He was so obviously enamored with her, and she immediately walked into his open arms.

Andrew leaned forward a little as he hugged Lauren, giving Jeni a clear view of Logan. Logan's gaze was on Jeni, singular and focused, like she was the center of his entire world, and she felt warm all over. A weight settled on her chest but in a way that was soothing, not unpleasant. Logan slid his hand along the bar, and Jeni met him. They briefly touched, skin to skin, behind Andrew's back. Jeni pulled back quickly, her fingers tingling.

Andrew stood and excused himself to the restroom and said he and Lauren were leaving afterward. Lauren slid onto Andrew's vacated barstool.

"Don't worry. I'm driving," she said to no one in particular.

"Thanks for coming," Jeni said. "You're obviously the only one he wants to talk to."

"Hey," Logan protested. "He was talking to me before you got here."

Jeni raised an eyebrow. "About his feelings and stuff?"

He deflated. "Not really. It was more me talking to myself than a two-way conversation but still. He called me first."

Logan pouting was adorable as hell, and Jeni stored it in her memory bank. She turned to Lauren, focusing on the serious matter at hand. "What does this mean? Did the chemo not work?"

"Not necessarily. Since I'm with a different service at the cancer center I can't ask his oncologist about it, even though I desperately wanted to call her when you texted me. I haven't seen the scan report, so I'm not sure how bad it was. But with his stage of lymphoma it's relatively common for there to be a little bit of residual disease after four cycles of chemo, and we have to give two more to get it all. I'm hoping that's all it is."

Logan nodded. "That's what he said when I met him here. Dr. Patel said he needed a little more of the same chemo."

"That's good, then," Lauren said. "If things looked worse, they'd be changing the plan completely." She put an arm around Jeni's shoulders, and she felt a little better.

When Andrew and Lauren left, Jeni and Logan moved to a booth in the back corner and sat on the same side of the table.

"I can't see you very well to talk to you like this," Jeni complained.

Logan tucked her close against his side. "But I can't touch you when you're across the table. This is better."

He leaned over and kissed her neck, sending goosebumps down her arm.

Okay, it was better like this.

"Are you okay?" he asked.

"Yeah. I just hate this for Andrew. I've gone with him to every single chemo appointment. He puts on a brave face, but I know he hates it. I just wish it was over."

"Me too. Hopefully it will be soon." He squeezed her shoulder. "You're a good sister. He's lucky to have you with him, supporting him."

"I wouldn't be anywhere else."

Logan smiled, but his eyes seemed sad. It was on the tip of her tongue to ask if he'd ever wanted biological siblings or if he'd become close with fellow foster kids, but he quickly moved on. "When are we going to tell Andrew about us now?"

Her shoulders slumped. "I don't know. How do you think he'll take it?"

He groaned. "I hate to say this but not well."

"Why not?" She twisted to the side to look at him.

Logan slid a finger lightly along the side of her face, pushing her hair behind her ear. "You know my, um, dating history."

Jeni pushed her lips out in front of her face. "Would we call that dating?"

"My point exactly." He cupped his hand around her neck, sliding his thumb back and forth along the sensitive skin there. "It's different with you. You know that, right? And I'm not saying that because I think the relationships I had with women before you were bad or wrong. But I'll be the first to admit that pretty early on into meeting those women, I knew it wouldn't go anywhere, so I moved on. You've stuck in my brain from the beginning. Even when you tried to get rid of me, I still kept you with me. I've wanted you almost since the first moment I saw you and never stopped."

"When you first saw me you'd just finished having sex with my neighbor."

He grimaced. "I said almost." A mischievous glint flickered in his eyes. "It was when you tried to steal my hummus that really sparked my interest."

Jeni laughed. "I was hangry. And you stole my parking spot."

"You keep saying that. I have no idea what you're talking about."

She took a sip of beer. "Uh huh."

Logan shook his head. "Anyway, I think I need to talk to Andrew and make sure he knows how serious I am about you. That you're not just a passing fancy or a body in my bed."

"I'm not even that, since you suddenly turned into a prude."

"Man, when it comes to sex, you're like a dog with a bone."

She nearly choked on her beer, and Logan seemed to realize what he'd said and laughed.

"Okay, bad choice of words," he said with a smile.

"If you'd just recently been introduced to how good sex can be, you'd think about it a lot too."

"I didn't say I wasn't thinking about it. All the fucking time."

"So, you're ready to get out of here then? I'll get the tab." She scooted to the edge of the booth.

But Logan grabbed her hand. "To be clear, you're thinking about sex with me, right? Not sex in general or with just anyone?"

The vulnerability and worry in his gaze surprised her. "Don't be an idiot. It's just you."

"But will it always? Just be me?"

She situated herself back into the booth. "Logan…" She trailed off, not knowing how to respond and be honest at the same time.

The look in his eyes became pained, and she'd do almost anything to make it stop. He pressed his forehead against hers.

Even if it wasn't exactly he wanted to hear, she said something true. "I can't imagine ever wanting anyone else."

"I think I'll want you forever."

"I can promise you I'll want you tomorrow." She'd want him for all the tomorrows, but there would come a day when he knew everything and he wouldn't want her. It would only hurt worse if she let things go too far now, so she didn't say it.

Logan closed his eyes. It hadn't been the answer he was looking for. But he still pressed his lips to hers softly, and she gripped his arm tightly, not wanting to let go.

His eyes were sad and his jaw tight when he pulled back. "Just say that every day, and I'll be okay."

CHAPTER TWENTY-TWO

There was something Jeni wasn't telling him. It went against his better judgment, but Logan ignored the feeling that kept creeping up in the back of his mind. Beggars couldn't be choosers, right? He had what he wanted, and there was a chance he'd be able to keep her forever.

Whatever hesitation she had about marriage and commitment, he just had to prove he was different. That he could be what she wanted and needed and he'd put her first. If he could only love her hard enough, she'd come around.

Or, at the very least, she'd never have a reason to leave. He wanted her to be happy and achieve her dreams. He'd never ask her to put them aside on his account, and with time, he'd show her that.

His phone vibrated on the desk, bringing him out of his thoughts.

Jeni: What should I wear tonight?
Logan: The Chiefs shirt I got you would be perfect.
Jeni: First, no. Second, it's Valentine's Day. We're not going somewhere fancy?

Logan: You wanted to wait to tell Andrew about us. It's not likely we'll see him, but I intend on touching you and kissing you all night so I figured it was best if we stayed in.
Jeni: Good. Fancy is overrated.

He'd thought she'd say that. Jeni wasn't one of those high-maintenance types, and he loved that about her. Most of the women he'd been with were hyper-aware of how they looked at all times. Perfect clothes and not a hair out of place. Jeni dressed nice when she wanted to, but was comfortable enough to be casual too and just be herself around him. That had to be a good sign, right?

Logan: My offer still stands. Chiefs shirt = sex.
Jeni: I hate you.
Logan: No you don't.
Jeni: No, I don't. Thanks for the flowers, by the way. They're beautiful.
Logan: You're welcome.
Jeni: Everyone at the office is asking who they're from.
Logan: Did you tell them?
Jeni: No. I almost told Sandra, but then I figured it might be kind of weird since she knows you.
Logan: Why?
Jeni: She'd probably ask questions about our relationship that I don't know how to answer.

Logan didn't know what to say to that. He didn't have a problem calling Jeni his girlfriend in public, so long as it wouldn't get back to Andrew until he had a chance to talk to him about it. But she had a point. If, from her perspective, their time together had an eventual expiration date, that could create an awkward conversation. Damn, this whole situation was weird.

Logan: Just tell them what I tell myself. We like each other and are spending time together, taking things one day at a time.

Jeni: That's good. You're one smooth talker, Logan Davis.

Logan: Can't wait to see you.

Jeni: Same.

Logan smiled down at the screen, despite that tiny voice telling him this wouldn't end well.

He hadn't been able to force himself out of bed early that morning, so he went to the gym over his lunch break. He started in the cardio room for a warm-up jog, and when he walked into the weight room, he found Andrew in their usual spot.

"Hey, man," Andrew greeted, pulling his earbuds out.

Logan dropped his water bottle next to a weight bench and gave Andrew a nod. "How you feeling?"

Andrew shrugged. "Pretty good. A little tired, but that's all the time lately."

"When do you start chemo again?"

"Tomorrow."

"Best to get it over with, I guess."

"Exactly."

"Just like before, you'll tell me if you need something, right?"

Andrew nodded. "I will. I appreciate it. Lauren and Jeni take pretty good care of me. I just need you to keep doing what you're doing. The usual guy stuff like this. Keep things normal."

"I can do that." Logan grabbed a weight and sat on a nearby bench to do bicep curls.

Andrew turned to the mirror and worked his shoulders. "Doing anything tonight?"

"Just hanging at the house," Logan replied between sets. Jeni's house, to be exact. "What about you?"

"Same."

Logan looked up from the bench. "Everything okay with Lauren?"

Andrew grinned and dropped his arms. "She's cooking me dinner."

"Ah. Good call." Seemed Andrew had the same idea as Logan. "More alone time, huh?"

"Man, I can't get enough of that girl." Andrew picked up another weight from the rack with a grunt. "It's never been like this before."

Logan knew exactly what he meant. "Sounds pretty serious."

Andrew smiled a little. "It is for me."

"I'm happy for you."

"Thanks. What about you? I'm surprised you don't have a date tonight."

Logan almost told him right then and there. He hated lying to his friend, and what would it hurt? Jeni said she wanted to wait until his chemo was over. A part of him wondered if that was the real reason or if it was because she didn't want to explain the nature of their relationship. Logan didn't intend to tell most people the specifics, but as her brother and his friend, Andrew deserved them.

Maybe it was best to wait until *he* knew what those were.

"Uh, I've been talking to someone lately. She's a little skittish of relationships, so we're taking it slow. I'm not really sure where it's gonna go."

"Yeah? Where'd you meet her?"

"Mutual friend."

Andrew feigned offense. "You have other friends?"

"My favorite wingman has been spending a lot of time with his new girlfriend. I had to make other arrangements."

Andrew laughed. "I'd say I'm sorry, but..."

"You're not."

"Not even a little bit."

Logan stood and studied the weight rack. "Good to know where I stand."

"Just wait till you feel like this about a woman. Believe me, you'll understand."

Logan just gave a nod and turned his back to hide his grin.

He already did.

~

"You sure know how to woo a woman." Jeni sat back in her chair. "And also how to make her feel uncomfortably full and not sexy at all. Is this your plan to distract me from sex? Feed me roasted cauliflower tacos and beer?"

Logan chuckled. "Is it working?"

Jeni seemed to consider this, her eyes dropping to his chest. "No."

Wasn't for him either. "You said it was your love language. I'm just taking advantage of that tidbit of information."

She looked away at his use of the L-word, and he wanted her back in the joyful, flirtatious place they'd been for the last hour while they ate and talked at her kitchen table. He'd finally asked about the color of her kitchen and she'd said it was like that when she bought the house.

"I considered painting it but then thought maybe it would rub off on me. Make me a little more cheerful or something."

Logan had just looked at her, probably with hearts for eyes. "You don't need to change a thing. You're perfect the way you are."

That had earned him a smile he'd remember forever.

Disappointingly, she hadn't worn the Chiefs T-shirt. Instead, she wore a white V-neck that contrasted against her skin, which remained tan even in February and showcased a lovely dip of cleavage. That, paired with her hair spilling around her shoulders and the way she kept pushing her glasses closer to her face didn't bode well for Logan's self-control. Every move she made was sexy as hell.

He needed another distraction. "Is it time for presents?"

Her eyes narrowed. "Dinner wasn't enough? You shouldn't have gotten me anything."

Logan rubbed his jaw. "It's sort of for both of us."

She pursed her lips, and he stood.

"Be right back."

By the time he returned from his car with the large box in his arms, she'd cleared the table and moved to the living room.

"What the hell?" Her eyes went wide. "That thing is huge."

He grinned. "That's what she said."

That got a laugh out of her, and Logan set the box on the coffee table.

"Just open it," he said.

She retrieved a pair of scissors to cut through the packing tape and pulled open the flaps. She sifted through the contents, and her eyes lit up with excitement. "A home brew kit?"

"We've both talked about trying it. I figured there was no time like the present."

Her smile widened as she pulled out the various items. "Wow, this has everything! A fermenter, tubing, wort chiller, kettle…"

He sat down and watched her hold every item, pride filling him that he'd put that look on her face. "I'm glad you like it."

She stilled her hands and looked over at him. "Like it?" She put down the thermometer, took two steps to stand before him, and leaned down, her hands on the back of the couch on either side of him. "I love it."

Logan sucked in a breath at her proximity, and the view down her shirt. He cleared his throat and said in a low voice, "It even has a special part to prevent unwanted blow off."

He couldn't wait to see what she'd do with that.

Jeni stilled. "I have the urge to say 'that's what she said,' but I'm not entirely sure what that means."

"Me either. Guess we'll figure it out as we go."

She moved forward, inch by inch, until her lips were so close he felt her breath against his. "I'm glad you made sure we're prepared for all scenarios. Even blow off." She licked his bottom lip.

Some incoherent noise left his throat.

She finally molded her lips to his, putting him out of his misery, and they kissed for several long moments. He'd never tire of her lips or her hands on his face, his shoulders, in his hair.

"This is the best thing ever," she said when she pulled back a little. "I love gifts that have a purpose. And ones that make beer."

Logan cupped her cheek and leaned forward to kiss her again. "How many gifts that make beer have you received?"

"This is the first." She put her weight on one arm and ran the fingers of the other hand lightly through his hair, sending a bolt of electricity down his spine. "I've had a lot of firsts with you."

He swallowed, hard. "I've had a lot of firsts with you too."

She frowned a little and sat beside him. "Really? Like what?"

Logan took her hand. "This will probably sound stupid. But it sort of feels like everything is new. Each time I touch you or kiss you, I feel something I've never felt before. I love it when you disagree with me and glare at me, like you're doing right now. I've never met another woman who shares my passion for the foster care community, other than Sandra—and she's forty years older than me. I love your competitive nature and soft side you try so hard to hide. I miss you when I'm not with you, and that's never happened to me before." He held up their entwined hands. "You know what I think it is?"

Jeni twisted her lips to the side. "I'm not sure I want to know."

"You probably don't, but I want to tell you anyway."

"Please. Don't say it."

"I'm in love with you."

She shook her head, her eyes closing. "Don't. No, you're not."

"I am. I can't help it." He slid his other hand along her neck, his thumb just below her earlobe. She kept her eyes closed but didn't pull away from his touch. "I've tried to stop, I really have. It didn't work." The words clawed their way free, from his heart and past his lips. "I'll never not love you, Jenifer Bishop."

"Don't," she mouthed, though no sound came out.

"It's okay," he whispered, kissing the corner of her mouth. "You don't have to say it back. This doesn't change anything. We're still taking it one day at a time. There's no pressure. I just have to say it out loud. It's killing me not to tell you. You have to know how I feel."

She opened her eyes, her golden-brown irises searching his face. He wished he could smooth the worry lines between her brows. "Promise?"

"That I love you? Hell yes."

"No. That nothing will change. That you still want to be with me but you're okay with the way we're doing it."

He wanted to promise her that, but the words lodged in his throat. "Can I ask you a question?"

"No."

"I know you had a terrible experience with your ex-husband. But hasn't this time with me shown you—at least a little bit—that no two relationships are the same?"

"Yes." Her response shocked him, but the look on her face told him she still hadn't changed her mind. "It's completely different with you than it was with Jackson. In the best, most wonderful way, and I love being with you. But you know what else I love? The thought that tomorrow, if I wanted to, I could move to France. I could quit, take a road trip to Canada, and go on an adventure. I could adopt six cats, just because I felt like it. I could go vegan and keep nothing in my house except raw vegetables and shelled nuts. When people get married and commit to each other at that level, they lose part of their independence. Maybe even the ability to get what they want out of life."

"Not if you find someone who loves you just the way you are

and accepts those things about you. Not if you find someone who shares the same dreams. Will you ever stop working to improve the lives of children?"

"You know the answer to that."

"Neither will I. As long as you're physically able, will you want to play softball?"

She looked away. "Yes."

"So will I. Do you love football, good beer, and tacos?"

"Sure. Right now, I do. But I can't say I always will. What happens then?"

"Then I wouldn't give a flying fuck. I'd quit my job, be sober, and boycott Mexican cuisine. You're more important to me than those things."

"Stop making good points. I'm not changing my mind."

Logan balled up his fists. "You're the most stubborn woman."

"I know you don't see it, but I'm thinking of you too. It's not just about meeting my needs, Logan. What about you? What if I can't give you everything you wanted out of life?"

"What could I possibly want that you couldn't give me?" He was at a loss.

Jeni blinked and looked at him for so long, he thought maybe she hadn't heard him.

He waited for several heartbeats, something in his gut telling him maybe this was dangerous territory. "Jeni?"

Then a single tear slipped from the corner of her eye. Then another and another. She tucked her lower lip into her mouth and looked away.

Logan's heart seized up, and he immediately scooted closer and put an arm around her. "What's going on?"

Her shoulders shook, the tears coming in earnest. A few sounds came out like she tried to speak, but each word fractured on a sob.

"I'm sorry," he said, feeling helpless. He had no idea what to do or what he'd said that drove her to instant tears. "Jeni, you're scaring me. Tell me what's wrong."

She'd bowed her head but tilted it up now to look at him. Her tear-stained cheeks and the pain in her eyes was a jagged knife right into his heart. What the hell was going on?

"I—" she started and then cried even harder. She put her head in her hands.

Logan rubbed his hand up and down her back. He was desperate to know what had sparked such emotion but hated seeing her like this. He didn't know how to make it stop. "It's okay. It's okay. You don't have to say anything now. We can talk about it later, okay?"

She sniffed and nodded, leaning into him heavily.

"I'm sorry," he said again.

Jeni hiccupped and seemed to attempt a deep breath before getting the halted words "not you" out.

He leaned back against the couch, pulling her with him to lay across his chest. It took a long time for her tears to abate, but he wasn't in a hurry. If anything, he'd relish these minutes she let him hold her in his arms. Because if what just happened told him anything, it was that she was seriously hurting and something about it made her believe they could never be together long term.

Logan kissed the top of her head, drowning in her a little more. Knowing what he was doing to himself.

It hurt to be with her knowing she didn't think it would last.

But it would hurt more to never have her at all.

CHAPTER TWENTY-THREE

Jeni thought she knew what it meant to be the center of Logan's attention. The night they'd slept together she'd felt his singular, intense focus, and she'd been positive she'd never experience anything more overwhelming again.

She was wrong.

Since they agreed to start their relationship of sorts, he was everywhere. Even if he wasn't with her physically, his presence was somewhere. All the time.

In the flowers on her desk, delivered fresh every week.

In the sweet text messages he sent just to say he was thinking about her or that he hoped she had a good day.

In their batches of beer fermenting in her garage that she saw any time she went anywhere (the first had been terrible, the second tolerable, and the third somewhat enjoyable).

He'd been so patient with her that night she broke down crying. Held her close and wiped her tears without forcing her to talk about what was going on inside her head. He still hadn't brought it up since, letting her do it in her own time.

He was the best man she'd never known.

Every time she caught herself getting used to it, she steeled herself and tried to stop her feelings from growing deeper. Logan was planting roots deep in her heart, and the more entrenched they became, the more painful it would be when they were inevitably ripped out.

One morning as they sat on the porch after he'd stayed the night (nothing exciting to report—Logan wouldn't budge an inch on his decision to take it slow on that front) she'd almost told him what upset her so much that day. Her deepest, darkest secret. Which wasn't actually a secret so much as a fear and an inadequacy in her ability to be what he needed.

But as they sat in the quiet that morning, Logan seemingly comfortable in the silence Jeni preferred while she drank her coffee, she decided she didn't want to lose him just yet. She wasn't ready to go back to being lonely.

So, she didn't tell him.

She couldn't bring herself to regret it. Things had been wonderful since Valentine's Day, so why mess with a good thing?

He was never far from her mind. What was he doing right this minute? Was he thinking about her? She pulled out her phone to send him a text when an elbow jabbed her in the ribs.

"Hey, can we go in there?" Lauren asked, pointing to Athleta. "I need new Netflix pants."

In a weird thought that was some sort of mixture between happy and depressing, Jeni looked at Lauren and realized that even when things with Logan ended, she wouldn't be as alone as she was before. She now considered Lauren a friend, and the two were spending the afternoon shopping on the Plaza. Not only was she a friend, but Jeni half-expected Lauren to become a soon-to-be member of her family any day now. Her brother hadn't said he planned to propose, but she could feel it. Twin connection or whatever. His last chemo was Friday, and his (hopefully) last scan early next week. If he was cancer free, what better way to celebrate than an engagement?

Jeni adjusted her glasses. "Sure, but only if you tell me what Netflix pants are."

"I'm a huge documentary nerd, and I like to be comfortable when I'm watching them. Netflix pants."

Jeni rolled her eyes. "You and my brother are perfect for each other." She'd never met anyone as obsessed with documentaries as he was.

Lauren smiled wide, as if that was the best thing she'd heard all day.

They walked into the store, Lauren making a beeline straight for the capri leggings. Jeni decided she could use a new sports bra and went in the other direction. When she spun around, she nearly walked right into someone.

"Oh, excuse me," Jeni said, shifting to the side.

"Jeni Bishop?"

Jeni looked up. "Gretchen? Is that you?"

"Yeah!" Gretchen Thomas, a friend of Jeni's from high school, held her arms out for a hug.

"What on earth are you doing here?" Jeni asked when they pulled apart. She hadn't seen Gretchen in years. She'd always liked her, but they weren't so close they kept in constant communication outside comments and likes on social media posts.

"My mom and I came down for a girl's shopping trip. She's not into exercise, so we split up when I wanted to come here. I'm meeting her at Panera in ten minutes. You should come. She'd be so happy to see you."

"Oh, that's nice. I'm here with a friend, but thanks for the offer. Tell her I said hello."

"I will." Gretchen tucked her short dark hair behind one ear. "So, how are you? You live here now, right?"

"Yeah, it'll be a year in July. It was a change, but I love it here. Different from small-town Nebraska, that's for sure."

Gretchen nodded solemnly. "I don't blame you from wanting to get away. Did you hear Jackson got married again?"

Jeni's mouth dropped. "He did?"

"Oh." Gretchen grimaced. "Shit, you didn't know? Sorry, I just assumed one of your sisters would have told you. He married Pixie Thurman, of all people."

"Jackson and *Pixie?*"

"Right?" Gretchen shuddered. "I can't stand her. He's happy though, looked like he was on cloud nine when I saw him at the grocery store the other day. Rumor is she's pregnant."

"Pregnant?" Jeni suddenly felt lightheaded. "Are you sure?"

"Well, no. You know how people talk in our small town. But they did get married awfully quick. It's been a few months now. I haven't seen her lately, so I couldn't say for sure."

"That doesn't surprise me," Jeni said. Jackson wouldn't want his wife far from the farm. Maybe for some women, that kind of life was appealing. For Pixie's sake, she hoped that was the case.

A cell phone rang, and Gretchen dug around in her purse. "That's my mom. I'd better go. It was so good to see you. We're here for another two days, maybe we could get coffee and catch up?"

"Sure. My number's the same."

"Great, I'll be in touch." Gretchen smiled and gave Jeni another hug before rushing out the door.

Jeni stood rooted to the spot after Gretchen left, her mind racing.

Jackson got remarried? And his wife was pregnant?

The first part she didn't really care about. She didn't have feelings for him anymore—he'd made certain of that with the way he treated her those last two years.

It was the news about the baby Jeni's thoughts kept tripping over.

For so long, he'd told her he didn't want kids. At the end, he swore up and down that wasn't the problem and that he hadn't changed his mind about that fact. She'd always suspected it wasn't true and wondered if that was one reason he'd begun to resent her.

Now she knew without a doubt—she'd been right.

～

Later that night, Jeni and Logan spent hours messing around on her couch. "Logan," she said breathlessly, and he looked up at her with flushed cheeks and hooded eyes. "I want you to make love to me."

He let out a half-groan, half-moan. "Jeni."

"What are you waiting for?" she asked, careful to keep her voice neutral and not accusing. She really wanted to know.

"I know. It's ridiculous. I'm making us both miserable, but like I said before, I'm trying to do things right by you."

"What does that even mean? I'm telling you I want you. You're not taking advantage of me or pushing me to do something I don't want to do. We've been dating almost two months now."

He gently pushed her off his lap and sat up, rotating his body to set his feet on the ground. His back curved forward, and he put his head in his hands. "It's hard to explain."

"Can you try? I mean, it's okay. I want to spend time with you no matter what we're doing. I'm just trying to understand what's going on in your head."

"I'm not sure I even know." He rubbed at his forehead before straightening to look at her. "I've given my body to other women, but not much else. I never told them my innermost thoughts, talked about my life, or shared emotion. With you, I wanted that connection from the start. Even when I didn't realize it, I wanted you. And not just to have sex with you but to know you inside and out. In every way. Sex can be so powerful. And with you, it was consuming to a level that frankly freaked me out." He passed his palm across his chest. "It feels like when we go there again, I'll lose myself in you so completely that there's a part of me I'll never get back. And I guess, with the way we're doing this thing, I'm worried it will break me."

"Oh," she murmured. Talk about a punch in the gut. "I didn't know you held sex in such high regard."

"Neither did I," he said quietly. "I know my actions before I met you didn't point to that. But you changed everything."

"You changed everything for me too," she admitted. Her prior experience didn't connect intimacy with sex like she'd expected. "It was something I tolerated, nothing more. But with you? It was like you and I were the only two people who existed in that moment. I've never felt so in tune another person."

"Me either. And we didn't even know each other that well. It was refreshing. And it gave me something to look forward to. I started to think, imagine how it will be when I really *know* her and she knows me. I couldn't fathom something so meaningful at the time. But I wanted to. I still want to."

Jeni curved her hand around his thigh. "You've learned a lot about me these past few months. But I still feel like there's so much I don't know about you."

He pressed his lips together. "I know. I'm not good at talking about myself, especially my childhood." He covered her hand with his. "You already know more than anyone else, if it helps."

"Will you tell me more?"

"Sure."

She watched him, waiting expectantly.

He frowned. "What, right now?"

"Why not? I don't want to push you, but I want to know everything about you too. Even if it's not pretty."

Logan tilted his neck to the side, like he was stretching the muscles there. He inhaled deeply, as if preparing for a difficult conversation. "Okay."

His right knee bobbed up and down, and Jeni lightly squeezed his thigh. He stilled.

"I'm not really sure where to start."

She slid her thumb back and forth across the denim. "I can ask questions. Would that make it easier?"

"Maybe."

"Why did you enter the foster care system?"

"My mom was a meth addict."

Only six words, but they said enough. "Is she still alive?"

"No."

"What was your life like before they took you from her?"

"We moved around a lot, living with whatever man she'd tied herself to. I have no idea who my biological dad is. I don't think she did either. Some of the men were okay, but others were mean as hell. Some hit me. When I was six, we ended up in this government assistance apartment complex. We lived there over a year, longer than we'd ever stayed anywhere else. There was an older lady named Paula who lived in the apartment next door to us. She was nice to me and let me come over when Mom was messed up or when she had men over. She fed me and let me watch cartoons and stuff. One day, my mom left me home alone, and I went to Paula's. My mom never came back. Paula let me stay with her and told the apartment manager she was my grandmother. That put off any questions for the time being."

"Was that the last time you saw your mom?"

"Yeah. They found her body a few weeks later. I would have stayed with Paula until she or someone else made me leave, but one night she died in her sleep. I was so freaked out that I just sat in the corner of her living room, her dead body in the next room, until someone found us. We didn't have any family that I knew of, so that's when I went in the system."

Tears burned beneath Jeni's lids, but she tried to keep them contained. "I'm so sorry. You were so young to have gone through so much."

She scooted closer, but he just sat there, unmoving.

"I moved through several foster families. I tried really hard to be a good kid. To do good in school and not fight when there were several of us in the home at once. That didn't always work out, but I so badly wanted to just find somewhere to stay and someone who wanted to keep me. It was all I thought about."

I want to keep you. Jeni swallowed the lump in her throat, and several tears escaped. She understood so much now.

His interest in social media. He'd been deprived meaningful human connection until he was adopted.

His sparsely decorated house. He'd moved a lot and learned to keep few possessions.

His lack of childhood friends. Probably didn't stay in one place long enough to make them.

"When I was thirteen, Sandra placed me in Ingrid and Robert's home. I know now she'd handpicked them for me. After six months, they asked if I wanted to be a permanent member of their family." His voice wavered. "I can't even explain how that felt. I'll never be able to repay them for what they did for me."

"It wasn't one sided. They gained a pretty wonderful son out of the deal."

"I try to make them proud every day."

"I'm sure you do," Jeni said. "What was your dad like?"

A small smile formed on his lips, and Jeni had never been so happy to see it.

"He was an accountant, so he was kind of a geek. Good with numbers and a little uptight. Made me wear a helmet when I rode my bike. Never let me take a sip of his beer. Expected me to make straight As in school. But he knew the meaning of quality time. He taught me to throw a baseball. How to treat women with respect. When to fight and when to let something roll off my back. And most of all, he was the biggest Chiefs fan I've ever met."

"I knew that was coming," Jeni said, tapping his shoulder with hers.

"The man never missed a home game. Those seats you sat in? They've been in his family since the seventies. He took me to games, and it was the first thing we truly bonded over. There's nothing like a father and son cheering together for the same team. For me, going to those games and watching away ones in our basement was about so much more than football. It was the first steady thing in my life, and it was about a man who gave me the time of day. Who thought I was worth his time. Anything good in me is because of him."

More tears slipped down her cheeks. "I'm so glad they found you."

He slid his thumb across her wet cheek. "Don't cry."

"I hate what you went through as a child. But you have to know what an amazing man you've become."

He shrugged, scrunching up his nose a little.

Jeni frowned. "I'm serious. I've never met anyone so generous or accepting. You're kind, funny, and hard-working. You didn't let your early life turn you into some angry person who doesn't give a damn. You're a man who wants to leave this world better than you found it."

"I just don't want other kids to go through what I did."

"You're doing your part to make sure that happens. Through Fostering Sweet Dreams and donating your game seats to families." She'd become more intentional about utilizing FSD's donations since learning Logan was behind the organization and saw how many kids were safely placed in foster homes solely based on the beds she arranged for.

"Sometimes it doesn't feel like enough."

"It's more than most people do. I know how you feel. There are times when I feel like I'm making zero impact, and it's my full-time job. It's a thankless career sometimes."

"That reminds me, it's been like a month since I last thanked Sandra."

Jeni smiled. "I love that you're still in touch with her. It would be the highlight of my life to see some of my foster kids grown up and doing well for themselves."

"I hope you will, someday."

She pulled her hand away and tucked both in her lap. "I'm a little nervous about my job, actually."

"Why? What do you mean?"

"At a staff meeting back in October, Sandra told us that there might be state budget cuts to the department. At the time, she wasn't sure if it would impact the foster services, but last week she said we were losing some funds. She and the higher ups are trying to figure out how to handle it."

"You're worried they'll let you go?" Logan looked affronted. "That would be a huge mistake. You're an asset to their program. I'll talk to Sandra."

Jeni shook her head. "No, don't. She's already stressed out and doing everything she can to avoid cutting positions. She made sure I knew I'm doing a good job, but she and I both know the facts. I'm the newest employee. I have the least experience and no seniority. If it came down to layoffs, I'd be the first one up. It's out of her control."

"But you love your job." Concern laced his eyes. "When will you know?"

"I'm not sure."

"What would you do? If they did let you go?"

Jeni shrugged. "There are plenty of private organizations around here that hire social workers. But I've always wanted to be part of a large government agency where I'd have the most opportunity. That seems the best way to work my way up and have the tools to impact system laws and reforms. It's harder to have the same impact in the private sector."

"Did these budget cuts affect the whole state?"

"I think so."

"So, to work for a government agency, you'd have to look in another state?"

"Maybe. Probably."

He rotated his upper body to face her full on. "When were you going to tell me about this?"

Jeni leaned back a little. "Um, I'm not sure. I'd definitely tell you if I got a job somewhere else and had to move."

His gaze tracked to the windows lining the wall and back to her. "You don't think I'd want to know there's a chance you might not be in Kansas City in a few months? Do I not factor into the equation even a little bit?"

Logan was a huge factor, but he was never supposed to be. She was supposed to keep her distance and never again let a man dictate her life choices. The fact that her lungs constricted and she couldn't breathe when she thought about leaving him was irrelevant.

"Nothing's happening right now. I might keep my job and none of this will matter. But either way, I've been clear about this from the start," she said. Had her opinion shifted with each passing day with Logan? With each kiss, each touch?

Yes.

Did she want to stay with him indefinitely?

Hell yes.

But sticking to the plan wasn't just about her own happiness. It was about his too. He thought she was what he wanted—she could see it in his eyes. And a selfish part of her wanted to grab onto that for dear life, everything else be damned.

Unfortunately, the rational part of her brain said that wasn't fair to Logan. The news about Jackson solidified that in her mind.

"Wow." He stood, gripping the back of his neck. "Yeah, you have. I guess I've just been hoping something would change at some point."

"I'm sorry. It won't."

Logan grabbed his phone from the coffee table.

"Are you leaving?" she asked quietly.

He walked to the door, and that was answer enough. "I need to think."

Jeni wanted to jump up and run to him. Wrap her arms around him and beg him to stay. But she sat there, still as stone, and whispered, "Okay."

Before she even took a breath, he was gone.

CHAPTER TWENTY-FOUR

What the hell was wrong with her?

More, what the hell was wrong with him that he loved her despite it?

Throughout the following week, Logan wavered between two options.

Change nothing, enjoy whatever time he had left with Jeni, and deal with the consequences of losing her later. Even if she kept her job and didn't move now, he'd seen the hard truth that she wasn't willing to let his presence in her life be a consideration.

For any decision.

The other choice was to cut it off now. It would be an attempt at self-preservation, though he wasn't confident it would be any easier to lose her now than later. It just felt like the first option was delaying the inevitable.

He'd spoken to her a few times since the night he left her house, but their conversations were short and stilted. They were both waiting for him to figure out what to do.

It wasn't until he had dinner with his mom the following Tuesday that his mind cleared. It was an unusually warm evening for late March, and his mom suggested they take a walk after dinner. They were strolling slowly through her neighborhood talking about mundane things when his phone rang.

It was Andrew. He'd finished chemo last Friday, and his scan was today. The last time Logan had received a phone call on scan day, it was with bad news, and a brick settled in his stomach.

"Mom, I'm sorry, but can I get this real quick?"

She waved a hand as if to say, *go ahead.*

"Hey, man. What's the word?"

"You're gonna have to put up with my ass for a long, long time, bro. Scan was clean. I'm cancer free."

"Seriously?" Logan's shoulders relaxed. "That's great news. Congratulations, Andrew."

"Thanks. I can't believe it."

"It will take some time to sink in, I bet."

"Yeah, probably. I'm at Lauren's house, and Jeni's coming over to celebrate. Can you come by?"

"I'm at my mom's right now, but maybe I could stop by after."

"Sounds good. In case you don't end up coming, I have some other news too. Lauren and I are engaged."

Logan's pulse slowed. "No way." He forced his tone to be upbeat. "Even bigger congratulations for that. I'm really happy for you two."

"Will you be my best man? I probably should ask you in person, but…" He paused. "I'm just excited, I guess."

Logan forced out a chuckle. "As you should be. I'd be honored."

"Good. Lauren will be glad I've secured one groomsman. She's already got four bridesmaids on the line."

"Damn. Good luck with that."

"Yeah. So, I'll see you later tonight? Maybe? I'll text you the address just in case."

"Yeah. See ya." Logan slid his phone into his pocket and let his fake smile drop.

"Good news for Andrew?" his mom asked.

"Yeah. Cancer's gone."

"Oh, I'm so happy. I know exactly how he feels right now. The relief is almost too much." She squeezed his arm.

"I hope neither of you ever have to go through anything like that again," he said.

They continued walking, and after about a minute, his mom slowed a little. "Was there more?"

"Yeah. He, uh, got engaged."

She didn't respond with excitement, and he looked over at her. She regarded him in that knowing way moms do. "Why does that upset you?"

"It doesn't. I think it's great."

"I know when my own son is blowing smoke up my ass." She pursed her lips.

"Mom." Logan did a double take. He didn't think he'd ever get used to her referring to him as her son so casually, so naturally. But more so, he rarely heard her say a curse word.

"Something's bothering you. What is it?"

He angled his head away, his gaze drifting along the houses and parked cars they passed. He never talked to his mom about women. But Jeni wasn't just any woman, was she? She was the only one he'd brought home to meet his mother. The only one who took a dive into his heart and never came up for air. She'd jumped off the deep end to take a chance with him, that's for sure. He'd never find anyone like her. And yet, she wasn't willing to share herself with him completely.

"Jeni never wants to get married."

His mom was quiet for a moment. "Why not?"

"She was married once before. Didn't go so well. I think she's kind of lost faith in the whole idea."

"That's understandable."

"I know." He let his hand drift over a mailbox as they walked. "Why did you agree to marry Dad?"

"Why wouldn't I?" A smile was in her voice. "I was head over heels for that man and jumped at the chance to be his wife. I didn't hesitate even for a second."

"You didn't worry about losing yourself? Or that by marrying him you might be limiting things, like your career or interests?"

She balked like the thought had never occurred to her. "No, never. We were a team, and we approached every decision as a team. He'd never have stifled me like that."

"Jeni's first husband did. He was selfish and forced her to live a life she hated."

"That's terrible."

"It is. It makes me want to track him down and—" He glanced over at his mom, and she tilted her face up with brows raised. "Uh, it just makes me really mad. I hate that she was so unhappy, but even more, I hate that she thinks marriage to anyone will be the same."

"Do you want to get married? I've never heard you mention it before."

They rounded the corner that took them back down his mother's street.

"Yeah, I do. But I'd never had a specific woman in mind before I met Jeni. And now I've fallen in love with her and realized she's my one. You and Dad were the model relationship, and your marriage was so solid. I guess I always figured I'd want that someday, and that day came when I found her. I want to share everything with her, like you and Dad did." His parents were the only people he'd known who'd demonstrated the meaning of true love. "People have come and gone a lot in my life—and gone more often than they stayed. I don't want that kind of relationship anymore, and I want that security, I guess. It feels like taking that step strengthens the bond between two people, and I think I need that commitment."

"With the life you've lived, that's understandable. More, you deserve that."

"Maybe. But I just want to be with her so much. I don't want to lose her. Even if it means never getting married."

"Have you talked to her about it?"

"Several times. I told her I'd never do what her ex-husband did and that it could be totally different with someone else. With me." His shoulders slumped, like a hundred-pound weight had settled there. "I've tried to understand her perspective, and it's not all that uncommon for people to not get married nowadays. Even though I want it, it's a lot, I guess. To ask her to go back on a promise she'd made herself and retry something that made her so miserable the first time."

"The hell it is," his mom snapped, and Logan jerked his head around to look at her.

"What's with you tonight?" First *ass*, and now *hell*?

Suddenly, she was no longer beside him, and he stopped, realizing they were back at her house. She stood stiffly on the sidewalk, her chin trembling.

"You listen to me, Logan Ray Davis." She poked a finger at him. "You are a once-in-a-lifetime sort of man. You are worthy of a woman who values you, and your wants and desires matter as much as hers. If marriage is important to you, that's what you should have. Don't sell yourself short for someone who won't give you their all. You are worth that and more. Do you hear me?"

Logan's arms hung loose at his sides, and he dipped his head a little. "I hear you."

"I want to hear you say it. Say, 'I'm worth it.'"

"Mom." He glared at her, but his heart wasn't in it.

"Humility is an endearing quality, but not knowing your own worth isn't. Say it."

He heaved out a sigh. "Fine. I'm worth it."

She continued to eye him suspiciously, and he fidgeted under her perusal, looking around. A family was in their front yard several houses down, but otherwise the street was empty.

"Have you been buying things for her? Doing a lot of little things for her?"

Logan frowned. "What do you mean?"

Of course he did things for her. He wanted to make her feel special. He often sent her flowers and messages to let her know he was thinking about her. And he'd sent her tacos that one time. He knew how it felt to be lacking affection from others, and he never wanted Jeni to feel the same. Was that what his mom was asking?

"When you first came to stay with us and you'd been here a few months and we opened up the conversation about adoption, you started doing little things for Robert and me," she said. "All the time. You made us art projects, put away your own laundry, and did the dishes when we weren't looking. No thirteen-year-old boy does dishes without being asked. A few times you even found wildflowers and brought them home for me. It was like you didn't think we'd want you unless you proved to us you were worthy. Like you thought you needed to be perfect or earn our love by the things you did and not just for who you were as a person."

Logan just stood there, his brow furrowed, unsure how to respond.

He remembered the day his parents asked if he was interested in joining their family. They were the first people who ever seemed to care for him beyond a desire to give him a safe place to sleep. He was thankful for that from the other foster families, of course. And from Paula. But Robert and Ingrid were interested in spending time with him and investing in him. To teach him things and watch him grow. When he realized that, he supposed he had upped his game a little bit. He wanted to show them what a good kid he could be and that he could give them something in return. That he could be the son they'd always wanted.

The process of formal adoption was long, and part of him was terrified they'd change their minds.

"I…" he started but wasn't sure how to finish.

"Love isn't earned, Logan. It's freely given. We wanted you to be our son before you started doing those things. You already were. I thought as you got older and we hopefully showed you what unconditional love looked like, you'd see the truth in that. But I wonder if you're doing the same thing you did back then, trying to earn her love with the things you can do for her instead of just for who you are."

Was he?

Maybe in some ways he'd always done that a little bit. approached women in a way that demonstrated what he could offer. Which used to be mainly pleasure.

But with Jeni, he'd tried so hard to show her more than his body. To *be* more.

"Your past and the terrible people that neglected you when you were a child have nothing to do with who you are as a man. That coming and going mindset? It's true. People will come and go in your life. Some stay and are meant to be there. Others move on, and they don't deserve another second of your time. There are givers and takers, and you're a giver through and through. You'll give and give until there's nothing left, and you deserve someone who fills you back up. Who helps you see, and believe, that there are pieces of you worth loving and worth keeping."

Logan's eyelids burned, and he blinked several times through blurred vision. His heart ached with how badly he wanted Jeni to be that person.

"Shit, Mom." He sucked in a breath and held out one arm.

His mom's chin trembled, and she lurched forward and hugged him. "I love you so much. I just wish you could see why."

"I love you too, Mom." She was so small in his arms. For a split second, he wondered where his birth mom's head would land if he could hug her now, as a grown man. He immediately pushed the thought out of his mind.

This was his mother.

She pulled back and looked up at him. "And Logan?"

"Yeah?"

"Watch your language."

Logan left his mom's house shortly after that, with a lot more on his mind than when he arrived. He drove around in the dark for a while before finally pulling up Andrew's text with Lauren's address. He made a pit-stop before heading there and pulled up to the curb twenty minutes later. Jeni and Andrew's cars were still there.

He grabbed the paper bag and walked to the door, knocking.

Lauren opened it, and music trickled through the doorway. "Hi! I'm so glad you came," she said. Her big green eyes dropped to the bag in his hand. "What'd you bring?"

Logan grinned. "Just something for Andrew."

"Well get in here then."

The living room was right off the entry, and Logan immediately found Andrew on the couch. Jeni was nowhere to be seen.

Andrew stood and held out his hand. "Hey, man, you made it."

Logan grabbed his hand and pulled him in for a loose hug, clapping him on the back. "It's a big day." He pulled back and shoved the brown bag at Andrew. "Got you something."

"Yeah?" Andrew took it and sat down. "It's heavy."

Logan stood behind the couch to watch as Andrew carefully set the bag down at his feet and reached inside.

"Bourbon, a comb, licorice, and scissors? The bourbon's awesome, but I'm not sure about the other three."

Lauren joined Andrew on the couch and took the bottle of whisky, turning it over in her hands. "I like this bottle."

"So did I," Logan said. "The rest are all things you couldn't use while you were on chemo, and soon you'll need them again. Your hair will grow back, the smell of licorice won't make you want to throw up, and you don't have to worry about bleeding out if you accidentally cut yourself. You can get back to cutting out paper dolls or doilies or whatever you like to do in your spare time."

Andrew and Lauren both laughed.

"That's super weird but awesome at the same time. Thanks," Andrew said.

"That's so thoughtful," came Jeni's voice from behind him.

Logan turned and his heart leapt, lodging in his throat. She stood in the doorway, a few feet away, the picture of perfection. She wore a black tank top and fitted jeans, her bare feet shifting on the hardwood. Her long, silky, brown hair was down around her shoulders, and her glasses sat atop her freckled nose to frame her beautiful gold eyes.

She searched his face, lingering on his eyes. "Hi," she said then smiled sadly and mouthed, "I miss you."

"Hey," he said, following up with a whispered, "Me too." They seemed to miss each other often, which begged the question why they were apart so much.

"Come sit down, you two," Andrew ordered.

With Lauren and Andrew on the couch, the only available places to sit were a loveseat and a comfortable-looking armchair. Logan chose the loveseat, expecting Jeni to take the chair.

Instead, she plopped down next to him, her thigh pressed against his.

He swallowed and glanced nervously at Andrew. Luckily, he was so focused on his new fiancée that he didn't seem to notice.

"So how does it feel?" Logan asked.

"What, being cancer free?" Andrew replied. "Now I feel the same as the rest of you non-cancer patients, I guess." Lauren elbowed him, and he grabbed her hand with a grin. "It feels fucking awesome."

"*You* are fucking awesome," Jeni countered. "That was a lot to go through and during law school, at that. I'm proud of you, old man."

"I agree," Lauren said. "But not about the old man part. I'm not marrying a senior citizen. Besides, I'm older than Andrew."

"Barely," Andrew scoffed.

She pursed her lips. "Still."

Logan stiffened at the mention of marriage. Did Jeni notice? He was too afraid to look at her, especially right in front of her brother. His feelings would be written all over his face.

"So, any wedding details yet?" Jeni crossed her legs and swung her foot back and forth.

"Just that we want something small and relatively soon," Lauren said, blushing. "We talked about June, right after Andrew graduates. We decided the wedding party and that's about it. That reminds me—Logan? My friend, Emma, will be a bridesmaid. She's single, and I think you'd really like her. I thought maybe we could introduce you two before the wedding."

Jeni's foot stopped moving.

Logan leaned forward and put his elbows on his knees. "Oh. Yeah, sure."

Lauren smiled.

He felt Jeni's stare on the back of his head like heated laser beams. Why had he agreed to that?

"Actually," he said, his voice coming out too loud. "Sorry. But I, um, don't think that's necessary."

Andrew cocked his head sideways. "Why? You seeing someone? Is it that girl you told me about on Valentine's Day?"

What was Jeni thinking right now?

Andrew and Lauren both looked at him with blank expressions, waiting. What was he supposed to do now?

"Well, yeah." He rubbed his palm across his thigh.

A firm hand pressed against his lower back. Jeni was either warning him to stop talking, or…he didn't really know what else.

Too bad. "We're kind of just friends but sometimes a little more, and she's incredible. She's different from any woman I've ever met, and we share so many of the same interests it's almost scary. She makes me mad and makes me laugh, and I honestly can't picture my life without her. She believes in things with such passion and won't move an inch in her opinions unless you prove her wrong, and then she'll admit defeat and say she's sorry. She's so beautiful sometimes it's hard to breathe when she's around, and I'm ridiculously in love with her."

Lauren and Andrew stared at him, Andrew's jaw almost on the floor.

Jeni's hand no longer touched him.

Logan cleared his throat in the silence. "So, thanks for thinking of me, Lauren, but I'm good."

Jeni jumped to her feet. "I need some air."

Logan leapt up and followed her, throwing a "Be right back," over his shoulder.

She burst through the front door and onto the front porch. Logan joined her and shut the door behind them. Jeni's hands went to her hips, and she took two steps down into the grass.

"Where are you going?" Logan asked from the porch.

She shook her head, walking in circles. "I can't...I don't..." She let out a frustrated growl. "Just—stop. Stop saying nice things and accepting me for who you think I am. Stop trying to make me love you!" she said brokenly, finally facing him with pained eyes. "Can't you see it's done? I tried to fight it, and it happened anyway. You made me love you, and now we'll both be miserable for the rest of our lives."

Logan stepped down to meet her, unable to enjoy that this was the first time she'd said she loved him. "Why? Why will that make us miserable?"

"B-because." Her voice trembled.

Logan took her hand. He could see the love in her eyes, warring with frustration and fear.

He did the only thing he could and dropped to one knee before her.

She covered her mouth, pulling her hand away and backing up two steps, her head slowly moving side to side.

"Jeni," he said softly, with a hint of desperation. "Marry me. Please."

Her chest rose and fell with each breath. "You're proposing?"

"Yes."

"That wasn't our deal."

"I know." He rested one hand on his bent knee. "I can't help it. I want more from you. I want everything."

Her voice was barely above a whisper. "Can't we just keep things the way they are?"

"I don't know if I can," he said. He was crossing her line and forcing them to a breaking point, but he didn't have a choice. "Not without knowing we'll move forward one day. I want your full commitment. The promise of your every morning and every night, for the rest of our lives. We want so many of the same things out of life, and I want us to do them together."

"It's not that easy. Marriage isn't that easy."

"It doesn't have to be easy for me to want it. To want you."

She gripped her hands tightly in front of her. "It just won't work. You don't understand."

"Help me then. I'm trying to understand, but I can't with this wall between us."

Jeni closed her eyes for a moment. "I built it for a reason."

"You built it based on one bad experience. And I hate that you had to go through that, but I'm not Jackson." Saying his name angered Logan every single time, and his voice rose in frustration. "We're not the same. Stop punishing me for his sins. I'm a different man, and I deserve a chance. I deserve a commitment from the woman who loves me. I deserve your trust that I'd never choose anything else above you. You're the most important thing to me."

"I can't." She pressed her hands to her stomach. "You'll hate me."

"How could I hate the woman I want to spend every second of my life with? I want to marry you and have children with you. I want us to have a family and build a life together."

Tears streamed down her face. "That's exactly why you'll hate me," she said, her voice breaking. "I can't give you children, and you'll hate me for it."

Logan stilled, his eyes widening. "What?"

She swiped at her cheeks. "After my car accident, there were complications from internal bleeding. They had to decide during surgery and did a full hysterectomy. I woke up to the news that I'll never have children. Jackson knew that when we got married, and he promised me he didn't care. That he never really wanted kids anyway. But after a few years, he started making comments like 'look how happy that family is' or 'I wish I had a son to pass the farm down to someday.' I know that's one of the reasons he started to resent me, in addition to my resistance to farm life. He hated me for it in the end, and you will too. Eventually."

Logan blinked, and his legs suddenly went numb. He went to both knees, stunned by the information.

She shook her head. "See? I knew it would be a dealbreaker. It always will be."

Jeni walked around him, but he caught her hand and stood.

"Whoa, hang on. You can't just leave. I'm surprised is all. You can't drop something so significant on me and expect me to just move on right away. Just…" He scrubbed his other hand down his face. "Give me a second."

She yanked her hand back and stepped onto the porch, reaching for the door. "I'm not going to stand here and watch as you realize I'm broken and can never make you a father. That I'm not enough for what you need and I can't give you the life you want. I knew this would happen. I tried to stop it from the very start, but you wouldn't listen. You wouldn't stay away. My heart is already breaking. Just leave, Logan, and let it go."

He stared at her, realization hitting him with a shock, like he'd taken a nosedive into ice-cold water.

"You don't know me at all, do you?" His voice was nearly a whisper.

"What are you talking about?"

"You really think that I, of all people, don't count a family as one that includes kids from foster care or adoption?" He grimaced with pain from the knowledge that she wouldn't fight for him. For *them*. Not even a little. "That's the kind of family I want more than anything. The only thing that's brought me any healing is starting Fostering Sweet Dreams and hearing how much fun the kids have at football games. If you think being with you and spending our lives surrounded by kids in the system isn't something I want, you're gravely mistaken."

Jeni simply stood there, her expression tight.

Unbelievable.

"I'm done," he said. "I won't try to convince you anymore. I've said everything I possibly could to show you that I want to be with you and only you. But apparently you don't feel the same."

His mom's words were in the back of his mind. He had to stand up for what he wanted and what he needed.

"I've always had a hard time believing I'm enough. But I know I deserve better than this. I want a woman who would put me first, just like I would you. Like I have. I can see now you're not that person. Like you said, you've made that very clear. I was just too blind to see it."

CHAPTER TWENTY-FIVE

After Logan left, Jeni swiped tears from her cheeks. She didn't know what to do. He said he'd be okay with a family of foster and adopted children. But how could it be true? She believed he wanted to be a foster parent. But what man didn't want to get his own wife pregnant and have a child with his own DNA? He might think he wouldn't care now, but one day, he would.

She walked back into Lauren's house, intending to grab her purse and get the hell out of there. But when she closed the door, she turned and smacked right into Andrew's chest.

"What the hell is going on?" he asked tightly.

Jeni took one look at his face and broke down.

"Whoa, hey." He immediately put his arms around her, and she buried her face in his shirt. "Why are you crying?"

"I l-love him." Jeni sniffled.

Andrew went still but didn't loosen his embrace. "You love...Logan?"

She nodded into his chest.

"Okay." Her brother took a few deep breaths. "Okay. I'm

trying to be cool, but I'm gonna need more information here. Was he talking about you? Just now?"

She nodded again.

"And that you're *sometimes more than friends?*" His voice had an edge to it.

Jeni yanked her head back. "Don't do that."

"The hell I won't." Andrew's arms were suddenly gone, and he pushed past her. "Is that motherfucker still out there?"

"Andrew!"

Lauren's voice entered the conversation. "Andrew. They both admitted to being in love with each other. Calm down and let her tell us what's going on."

He yanked open the door and stuck his head out. A few seconds later, he pulled back and shut the door. "Fine. You're right."

"He's already gone, isn't he?" Jeni guessed. She took her glasses off and rubbed her eyes.

"Yep. He got lucky."

Jeni and Lauren exchanged a meaningful look. The three sat back down in the living room, and Andrew raised an eyebrow, waiting.

"I'm sorry we didn't say anything," Jeni started. "But you have to agree you've had enough on your mind."

Andrew remained silent, which he usually did when he knew she was right but wouldn't admit it.

"We've spent a lot of time together over the last several months. What he said was true—we have a lot in common. We both care about the foster community. We love playing softball and watching football. We've both always wanted to try home brewing, and we've been working on that together. Our third batch wasn't half bad." She grinned, but it disappeared almost as quickly as it came on as she realized they probably wouldn't brew another.

"Not only have you been seeing Logan behind my back, but

you have access to free beer and didn't tell me?" Beside him, Lauren mumbled something under her breath, and Andrew looked at her. "That *is* important."

"I'm sorry," Jeni said. "I didn't think you'd be happy about it, and I didn't want to stress you out."

"Why didn't you think I'd be happy?"

"Logan's not exactly a saint. You're my brother. What else needs to be said?"

Andrew rubbed a hand over his bald head. "I'm not thrilled by the idea. Yes, Logan likes women. But I know him better than most, and I know he's a good guy. Obviously you've figured that out too, or else we wouldn't be having this conversation."

"No one's ever made me feel the way he does. He's incredible."

"So, what's the deal? What happened out there? Did you have a fight?"

"He asked me to marry him."

Andrew shot to his feet. "*What?*"

Lauren's eyes widened a little, but she grabbed his hand and pulled him back down. "Things are pretty serious then."

Jeni rubbed at her sternum. "That's where he and I disagree. He wants serious, and I don't. He's asking for commitment and marriage. I can't give him that."

Andrew's expression softened. "Yes, you can."

"No, I can't."

"It's not a matter of ability, Jeni." Andrew glanced at Lauren and wove their fingers together. "It's a choice. If you turned him down, it's not because you can't. It's because you won't."

Jeni glared at him. "You're right. I won't. I won't agree to something I know he'll regret."

"What makes you so sure he'd regret it? I know what you're afraid of. I know what you went through and that you partially blame yourself, which is ridiculous. I also knew Jackson, and I know Logan. And they couldn't be more different. It's not fair to assume the outcome will be the same. Does Logan...know?"

She knew what he was asking. "He does now."

"And he still wants to be with you?"

Jeni blinked back tears and shook her head. He wouldn't want to be once he had time to think it through. She stood. "I'm not having this conversation again. It's no one's decision but mine. It's not yours, and it's not Logan's."

"I'm not trying to make the decision for you," Andrew said. "I just know you, and you push away when you're upset about something. You get stuck inside your head and isolate yourself. Sometimes it helps to talk things through. Get a different perspective."

He was probably right. But the pull to be alone was strong, and she didn't have the energy to fight it. "Maybe it would. But it's not happening. Not right now. I just want to go home."

Andrew's disapproving expression made her feel like a small child. She was running away, but sometimes that was for the best. There was nothing wrong with being alone. The first few months in Kansas City were a time of healing for her. Living on her own, being independent. Spending time in the quiet without anyone to answer to.

There was also nothing wrong with wanting to keep the man she loved from making a huge mistake. Even if part of her desperately wanted him to.

She slung her purse over her shoulder. "I'm sorry to ruin your night." She walked to where Andrew and Lauren sat and pressed a kiss to Andrew's head. "I'm so happy you're done and that you kicked cancer's ass." She looked at Lauren. "And that we're going to be sisters soon. I'm not sure you feel the same, since I'm obviously messed up. But I'm excited, all the same."

"So am I," Lauren said. "Will you call me? If you want to talk?"

Jeni gave a sort of noncommittal half-nod, and Andrew snorted. Jeni slugged him in the shoulder.

He didn't react. "We'll track you down, you know."

"I know," she said and left.

Her brother was one thing she could count on. No matter what happened, they'd always be there for each other.

She wished she could apply the same mindset to her relationship with Logan, but it seemed different. Family was like a pre-arranged support system. They were annoying and sometimes overbearing, but they loved unconditionally. She could tell them how she really felt, even yell and offend them, and they'd still love her. She never worried about losing them or that her decisions would sever any ties. They might disagree at times, but they'd always welcome her back home with open arms. They'd drop anything to help her if she asked. Even her dad, who'd stayed behind at the farm for most of Andrew's treatment. He showed support from afar but if it came down to it would find a way to be with her or any one of her siblings.

Why didn't it feel the same when it came to marriage? Was it because when she was with Jackson he put his own needs above hers? His love hadn't been unconditional. She wasn't sure he ever loved her at all. Her inability to have children was a shortcoming he couldn't get past, as was her desire to live outside the small-town farm community they grew up in.

Whatever the reason, she couldn't shake the fear that if she agreed to commit to Logan, at some point the outcome would be the same. Their lives would change, and their relationship wouldn't make it through.

As she drove home, she wondered how things would be different if somehow she could change her past. If she could have children and she hadn't had such a bad experience with Jackson, would her answer be different?

She swallowed the lump in her throat, and several traitorous tears slid down her cheeks.

"Yes," she whispered to herself.

If things were different, she'd marry Logan in a heartbeat.

$\sim$

Three weeks later, Jeni stood in her garage, bottling the first beer she brewed all on her own. The April weather was beautiful, and she left the garage door open to let in the breeze. A car pulled into her driveway, and Jeni looked up from her task, swiping hair back from her face with her forearm.

Lauren stepped out of her Honda. "Andrew said I might find you here."

Jeni hadn't spoken to Andrew, or anyone really, since the night at Lauren's house. She hadn't wanted to talk, especially since receiving the news her position would be cut from CPS. She had two weeks left and had no idea what she'd do when her time was up.

"He sent you to try and cheer me up?" Jeni lifted an eyebrow.

"No, he sent me for beer."

Jeni snorted. "Well, get over here and help then. I could use someone to cap these after I fill them. Take as many of you want, but they can't be opened for two more weeks."

Lauren came closer, and Jeni showed her how to use the capper. Jeni went back to filling the bottles, setting them on the workbench when full.

"So, how are you?" Lauren asked.

"Fine."

"Really?"

"No."

Lauren squeezed the lever and inspected the finished product. "Not bad," she said. "Wanna talk about it?"

"I don't know."

Lauren tipped her head in acknowledgement and remained silent, waiting for the next bottle. They worked side by side without speaking for several minutes.

"I got laid off," Jeni blurted out. She hadn't told anyone, not even Andrew. "And I miss Logan. I'm lonely. I don't know what to do."

"You got laid off? When?"

"My boss told me last week. Budget cuts." Jeni didn't blame Sandra even a little bit. The woman had cried when she broke the news, for goodness sake. "They didn't have a choice. I'm done in two weeks."

"I'm so sorry. Do you know what you're going to do?"

"No."

"Want me to look into social work positions at the cancer center?"

Jeni squinted. "Maybe? I don't know. I really like working with kids."

"I could ask at the children's hospital where I volunteer."

That could work. "That would be great, thanks. I haven't really started looking yet. I think maybe I keep hoping something will change and Sandra will call me up to tell me they found something else for me at CPS."

She wished there was another organization like FSD she could get involved in. After having seen the reach of the dona- tions, she'd learned what a major impact nonprofits like that had —but with Logan at the helm, there was no way she'd seek a position at that one. So far, she hadn't found another that appealed to her the same way.

"Maybe she will. But I'll ask, just in case."

"Thank you." Jeni handed Lauren another bottle.

"And the other thing—want to talk about that?"

Jeni paused and dropped her head. "I don't know what the hell I'm doing or if I'm making the right decision when it comes to him. It feels like I'm not. In my heart, I know he's different than my ex-husband. I know no two relationships are the same. And what I feel for him is so much stronger than what I felt for Jackson. So much that it terrifies me."

"Why? What about it scares you?" Lauren finished capping the new bottle and put the tool on the table, giving Jeni her full attention.

"It used to be fear that any man I married would try to control me. But the more time I spent with Logan, the more I saw that's not true." Jeni's shoulders slumped. She thought of his mother and Logan declining his dream job to move home and be with her during her cancer treatment. He'd proved that he put the people he loved before anything else. "Now though, I'm just scared that it will end. Because a lot of marriages do. And that I won't recover like I was able to with Jackson. I went into my first marriage thinking it would be forever. Isn't that what everyone thinks when they get married? Now I'm wiser, and I know it's not a guarantee for life. What would it do to me if something came up and Logan and I couldn't make it work? My heart wouldn't survive."

"From what I know, your situation with Jackson was unique. You were both young and probably immature. You didn't know what life was yet. You were looking for a way out and found it in him, and maybe the foundation of that relationship wasn't strong to start with. When you take the time to get to know someone and experience life with and without them, you get to make a choice. Is life better with them or not? If it is, it's probably worth taking a chance to spend it together."

"I know my life is better with Logan in it. But I don't know if the reverse is true. I'm scared I can't make him happy, and that some...physical issues I have will eventually drive a wedge between us."

"Have you talked to Logan about that?" Lauren asked gently.

"Not since that night at your house. I don't think he wants to hear from me."

"I doubt that. You don't stop wanting or loving someone just because you had a fight."

"I'm not so sure." Jeni swallowed. Logan had seemed pretty upset when he left that night, and she couldn't blame him.

"Andrew and I have had more than one fight since we met. Hasn't stopped us."

Jeni scoffed. "That's because it's Andrew."

"Why does that make a difference?"

"I don't know. Because Andrew's my family, I guess. He's been there for me for my whole life, and I don't see that ever changing. That's what family does." It was the big difference between family and relationships. The first was an unbreakable bond. The second could fall apart at any moment. Her family would never hold it against her that she couldn't have children. But a husband might.

Lauren let out a noise of disgust. "Not my family."

"What do you mean?" Jeni didn't know much about Lauren's life outside her job and her relationship with Andrew.

"Far as my parents were concerned, their lives would be easier if I wasn't around. They had me young and each married other people. Started other families. I was like the awkward bastard child for both of them. It wasn't until I moved here and met friends at the cancer center, and Andrew, that I found what I considered true family. It's not all about whose blood runs in your veins. Sometimes it's about the choices you make. The people you choose to surround yourself with can be your family."

Jeni looked down at her hands, thinking.

"What's Logan's family like?" Lauren asked.

"It's mainly just his mom. But she's wonderful. He's adopted, actually. He had a pretty rough childhood without a father and a neglectful mother and spent a lot of time in the foster care system. The Davises adopted him when he was thirteen, and they were the best parents anyone could ask for."

Lauren tucked a strand of hair behind her ear and glanced outside. "Do you think his adoptive mother's love toward him is conditional?"

Jeni balked. "No," she answered immediately. "That woman adores him and he, her. Their relationship is rock solid."

"And yet, it's a choice for both of them, isn't it? He wasn't born into that family."

"I guess." Jeni fixed her eyes the empty beer bottles near her feet.

Lauren was quiet for a moment. "You want to know what I think?"

"I'm not sure."

"That's fine. I'll tell you anyway. Sisters speak their minds, right?" Lauren crossed her arms and leaned a hip on the bench. "I think you're not giving Logan enough credit. If he knows everything about you, including the details of your past relationship and the physical issues you mentioned, and he still says he wants to be with you? If you trust him, you've got to believe him. He's a grown man and can make his own decisions. You have no right to question that. Now, if you think he's straight up lying, then there's an obvious trust issue there, and that's no foundation for a relationship. But I don't get the feeling that's the problem here. Do you trust him and trust his judgment?"

"I trust *him*. His judgment is questionable though. I mean, he likes the Chiefs."

Lauren chuckled. "I also think you're not giving yourself enough credit. You've got a lot of great qualities. You're a great catch, regardless of what happened in the past. Seems like the problems in your first marriage stemmed from some circumstances beyond your control. You need to stop assuming you have some great shortcoming that renders a successful relationship impossible. If everyone thought that after a bad experience, no one would ever get married, and the human race would die off."

"I don't know how people do it." Jeni rubbed at her forehead. "The idea of doing it again is terrifying."

"I understand." Lauren said. She pulled her long, auburn hair over her shoulder. "Hey, you played softball, right? Andrew said you were the best in the state."

"Yeah," Jeni said, a little disoriented at the change in topic. "I still play a little."

"Then I'm surprised you don't gravitate toward the idea of being part of a team. That's one thing I'm most excited about—that Andrew and I get to navigate this life together. I don't have to do it alone like I have most of my life. Marriage is just like being on a team. And you both have different strengths, so when you share the same goal you can do so much more together. It's like, if you're the best batter but he runs faster, you hit and bring him in to run, and you both get farther than you would on your own."

Jeni blinked, letting the words sink in.

The analogy hit her smack in the middle of her chest. She didn't know if it was because she and Logan had been in that exact scenario—she bats, he runs—or if it was something else, but whatever the case, it clicked.

Being part of a team. Why hadn't she ever thought about it like that?

Every member of her high school team had the same goal in mind. They put in the hours and work to give them the best shot of getting there. Jeni didn't always like every person on the team or agree with everything they said, but they all learned to put aside those differences when they stepped onto the field.

When it really mattered.

They made sacrifices for the good of the team, even if it meant losing personal recognition. They knew who was best at what and capitalized on those strengths. They worked together to fill in the weak spots, and they always, *always* had each other's backs.

And most important of all: if each position wasn't filled with just the right player, everything fell apart.

CHAPTER TWENTY-SIX

Logan's phone rang. Again.

It was the sixth time in two hours. He shoved the box spring into the bed of his pickup truck before he answered.

"Hello?" He leaned his back against the vehicle while he listened. "Uh, I think I have an infant car seat, but I'll have to check. I'm making a delivery right now, so I'll have to let you know. It will probably be an hour before I can get back to the garage. Okay, I'll call you back." He huffed out a breath and climbed into the driver's seat. He hated the frustration he felt right now. This organization was supposed to bring him joy and healing, not stress.

It just blew up so quickly. Faster than he'd anticipated and he didn't have the time or manpower to do it on his own anymore. Not only did he need to keep his day job for financial reasons, but he also loved it. The foundation was supposed to be a side gig, not a full-time job.

But what choice did he have? As long as there were kids who needed beds or a safe car seat, he'd keep doing it. Even if it ran him into the ground. What he really needed was to hire someone to run the day-to-day operations for him. The volunteers who helped out were inconsistent and just weren't cutting it.

His phone vibrated on the dash. Logan considered not answering, but what if it was Jeni this time? Every damn time his phone rang, a little part of him hoped for it.

He'd thought about calling her several times but always decided against it. He'd put himself out there enough times. It was her turn. If she wasn't willing to meet him in the middle and even discuss a future together, he was better off without her.

Didn't mean it didn't hurt like a fucking gunshot straight through his heart.

Logan grabbed the phone and checked the screen. It wasn't Jeni, but it was the next best thing. "Hey, Andrew. Long time, no see."

"You can't see me."

"Wiseass." Logan grinned. "Okay, long time, no talk."

"The last time I saw you I learned through a door that you were, and I quote, 'more than friends' with my sister."

Logan grimaced. "Yeah. Sorry about that. I wanted to tell you."

"Why didn't you?"

"Jeni said no."

"I'd argue more, but I get that."

"I really am sorry."

"I've had a few weeks to let it sink in. I was actually calling to check on you. See if you wanted to hang out. Talk or something."

"Yeah? We're still friends?"

"For now. Jeni's a mess, and I need you to fix that."

"I wish I could."

Andrew's sigh was audible through the earpiece. "Yeah, I get that too. I've been mostly worried about her, and then I realized I'm being an ass and you're my friend and you might be a mess too. What are you doing? Want to get a beer?"

"I'm delivering a bed to a foster family, and then I have to go back and check for a car seat. The foundation has been insane lately. I probably won't be home until after eight."

"Okay if I stop by?"

"Sure. I'll call you if I think I'll be later than that."

"Sounds good."

"And Andrew? I am. A mess."

Andrew laughed once without humor. "Yeah. Love does that."

Two hours later, Logan and Andrew sat on Logan's back porch, drinks in hand, watching the sky darken. They hadn't said much yet. Logan wasn't sure where to start, but he figured apologizing again couldn't hurt.

"I wasn't a good friend to you. Seeing Jeni behind your back like that. I should have asked you first."

"Asked me? Like for permission?"

"Well, yeah. Or at least asked if you were okay with it. I know you probably don't think I'm worthy of her, with the way I used to—"

"Stop."

Logan halted his words and looked at Andrew.

"You're one of my best friends. I think very highly of you."

"You do?"

"Sure. You're a great guy. You don't always act like you think so, but I know you're more than the Casanova role you play. Besides, who am I to judge? I'm no saint."

"Oh. Well, that's good to hear."

"Would I have liked to know you were interested in my sister? Yes. You crossed a line there. But I've had a lot on my mind these last few months. I understand why you didn't want to add that into the mix. Depending on the day, I might have flipped my shit on you. Chemo messes with your brain, man, I'm telling you."

"I bet. Because of that, I'd have let you hit me. Once."

Andrew laughed. "Once is all it would take, my friend."

"Eh, I don't know. Chemo makes you tired too."

"Sure, okay. You want to use my chemo as a handicap, go ahead."

Logan smiled. He hadn't realized how much he'd missed Andrew.

Andrew must have been thinking something along the same lines. "I sort of blame myself too. I haven't really been around much. If I hadn't been spending all my free time with Lauren, I'm sure I would have figured out what was going on between you two."

"You found your girl. Can't fault you for that."

"Yeah, but that doesn't mean I can forget about my friends."

"You didn't. You're here, aren't you?"

"Yeah. I'm here." Andrew took a sip of beer. "So really. How are you?"

"I've been better."

"What happened exactly? Jeni only told me bits and pieces."

"You want it from the beginning?"

"Sure."

So, Logan told him everything. Well, everything except the mind-blowing sex. Probably best to keep that to himself. But he did tell him about the night of Andrew's diagnosis and how they talked most of the night. And about the time he 'saved' her from the rest of their family, to which Andrew nodded in understanding. He told him about realizing he wanted to date Jeni, her resistance to the idea, and crashing dinner at Jeni's house so he could spend more time with her.

He told him about the Chiefs game, softball, and having dinner with his mother. How Jeni found out about his involvement in the foster community and that she knew about his life before adoption. He kept that part brief because he'd never talked about it in detail with Andrew before. Even though he'd opened up to Jeni, it didn't mean his past was suddenly open to the public.

He told Andrew about the time she called him for the little boy hiding under her desk and how they started brewing beer together.

"We'd both always wanted to but just never done it. We spent a lot of time together, sometimes just as friends and sometimes… not." Logan cringed a little at that, but Andrew's fist didn't fly at his face so he counted that as a good sign. "But no matter what, she insisted that whatever we were doing was temporary and she never intended to get married again."

"That sounds like her."

"Like an idiot, I thought I could change her mind. Show her that I wouldn't hurt her and that she was a priority. Now I know her fear of commitment goes deeper than that. She said she doesn't think I could ever be happy with her because of…" Logan trailed off, suddenly worried. Andrew knew about that, right?

"Because she can't have kids?"

Logan's shoulders relaxed. "Yeah. Which couldn't be further from the truth. I didn't ask her to marry me for her uterus."

"Really? That's why I asked Lauren."

Logan caught himself just before he took a drink and laughed. "Different strokes for different folks." He thought it best not to tell Andrew which body parts of Jeni's he gravitated to most.

"I think it's different for women," Andrew said. "Having children is a different experience for them. Not having that option is hard for her, I think."

"You're right. Absolutely. I want kids, and I know she does too. But I have no requirement for how we do that. Even if she could have biological kids, I'd want to foster and maybe adopt. She would too. I'm just as happy for those to be the kids that fill our home. I wouldn't be the person I am today if my parents hadn't done the same for me."

"Did you tell her that?"

"Yes."

Andrew sighed heavily. "She's stubborn. When she has her mind set on something, it takes an act of God to change it."

"I know. But I've seen it happen, so I know it can."

Andrew crossed one ankle across the opposite knee and regarded Logan steadily. "In this case, I hope she comes around."

"You do?"

"I like you for her. I'm kind of surprised I didn't think of it first. She hasn't dated at all since her divorce, and I've been worried about her."

"I don't know if I'd call what we were doing 'dating.'" At Andrew's narrowed eyes, Logan quickly backtracked. "Not because—um, I mean because she won't let us label it like that. It's not like, just physical or anything..." Oh, hell.

"Stop. I get it," Andrew interrupted.

"Thank fuck." Logan took a long drink. "Is this always going to be weird?"

"Not if you marry her."

"I'm trying. She won't let me."

"Keep trying."

Logan was all for fighting for the woman he loved. But there was a point where it crossed the line from persuasive and romantic to pathetic and hopeless, and he felt like he was standing right on it. He risked a black eye to say the truth. "I've done my part. I put it all out there and said all I can say. It's her turn, man. She's gotta decide."

Andrew was quiet for a moment. He tipped his head back, his eyes on the stars making their appearance in the sky. "Well. Let's hope she makes the right decision."

Logan began to lose hope. Two weeks had passed since Andrew came to visit and still no word from Jeni. He was tempted to track her down and beg her to reconsider. Or to tell her *he* would and they could go back to the way things were.

But when he really thought about it, he always talked himself out of it. He'd end up in this same place time and time again. A vicious cycle of half commitment, which was really no commitment at all.

If there was hope for them, he had to know she'd come to the decision on her own. That she wanted him more than her fear of past failures and the unknown of their future together.

He hit the gym hard after work that day in an attempt to release his frustration and sadness. He came home and ate in front of the television. Another riveting Friday night. He'd spent more evenings alone the past few months than he had the entire year before he met Jeni but surprisingly, he wasn't bothered. He didn't feel the need to go out and meet someone new. Finding that physical connection with women he barely knew no longer held the same appeal.

Maybe it never had. He just hadn't known any different.

Just as he considered the allure of exclusive familiarity and intimacy between two people, his phone rang.

His heart leapt, but when he looked at the screen, it wasn't Jeni. It was someone even more unexpected. He hesitated for several seconds then answered the call.

"Cassidy?"

CHAPTER TWENTY-SEVEN

Jeni took a deep breath and said a prayer.

Her foot tapped the gas pedal, and she turned the corner, her eye catching on Logan's house at the end of the street.

Her chest constricted. She hoped she wasn't too late.

She'd wanted to run to him the day after she and Lauren spoke. But she also wanted to think things through and decided it would be worse to make a rash decision. She had to dig deep and really decide what she wanted and what she was ready for.

Jeni approached his house and slowed, noticing the red Camaro parked in front of his house for the first time. It looked a lot like—

Surely not.

But when she sidled her Hyundai up to the curb, her eye caught movement near Logan's front door. It was open, and Cassidy and Logan stepped outside together. He enveloped her in a hug, and Jeni flinched as pain sliced through her heart.

Her thoughts whirled, her brain taking only a few seconds to catch up.

She was too late. He'd moved on.

"How could you?" she whispered, her eyes on his hands pressed against the upper back of another woman. Jeni directed the quiet words in Logan's direction, but she may as well have said them to herself. She was to blame for this.

Why hadn't she at least called? Texted him last week to tell him she was thinking things through and begged for a little time to figure her shit out?

Instead, she'd done exactly what Andrew predicted. Pulled back and isolated herself. She'd missed Logan desperately the entire time and had the audacity to hope he missed her too. Maybe he had, at first. Who knew. But who could blame him at this point for moving on? Not only had Jeni been difficult ever since he met her, but she'd basically dropped off the face of the earth after rejecting his marriage proposal.

Her chin trembled, and her chest burned. She was such an idiot.

As she sat there unable to tear her eyes away from the man she loved, Logan tilted his head up and looked right at her. Jeni straightened her spine, and her eyes went wide. She jerked the wheel and floored it, peeling away as quickly as possible.

Jeni couldn't help but glance once in the rearview mirror, just in time to see Logan jog to the middle of his yard and watch her drive away.

An hour after she got home, Logan called.

Jeni was too embarrassed to answer. She'd been in front of his house like a total creeper, staring at him moments after he'd probably had sex with another woman.

If she thought she'd protected herself with her stupid relationship rules these last several months, she was sorely mistaken. It felt like someone had taken a torch gun to her heart, sending it up in flames and ash.

Thirty minutes later, she'd calmed down a little. So, he'd been with Cassidy. He and Jeni weren't together right now, a situation she'd put them in, and he could do whatever he damn well pleased. Far as he knew, they were over for good, and she couldn't fault him for being with another woman.

It tore her up inside, but she couldn't be mad about it.

She had to at least try to talk to him. Maybe even say what she'd planned when she went to his house in the first place. She picked up her phone and called him back.

His voice was calm and deep when he answered. "Hey."

"Hi." She adjusted her grip on the phone. "I'm sorry about earlier. I wasn't, like, camped out in front of your house or something. I was coming over to see you, and you two came out just as I pulled up, and I kind of froze up. I didn't expect to see her there, and I didn't mean—"

"Jeni."

She closed her mouth and swallowed, trying to calm her racing heart.

"I called to tell you that it's not what you think. I almost didn't call at all, because I don't need to explain anything to you."

Jeni's breath stuttered. "You're right. You don't owe me an explanation."

"I want to though. I'm not sure why."

She braced herself, unsure if she wanted to hear it.

"Cassidy's mom was just diagnosed with breast cancer. She and I worked together when my mom was going through treatment, and Cassidy remembered. She wanted to talk to someone who had been through it with a family member before."

Jeni was ninety percent sure that's not all Cassidy wanted. "I mean, I'm sorry to hear that, of course. I just…I thought…"

"You thought what?"

"You know what I thought."

"That I slept with her?"

She pressed a shaking palm to her forehead, lowering her

chin to her chest, phone still to her ear. "Yes. And it made me so jealous that I could hardly breathe. I thought you'd moved on, and apparently I'm such a possessive bitch that even now I'm wondering if she asked you for sympathy sex after you were so wonderful and talked to her at such a hard time in her life."

"As a matter of fact, she did."

Jeni leaned forward, burying her face between her knees. "Don't tell me anything more. I can't take it."

Logan remained silent for a moment. "I didn't."

The lump in her throat was so tight she could barely get words around it. "You didn't?"

"No."

"Why not?" She squeezed her eyes shut. "I'm sorry. Forget I asked that."

He didn't say anything.

"Is she still there?"

"No."

"Can I come over?"

Jeni closed her eyes and knocked. She adjusted the paper bag in her left hand and fidgeted with her purse strap with the other. The door opened, and her heart swelled three sizes. Butterflies filled her belly, half from nerves and half with longing for the man standing before her.

"Hi," he said.

"Hi."

"Come on in." Logan stepped back and opened the door wide.

Jeni walked inside, inhaling his familiar scent as she passed. Another appealing smell followed soon after. "It smells good in here."

"I just had tacos."

"Oh." Why was that painful? So, he had tacos without her. They were *tacos*, for crying out loud.

But had he shared tacos with Cassidy? *Stop. Let it go.*

Jeni went to the living room and stood awkwardly in the middle.

Logan followed her and stopped a few feet away.

"Would you, um, sit? Please?" Jeni asked.

"Okay." He sat in the middle of the couch and leaned forward a little, his forearms resting on his knees.

Jeni's gaze tracked along the muscles and tanned skin of his forearms, and her mouth went dry.

Focus.

She gently set the bag on the coffee table and reached inside, grabbing a bottle. She retrieved a bottle opener out of her pocket and popped the top off, the cap landing on the table with a clink. She handed it to him.

He regarded the unlabeled bottle. "What's this?"

"Beer. I made it on my own a few weeks ago."

Logan's brows rose slightly, and he took a sip. His nose scrunched immediately, almost as if it were involuntary. "It's, um…"

"It's complete shit."

He cocked his head sideways and sniffed at it.

Jeni knew how bad it was. She'd tasted it. "Like, it's really, really awful."

"What did you do wrong?"

"I don't know! That's what makes me so mad—I have no clue. I thought I did it exactly the same as when you and I did it together, and it came out terrible."

"Oh. Well…I'm sorry?"

"Why are you apologizing? You weren't even there."

He frowned a little. "I'm not sure."

Jeni's thoughts were all jumbled. It was just so good to see him, and it was hard to focus when he was this close. "There's a reason I'm here, you know. I have a point to make."

"Okay."

"Two of them, as a matter of fact."

One corner of his mouth twitched. "Can't wait."

"Actually, they're more like questions rather than points. But whatever."

Logan arched a single brow.

Spit it out, woman. "I was hoping you might give me a job."

"Come again?"

"I got laid off."

His expression remained the same. "I know. Sandra told me."

"She did? When?"

"A few weeks ago."

"You didn't say anything?"

Logan sighed. "I wanted to, but we haven't exactly been on speaking terms. I didn't know what I could do or even if you'd want to talk to me. I was pissed at Sandra at first, but I can't stay mad at that woman."

"It wasn't her fault," Jeni said. "We both know that."

"Still. I'm so sorry."

"Don't be sorry. Be my boss."

He angled his head. "How, exactly?"

"I know I said I wanted to work for a government agency, but that was when I thought it was my only way to have wide reach and make a big impact. After working with you and Fostering Sweet Dreams, I realized I was wrong. I've thought about it a lot, and I think I'd really love a job like that. Not only do you reach a ton of families, but I also realized it's not always about the numbers. Every family and every child matters. And I have a lot of ideas about how to help with organization, fundraisers, and community awareness. You said yourself you're drowning in your donations and having trouble keeping the finance side up-to-date. You need a director to oversee the organization. I know it's a nonprofit and it wouldn't pay much, but it's not like I made much as a social worker. I'd love to be a part of that mission. I used to think CPS was all I wanted, but now I think for me, this might be even better."

Logan sat unnaturally still, watching her.

Now that she'd gotten the first part out, she took the time to really study him. He needed a haircut, and he looked tired. Were those circles under his eyes?

He rubbed the back of his neck then dropped his hand. "Okay."

"Okay?" she echoed.

He nodded. "Yes. I'll hire you. You're right. I need someone. Not just to help me out but the organization deserves the full attention of a formal director. The families we serve deserve a more organized service. You're already familiar with everything, from the foster families to the nonprofit. Win-win."

"Wow." Jeni shifted on her feet. "Great then." She cleared her throat, unsure where to go from here.

"What's the other question?" he prompted.

Jeni opened her mouth, but no sound came out. She'd started with the easier of the two, and while she was pleased with how that one worked out, the question that remained was the real reason she was here. She needed the job, but she wanted this more.

Her entire heart depended on it.

"I was hoping you might marry me."

Logan's eyes went wide, and he froze. She might have thought he stopped breathing if it weren't for the slight tremble in his hands.

"I'm sorry I've been so difficult," she continued. "I was letting my past experiences determine my future, and I refuse to do that anymore. These few weeks without you has shown me how empty my life is without you. I know I *can* do whatever I want on my own, but now I don't *want* to. From something as simple as making beer to playing softball and serving children in need—it's all better with you. I want to watch football with you and eat tacos with you, and I damn sure want to make love to you. A lot. And you know what else?"

His response was a little delayed, like he came out of a trance. "What?" he rasped.

"I'll never not love you, Logan Davis. I'll never not want your lips on mine or your arms wrapped around me. I'll never not tease you about cheering for the worst team in the NFL. And last but not least, I'll never not choose you. I'm sorry I took so long, but I choose you as my partner, my teammate, and my husband. If you'll have me."

Logan swallowed visibly and sat back against the cushions, looking stunned and a little bewildered. "What do you love about me?"

She hated that he needed to ask that, but she hadn't really been forthcoming with her feelings. Not even to herself and certainly not to him.

"Everything," she said with conviction. "I love your heart and compassion. Your dedication to put your all into everything you do. I love that you chose a career in sports and one that brings people together. Your sense of humor. Your taste in movies and the fact that you'd get bored sitting through a documentary because I hate them with a passion. I love watching you play softball and goof off with Andrew. Your laugh is the best sound I've ever heard, and your smile completely ends me. I love your loyalty to your family and friends and the fact that I know you'll be an incredible father. But I also know you'll never neglect *us*. Should I keep going?"

A sweet smile was on his lips, but his eyes remained tentative. He rubbed a hand up and down his forearm.

He had no idea what that part of his body did to her, did he?

"How do I know you mean it?" he asked. "That you won't freak out and throw in the towel the first time things get rough? Or the first time we disagree and someone has to compromise?"

"You don't, I guess. I know I haven't done anything to make you believe that. But I know in my heart this is what I want. I want you, and I need you, and I'll fight for you. I understand if you need time. We can take it slow, and I'll show you. Prove to you I'm not a quitter, and I'm in this one hundred percent. However long you need—"

Logan stood then, and she stopped speaking. He rounded the table, his blue eyes boring into hers. He shook his head, and her heart plummeted, threatening to break into a million tiny shards of pain.

"I don't need time," he said. "If you're serious and you mean this, we're getting married. Like, now."

"Now?" she squeaked.

He took one step forward, and only a few inches between them remained. He radiated warmth and life, and looking at him right now was like standing in the sun, face turned toward the sky.

"Well, not *now* now," he said. "But tomorrow, maybe. Next week. Actually, I don't really care when, just as long as you're in."

She nodded. They still weren't touching, but she didn't want to make the first move. Her skin tingled and her heart raced, and her gaze moved across his face to take in his beautiful eyes, messy hair, and addictive lips. "There's one more thing."

"Oh?"

Jeni moved back a little and took off the long-sleeved shirt she wore, revealing the Chiefs T-shirt underneath.

The smile on his face in that moment was everything. It devastated her and restored her all at once.

"You must know how much I love you to wear this."

"Nothing else you could do would mean more to me," he said with a grin.

Jeni's eyes tracked down his body. "Remember what you said? When you gave this to me?"

He lifted his eyes from her chest and the emblem emblazoned there, gaze burning.

"I can't recall, exactly," he said in a husky voice.

"I believe the gist was you'd consider my earlier proposition if I wore it."

Logan coughed a little. "Um. Aren't those propositions null and void? Now that we're engaged?"

He had a point. "Yes. But that doesn't change the fact that I want you. Do you want me?"

Instead of answering, he asked another question. "You want to be with me for real?"

"Yes."

"Forever?"

"Yes."

"We're getting married someday?"

"We're getting married someday."

"Soon?"

"I said ye—"

Jeni's response was cut off when Logan lurched forward, his hands on either side of her face, his mouth suddenly on hers in a kiss that was forceful and passionate and exactly what she needed. She sucked air in through her nose and pressed against his hard chest, her arms curving around his shoulders and back.

The worry and heartache that had built inside her over the last several weeks melted away with each touch and each press of his lips. His hands slid down to circle her waist, and she pulled her face back a little, lifting her hands to trace the wavy hair along his temples.

"I want you to keep the shirt on." His voice was low and deep.

Fire exploded in her belly. She bit her lower lip. "Okay."

His eyes dropped to her mouth and stayed there for a

moment, and Jeni thought her heart might beat right out of her chest. He met her eyes again and tipped his head to the hallway.

She nodded eagerly, and seconds later they were in his bedroom, on his bed, limbs tangled and lips searching. His heavy breaths matched hers as various pieces of clothing came off— except the bright red T-shirt.

Logan hovered above her, the muscles in his arms and torso flexing with each move he made. Her skin was like a live wire, lighting up with every touch of his fingertips.

"I can't be slow this time," he said, his palm on the column of her throat, firm but not painful, fingers on her jaw as he nipped at her ear.

"Good," she managed to get out. It was difficult to focus with his other hand roaming, but she was coherent enough to recognize that Logan Davis unhinged was something she wanted to experience. "I don't want slow."

He groaned, the deep vibration echoing through every cell in her body. His lips crashed down on hers, his tongue sliding inside her mouth. She arched up, wrapping one leg around his hips, searching.

Searching…

"I love you.

"I know."

…and finding.

Logan pressed his forehead lightly against hers. "I'm gonna love this body every day for the rest of my life."

He slowly slid his fingers underneath the red shirt and across her ribcage, and she sucked in a shaky breath. She still hadn't fully recovered from what just transpired.

"When you do, you love more than my body." She took his

hand and pressed it to her chest, right over her pounding heart. "I feel it in here. In my veins and in my bones. In my soul."

His face transformed to something serious, almost severe with emotion. "That's kind of the whole point."

His words went straight to the deepest part of her.

"I never knew," she whispered.

"Neither did I."

He kissed her, slow and deep, for several moments. When they parted, he smiled down at her. "So, are you a Chiefs fan now?"

"Nope."

"Come on." He raised a brow. "Not even after that?"

"Let's see what you can do when I wear green."

"Won't be the same for me."

"Are you saying it wasn't me but the Chiefs that turned you on? That's a little weird."

"It was *you* in the Chiefs shirt."

"Still."

He chuckled. "Rethinking this whole marriage thing?"

"I don't know. Throw something else into the pot to sweeten the deal."

Logan pushed up on his arms, muscles taut. She almost said that visual was enough, but then he lowered his head and whispered the sweetest words in her ear. "Tacos and beer."

She moaned. "Hard or soft tacos?"

Logan considered. "I'm thinking hard."

Jeni grinned up at the man she loved, and he smiled.

"That's what she said."

ACKNOWLEDGMENTS

This book took a couple of tries and some excellent advice from Denise Williams, Heather Gearhart, and Torie Jean, but I cannot tell you how happy I am with Jeni and Logan's story. These two were in my head from the first few chapters of writing Perfect Distraction and I couldn't wait to get my hands on them so they could tell their own love story. Jeni ended up a little sassier and Logan a little softer than I planned, but I love them both so much.

Thank you Jeni Chappelle for editing this book, and Elizabeth Turner Stokes for the gorgeous cover. Thank you Rae, Skye, Sarah, and Lindsay for giving me tips on self-publishing (jeez, it's stressful!). On that note, an extra thank you to everyone who bought this book. You may not have known I self-published this one, but I honestly loved the story so much I just had to put it out there. Thank you for giving it a chance.

Thank you to Dara, who gave me invaluable information and insight into the foster care system. Any errors or misrepresentations are on me. And thank you for being so lovely supporting my books even though we know each other through Anne (who I also owe huge thanks to—Anne, you're one of my top betas. You make me feel worthy of writing and give great feedback). Thanks to Kristy Payne who generously allowed me to base Logan's organization off the real (and much better organized) Fostering Sweet Dreams located right here in Oklahoma. If you're interested in donating to that organization, visit https://fosteringsweetdreams.com.

I have the best betas/early readers who support me endlessly and give me so much encouragement: Fransen, Abby, Ashtin, Lindsey, Staci, Jo, Ashley, Anna, Anne, Lyn, Amber, Misty, Tobie, Beth…and can I be honest and tell you I'm guaranteed to leave someone out here? As authors we're told to keep track of people to thank from the very beginning, but for a long time I didn't know if this book would ever make it to publication and I admit I didn't keep a list. I'm positive I'm going to leave out someone important. Please forgive me.

Thanks to BIG Brew Co for always being willing to hosting my release parties and sponsoring my Books and Brews promo event. You're good people and you make excellent beer.

Thank you to the Bookstagram community for being so creative and supportive of authors and romance novels in particular. We're a genre that often gets criticized and insulted in the larger literary world, but your love and never-ending dedication to romance novels keeps us going. As long as you keep reading love stories we'll keep writing them.

As always a big thank you to my parents and my husband who believe in me and support me and take my kids somewhere else so I can write. Love you.